We hope you enjoy this book. Please return or renew it by the due date.

You can renew it at www.norfolk.gov.uk/libraries or by using our free library app.

Otherwise you can phone 0344 800 8020 - please have your library card and PIN ready.

You can sign up for email reminders too.

Pam EVANS

The Tulip Tearooms

HEADLINE

First published in 2022 by
HEADLINE PUBLISHING GROUP

First published in paperback in 2022 by
HEADLINE PUBLISHING GROUP

1

Cataloguing in Publication Data is available from the British Library

ISBN 978 1 4722 5680 5

Typeset in Bembo Std by Palimpsest Book Production Ltd, Falkirk, Stirlingshire

Printed and bound in Great Britain by Clays Ltd, Elcograf S.p.A.

HEADLINE PUBLISHING GROUP
An Hachette UK Company
Carmelite House
50 Victoria Embankment
London EC4Y 0DZ

www.headline.co.uk
www.hachette.co.uk

The Tulip
Tearooms

Chapter One

One Saturday evening in the spring of 1946, a soldier with an overseas tan and a kitbag slung over his shoulder walked out of London's Hammersmith underground station and was embarrassed to feel a lump gather in his throat and his eyes burn with tears. It was five years since Harry Riggs had last been here in his home city, and the strength of his emotions took him completely by surprise.

Harry wasn't normally a sentimental type; he had trained himself not to be in the tough environment of the wartime army, and he had even managed to put on a brave face when he'd been feeling broken by the loss of much-loved comrades in action. Yet now, on arriving home, he was reduced to tears. Admonishing himself for his weakness, more suited to an emotional adolescent than a battle-hardened soldier of twenty-four, he brushed away his tears with the back of his hand, cleared his throat and walked on with his head held high.

It was raining lightly and London looked dismal in the gathering dusk, shabby and broken by war, bomb-damaged buildings left decaying as they were, dust, dirt and peeling paint everywhere. He guessed it would take years and a great deal of government money to put London right after the German onslaught, but it was home and he loved every scruffy inch of it. He walked on through the Broadway, which was bustling with people heading for the train station, others queuing at the bus stops, all spruced up and probably on their way to their weekend entertainment in the pubs and dance halls. Saturday evenings had always been the big night out for the people around here. It was well known that even during the worst of the Blitz the pubs, clubs and dance halls had been packed most nights of the week. Harry and his mates had got to hear about it even while in foreign fields, where any scrap of news from home had been eagerly welcomed.

As he turned into the quieter side streets, then on into Dexter Street and paused outside number ten, he could feel his emotions starting to overwhelm him.

He knew that the door key would be tied to the end of a piece of string and he could pull it out through the letterbox, then use it to let himself in, but, after all this time, that might be too much of a shock for the family. He'd written to say that he would be back sometime soon but hadn't been able to tell them exactly when. Now, he walked up the path to the front door and gave the door knocker a good hammering.

His mother Marg, a small, dainty woman with soft brown eyes and greying hair, a neat pinafore worn over her clothes as always, opened the door. For a split second he wondered if he'd done the right thing in surprising her because the colour drained from her face and she began trembling visibly.

'Harry?' she said shakily at last, the beginnings of an uncertain smile lighting up her face. 'Harry, is it really you?'

'Yes, Mum,' he said, hugging her and holding her close to

him, his brown eyes hot with tears of joy. 'After all this time, it really is me. I'm home at last.'

Before long, the house was buzzing with excitement, everyone wanting to talk to their war hero: Harry's father Michael, grandparents Nell and Cyril, who were staying here temporarily, having been bombed out of their own home during the Blitz, and his little sister Ruby, who wasn't so little any more, he noticed.

'What have you done to my kid sister?' he asked jokingly, as his father got from the sideboard the sherry he had been saving for this very occasion, and poured everyone a glass. 'She was just a nipper when I went away.'

'It's called growing up,' said his father drily. 'It happens to us all eventually.'

'I'm seventeen now,' announced Ruby proudly. She was a pretty girl, with rich brown eyes and hair, like her big brother. 'A proper adult. So, you won't be able to boss me around any more, Harry.'

'Don't count on it, kid,' he laughed, giving her a brotherly hug, his heart full of love for these people he hadn't seen for such a long time. 'You'll still be my little sister when you're thirty-five, and bossing you about comes with the job.'

'I don't know so much about that,' she said, blushing. He was the big brother she had always looked up to, but he'd been away for a long time and seemed almost like a stranger to her now. She was keen to impress him but feeling more than a little shy.

As they sipped their drinks, everyone talking at once, Harry mentally tuned out, revelling in the simple pleasure of being home and reunited with his loved ones. His parents weren't just kind and caring towards their own family, but were well known in the community for their warm hearts. If there was any trouble in the neighbourhood it was to Marg and Michael Riggs people turned for help. Mum and Dad, so loving and dependable; Ruby, all grown up and with a whole new attitude to life; and Grandma and Granddad, too, still smiling even in the face of adversity . . . Oh, it was so good to be home!

'Did you kill many Germans, Harry?' asked Ruby, later on when the family were over their surprise at Harry's return and were sitting around talking more comfortably.

'Ruby!' admonished her mother. 'What a terrible thing to say! You shouldn't ask that sort of thing of a man just back from the war.'

'Oh, sorry,' said Ruby, blushing furiously. 'I didn't realise we weren't supposed to . . . I was only wondering.'

'It's all right, kid,' said Harry quickly, although his stomach churned at the memory of how it felt to take a life. It was not something he would ever forget. A lot of the lads reacted badly and had had to remind themselves that they were just obeying orders. 'I did what I had to do, Ruby, and some of it wasn't pleasant, but I'd rather hear about what you've been doing. It's time to put the war behind us.'

'Oh, right,' she said, angry with herself for saying the wrong thing. 'Well, I left school and work in the offices of an engineering factory now. I go to night school to learn shorthand and typing, and I hope to be a secretary eventually.'

'Ambitious, eh? Good for you,' Harry said with an encouraging smile. Girls of her ilk usually took the clerical route, while those seeking the fatter pay packet worked on the factory floor. There was rarely any thought of a career for girls like Ruby, with no particular talent; just a job until they got married. He guessed she would have been persuaded against the factory floor option by their parents because the work was often hard and monotonous. 'And do you enjoy the job?'

She shrugged. 'Yeah. It's all right, I suppose, but a bit boring at times. The best part is getting my pay on a Friday. I like it all right then.'

Harry gave a hearty laugh. 'That's everybody's favourite bit,' he said.

'They've got a good social club at work, though,' she told him. 'And they have dances sometimes on a Saturday night. There are quite a few people of my age working there so I've made some new friends.'

'Out dancing, eh?' said her brother. 'You are growing up. You'll be courting next.'

The girl turned scarlet and said, 'Oh, no! Nothing like that for me at the moment.'

'I should think not,' said her mother.

Harry turned to his father. 'Still working for the railway, Dad?'

'Yeah, still making sure that people can get about,' said Michael, who was a railway engineer. 'Glad to see the end of the bombing, same as everyone else.'

'I bet,' nodded Harry.

'I suppose you'll go back to your job at the factory after demob, won't you, son?'

Harry didn't reply at once. 'Not really sure, Dad, at the moment. Before I went away, the guvnor said there would definitely be a job for me if I wanted it when I got back from the war,' he said eventually. 'But I've got some other ideas so I might not take him up on it.'

'Sounds interesting,' said Michael. 'What sort of thing do you have in mind?'

'Just a few thoughts at the moment, Dad, so I'll keep them to myself for now, if you don't mind. After all, they might not come to anything.'

'Of course, I don't mind, son. When you're ready we'll have a chat, if you like.'

'Yeah, sure.'

'Sounds intriguing,' said Cyril, Harry's grandfather, whose interest in the family hadn't dimmed with age.

'Not 'alf,' added Nell, his wife, her lively blue eyes showing no sign of fading, although her hair was pure white. 'We'll look forward to hearing all about it when you're ready.'

The conversation turned to local gossip as well as family news, the dire shortage of everything, and then the event Marg had been planning for years: Harry's welcome home party.

'You don't have to go to all that trouble, Mum,' he told her. 'We'll just have a few drinks down the pub to celebrate. That'll do for me.'

'We're having a proper welcome home party, with all our friends and relatives,' she said. 'And I don't want any argument about it.'

'There's a welcome home do nearly every weekend around here as the boys arrive back, and your mum has been looking forward to yours since the day you went away. We've got bottles of booze stashed away all over the house in readiness,' said Michael. 'So I think you'd better get used to the idea and stop protesting.'

6

'Righto, then. Thanks, Mum,' Harry said, smiling. 'I'll really look forward to it.'

'You won't be disappointed, I can promise you that,' she said.

This was one of the happiest days of her life. She had her boy back home fit and healthy, and it didn't get better than that.

Harry found it rather strange being in bed in a room of his own again. He'd become so accustomed to sleeping in a barrack room with a crowd of noisy blokes that, alone at last, he found himself missing his mates. Five years was a long time. They weren't all the same men throughout the war, of course – some had been killed, others had been sent to different units or shipped back to Blighty for various reasons – but the spirit was still the same. They were young men thrown together in dreadful circumstances, they had made the best of it and become closer than brothers. Harry would never forget any of them.

Mum had mentioned that his best mate Mick, who lived next door, was also home on demob leave so Harry decided he would catch up with him and any other of the boys who were around, enjoy some time with the family and give serious thought to his life after he was finally done with the army.

Before call-up he'd had good prospects working in an engineering factory, and at first he'd fully intended to go back there. But meeting new people from many different backgrounds in the army had changed his perspective, and his old job no longer appealed to him. He fancied the idea of an occupation that would make a difference to society, and would in turn make him feel a part of something, but he wasn't yet sure if he could take this idea any further so he'd decided to keep quiet about it for the time being.

In the meantime, he'd enjoy the soft pillows, clean sheets and silky eiderdown; sheer luxury after itchy army blankets and a lumpy mattress. He'd have a lie-in tomorrow, too. Lovely, he thought, snuggling down but, try as he might, he couldn't get to sleep. As well as the excitement of being home at last, there were too many memories disturbing his peace of mind.

'How's your love life, Harry?' asked his pal Mick the following evening over a pint in the local pub.

'Non-existent, mate,' Harry replied.

'Same here,' said Mick. 'The war mucked everything up good and proper for a lot of us. The girl I was seeing when I got called up promised to write to me.'

'And she didn't?'

'Just once, to tell me she'd met someone else. It wasn't serious between us but it was still a rejection. Not much you can do to cheer yourself up either when you're stuck in the middle of nowhere with a gang of blokes.'

'Oh, bad luck, mate,' said Harry.

Mick shrugged. 'That's women for you. You never know where you stand with them.'

'I'm sure they're not all unreliable,' said Harry. 'But I don't have a girlfriend either. So, we'll have to visit a few dance halls to see what's around in the way of opportunity.'

'Yeah, I'm all for that, Harry.'

'Mum is putting on a welcome home party for me on Saturday night, and naturally you're invited, but we could go out the following week if you fancy it,' suggested Harry. 'Saturday night is when the girls go out dancing, isn't it?'

'Yeah, definitely the best night to find women,' agreed Mick, attracting the attention of the woman behind the bar and ordering another round.

'Are you going back to your old job after demob?' Harry asked his friend.

'Yeah, are you?'

'Not quite sure, Mick. I might not,' Harry replied. 'I wouldn't mind a change.'

'Oh, really? Doing what?'

'Dunno yet,' he fibbed.

'I reckon you'll have plenty of time to make up your mind,' said Mick. 'I read in the paper that at the end of the war, there were five million servicemen and -women needing to get demobbed so Gawd only knows how long it'll take them to get to us.'

'But that was months ago, so they'll have made some progress by now,' Harry pointed out. 'Still, we'll have to wait our turn like everyone else.'

'After what we've been through, it won't be much of a hardship, will it?'

'Never a truer word, mate.' Harry sipped his beer. 'So, where were you?'

'France mostly,' he replied. 'How about you?'

'Middle East.'

'See any action?' asked Mick.

'Some,' Harry said. 'You?'

'A bit.'

Harry had noticed that servicemen either couldn't stop talking about what they'd done on the battlefield or they said nothing at all. Both he and Mick seemed to be of the latter variety so they moved back to the subject of their non-existent love lives.

'We'll enjoy ourselves at the party on Saturday, women or no women,' said Harry. 'There will be some girls there, but most of 'em are cousins or too young for us.'

'It doesn't matter,' said Mick. 'I'm not planning on staying sober after the first hour or so anyway.'

Harry laughed. 'I don't blame you,' he said.

'My mum put on a do for me when I first got back and I was blotto by nine o'clock.'

'I'm hoping to stay sober for longer than that,' said Harry lightly. 'Not too much longer, though,' he added, laughing.

Harry was enjoying himself far too much at the party to bother a great deal about the alcohol. A 'Welcome Home Harry' banner was draped across the front of the house and the gathering was a really happy get-together, with relatives from all over London, friends and neighbours, everyone letting their hair down. The furniture was moved to the sides of the room and people jigged around to the latest hits on the gramophone. Ruby was in charge of the records, helped by Philip, the boy next door on the other side from Mick's family, who was a similar age and was winding the gramophone handle. 'Aren't You Glad You're You?' by Bing Crosby was a real favourite.

Later on, as people became inebriated, the records were abandoned and the partygoers belted out old sentimental songs in a boozy manner. 'Nellie Dean' was very popular, and they finished the party with 'The Hokey Cokey' and 'Knees Up Mother Brown'.

'Lovely party, Mum,' said Harry after they had seen the last guest out. 'Thanks ever so much for putting it on for me.' He turned to his father. 'And you, Dad, of course.'

'No need to thank us, son,' his mother assured him, washing glasses at the sink. 'We've been looking forward to it for years so the preparation was no hardship. Everyone seemed to enjoy themselves and that's thanks enough for us.'

'Your mum is right, son,' added Michael.

'You go up to bed, Harry,' said his mother, who was so pleased to have her son home she was in the mood to spoil him. 'Your dad and I will clear up here. You can go as well, Ruby.'

Ruby didn't need telling twice that she could skip the chores. 'Thanks, Mum,' she said, and headed speedily for the stairs.

Harry knew his mother would do most of the clearing-up because that was the way things worked around here, but he did as she asked and headed for bed, smiling. She wanted to spoil him and he would let her, but he'd find ways to thank her in due course.

'Don't expect to find the girl of your dreams at the first dance we go to, Mick,' Harry advised his friend over a pint at the pub the following evening. Mick, however, seemed to think it was a foregone conclusion and was already planning a date.

'Why wouldn't I?' he asked. 'I'm no film star, but I'm not a bad-looking bloke. There must be plenty of girls around who'd like to go out with me.' He was stockily built with light brown hair and hazel eyes; ordinary but not unattractive. This evening both he and Harry were wearing army uniform.

'There's sure to be, but these things take time,' Harry reminded him.

'Not necessarily. And it won't be for lack for trying if I don't get fixed up,' said his friend. 'I'm determined to find someone.'

'You definitely won't if you seem as desperate as you are now when we actually approach some girls,' said Harry. 'I don't know what the urgency is all about.'

'Then there must be something wrong with you,' Mick declared. 'A man needs a girl on his arm and it's been a very long time.'

'In his bed, you mean.'

'Yeah, that as well . . . it's only natural.'

'I suppose so,' Harry agreed. 'But that takes time, and marriage for most women.'

'Not all of them, thankfully,' Mick said. 'There must still be a few girls around who just like a bit of fun.'

'Maybe so, but it's a well-known fact that being overly keen puts them off so you need to calm down a bit.'

'Point taken,' said Mick. 'Did you go out with any foreign women while you were abroad?'

'One or two,' said Harry. 'Never a success, what with the language and different customs.'

'I never had any luck with that either,' said Mick. 'But some of the lads did.'

'I've always had this idea in the back of my mind that one day I'll meet someone really special – the woman of my dreams – and it will be love at first sight,' said Harry.

'I wouldn't hold your breath,' said Mick with a dry laugh.

'You're probably right, but there's no harm in having a dream and I've always been an optimist.'

'Let's hope you get lucky at the Palais, then.'

'It would be nice but I'm not banking on it,' grinned Harry.

Lola Brown answered a knock at the door on Saturday afternoon. Two of her father's cronies stood on the doorstep, both dressed in loud pin-striped suits with brightly coloured satin ties.

'Is your dad in?' asked one of the men.

When Lola nodded, without waiting for an invitation the man pushed passed her rudely, followed by his mate. They were greeted warmly by her father Charlie, who took them into the front room and shut the door, having told Lola's mother Rita to bring them tea and make sure they weren't disturbed.

'Tea for three coming up, dear,' said Rita in her usual obedient manner.

'I wonder what they're talking about,' said Lola's younger brother, Frankie, who was nearly thirteen.

'Their next crime, I should think,' said Lola disapprovingly, her blue eyes bright with anger. 'That's all they ever talk about. Spivs and thieves are the only sort of people Dad mixes with, he being one of them.'

'Don't talk like that about your father, Lola,' admonished her mother. 'He does his best for us. We have things other families don't because he takes risks. You should be grateful to him, not criticising all the time.'

'He's a crook, Mum, and so are all his mates. He doesn't even try to hide it and even boasts about it,' said Lola. 'I just can't approve of that sort of thing.'

'That's all just talk,' said Rita dismissively. 'Your dad likes to

13

play the big man but he isn't really bad. I should know – I've been married to him for long enough.'

'Long enough for him to convince you to believe everything he tells you.'

'No,' argued Rita. 'Just long enough to know when not to ask too many questions.'

'I'd sooner not have extras that have been gained illegally,' said Lola. 'God knows what he gets up to when he's out of this house.'

'It's just a bit of black market,' said Rita.

'I think it's a lot more than that, Mum,' said Lola, who, at eighteen, was old enough to know what was what.

'You're not suggesting he's involved in actual crime surely, robberies and so on?'

'I've no proof, but I wouldn't put it past him,' said Lola.

'Oh dear, I do hope not,' said Rita, sounding worried. 'I can cope with a bit of dodgy stuff but I'm not so sure about anything actually criminal.'

'Black market *is* criminal, Mum,' said Lola, with exaggerated patience.

'Yeah, I know, but it isn't as if anyone gets hurt.'

'I wouldn't be so sure about that,' said Lola. 'Where you get greed, you get violence. I don't know why he can't get a proper job like other people's dads.'

'He can't take discipline, that's why,' said her mother. 'It nearly killed him when he had a regular job before the war. A bit of dealing in his spare time was the only thing that kept him sane then. Self-employment suits him and he works hard in his own way, always out trying to do business.'

'In the pubs and clubs mostly,' said Lola disapprovingly. 'So, no real hardship. He feels at home in those sorts of places.'

'That's where the people he deals with operate so he has to go there,' said Rita. She never failed to defend her man, almost as though it had become a habit. 'It's all about contacts. And I think his is a very competitive world. He has to work really hard for every little bit of business. And some of it's legit . . . I should think.'

Feeling a wave of sympathy for her long-suffering mother, Lola said quietly, 'I'm probably exaggerating, Mum. Take no notice of me. Let's get the tea into them and have a cuppa ourselves.'

'All right, dear,' Rita said.

Watching Rita fill the kettle and put it on the gas stove, Lola thought how much nicer Mum would look if her appearance wasn't dictated by her husband. She was a peroxide blonde, her hair home bleached and patchy; there was far too much rouge on her cheeks and her lipstick was drawn clownishly outside the shape of her lips. Her husband liked her to look this way. He said she was glamorous, and because it pleased him she went along with it.

Lola wondered if it would have been better for her mother if she had been forced to go out to work during the war. She might have gained some confidence and self-respect then. But because she'd still had a child of school age, she hadn't been obliged to do so, and had stayed at home, totally reliant on her husband.

Many a time Lola had thought about leaving home to free herself from the man she disapproved of so strongly. But she couldn't bring herself to leave her mother and brother. It wasn't as if Dad was physically cruel; just very dominant, often verbally insulting to his wife, hideously conceited and a law breaker. But family was family, so Lola had to make the best of the situation.

At least they had Uncle Bert, who was her father's brother and the salvation of this family, with his kind and supportive ways. Anyone could see how fond he was of them all, especially her mother, and that gave Lola some comfort. Her uncle was the exact opposite of his brother, being totally law abiding; the sort of man who would never do anyone out of so much as a farthing.

'Where's that tea?' shouted Charlie.

'Just coming,' said Rita.

'I should bloody well hope so too,' Charlie yelled back.

At that moment the back door opened and Uncle Bert came into the kitchen. 'What's all this shouting about?' he asked.

'Dad's entertaining and he wants tea taken in,' said Lola.

'Tell him to come and get it,' said Bert, who was a widower in late middle age, tall, like Charlie, with brown hair balding at the temples and warm hazel eyes. 'There's no reason why any of you should run about after him.'

'Tea,' shouted Charlie.

'Come and get it, you lazy sod,' Bert called back.

There was a silence, then Lola's father appeared, muttering about having to do everything himself in this house. Happy days, thought Lola with irony. Still, Uncle Bert always cheered everyone up. She herself had something to look forward to later on, too, because she was going out dancing tonight with her friend Doreen from work. Dancing was one of Lola's favourite ways to spend an evening, especially jiving, which was so popular now. She loved the lights and the music, the crowds, the whole atmosphere of a dance hall. There was always the possibility of meeting some lovely young man, too.

* * *

'Now don't forget, Mick,' said Harry as the two friends queued for their tickets at the Palais, both looking smart in army uniform, 'keep your distance with the women. Don't seem too eager or you might put them off.'

'You look out for yourself and leave me to do it my way, mate,' said Mick.

'Just trying to help,' said Harry with an ironically raised eyebrow.

'I don't need help, thanks very much,' said Mick. 'I know how to handle women, don't worry.'

'Good for you,' said Harry as their turn came at the box office and they bought their tickets and headed for the ballroom. 'So, let the fun begin.'

'I really hate this bit,' said Lola to Doreen as the two friends stood at the edge of the dance floor among all the other women hoping for a partner. 'It makes me feel cheap and desperate.'

'Mm, there is an element of that about it I must admit but this is the way it works so we have to do it. And you won't be standing here for long,' said Doreen. 'You always get plenty of partners.' Doreen herself, though an unremarkable brunette, had such a ready smile that she was never short of company for long.

Lola couldn't deny the truth of Doreen's words. Easy on the eye with her blond hair and blue eyes, she usually attracted a fair amount of male interest. Never that someone special, though, not yet.

* * *

'I've just seen the girl of my dreams,' said Harry to his pal.

'Really? Where?'

'Over there,' said Harry, nodding towards Lola. 'The blonde in the blue dress. Isn't she lovely?'

'Very nice too,' agreed Mick. 'You'd better look sharp, though. A girl like that won't be standing there for long.'

'You're right,' said Harry, and hurried across the dance floor as the band struck up a quickstep.

'Do you live around here?' Harry asked Lola after they had exchanged names while dancing.

'Not far. Just the other side of town. About ten minutes' walk, but I usually take the bus to come to the Palais.'

'Lazy,' he said, teasing her.

'High heels,' she said by way of explanation. 'Anyway, if we all walked everywhere there'd be no jobs for the transport workers, would there?'

'That is definitely the worst excuse I've ever heard,' Harry said, laughing.

She smiled too. It didn't matter what they said because there was magic in the air and they both knew it even at this very early stage. They danced every dance together and during the last waltz he asked if he could see her home.

'I'd really like that,' Lola said happily.

'You're not going to invite me in to meet your family then?' Harry teased her as they stopped at her front gate.

'At this time of night. Not likely! They'll be in bed and

asleep by now,' Lola said firmly. 'Anyway, I've only just met you so it's much too soon.'

'How long do I have to know you before I get invited in then?' he asked.

'There are no set rules but definitely longer than one evening,' she said, laughing, although she rarely invited people home because her father made no secret of his illicit dealings to any company and it embarrassed her. She certainly wasn't going to risk that situation with Harry at this very early stage. He might be completely put off her. 'Are you as pushy with all the women you meet?'

'No. Only you,' he said.

'Why me?'

'Because you're special.'

'Oh, really?' she said, loving it. 'In what way?'

'Every way,' he said.

'Well, you certainly know how to make a girl feel good.'

She put up no resistance when he kissed her and was delighted to say 'yes' when he asked if he could see her again.

There was no long-drawn-out lead in to their love affair. From that first kiss they fell desperately in love and were together at every possible opportunity. Harry was on leave from the army, so he was free to meet Lola from work and walk her home every day. They saw each other every evening too, and at weekends, so Lola was rarely in. They spent their time together out dancing, or at the pictures, or just out walking.

When she was invited to Sunday tea with his family, Lola

realised for the first time the extent of the difference in their backgrounds.

Harry's home was tastefully and traditionally furnished in browns and beiges, with conventional pictures on the wall, unlike the gaudy furnishings in her house, the surfaces crowded with brightly coloured ornaments and nothing matching because most of it was stolen. Harry's parents were absolute darlings, as was his sister Ruby, and they all made Lola feel immediately at home, with their warm-hearted and genuine interest in her.

'So, what does your father do for a living?' enquired Michael.

'Er, he's a salesman,' said Lola, thinking that it was partly true because he did sell the stuff even if it was of questionable origins.

'Door to door?' asked Michael in a friendly manner.

'Partly,' she said, because she didn't want to admit to these obviously extremely law-abiding people that her father sold most of his wares to dodgy dealers in pubs.

'Very admirable too,' said Mr Riggs, the railway engineer. 'It takes courage to do that.'

Lola nodded politely. It occurred to her that there wasn't a class difference between the two families so much as an attitude towards life. Both were working class, but the Riggs family had taken the respectable route while her father had fallen by the wayside good and proper.

'Dad isn't short of courage,' she said truthfully.

Thankfully the conversation moved on. Lola had been terrified that Mr Riggs was going to suggest a meeting of the two families. That really would be a disaster, with Dad boasting about how he outwitted the police and earned good money illegally.

Unfortunately, Lola wasn't quite out of danger because, afterwards, when Harry was walking her home, he said, 'So when do I get invited to tea at yours?'

'Oh, shouldn't you wait to be asked?' she said, making a joke of it.

'Probably, but I think I might have a long wait so I thought I'd speed things up a bit,' he said. 'If you don't soon invite me, I might start to think you're ashamed of me.'

'Never,' she almost shouted because he was so far from the truth.

'That's a relief.'

'I'll organise it soon, I promise,' she said, seeing the end of this relationship in sight and feeling desperate about it.

Lola knew she couldn't avoid Harry coming to the house for much longer. Although they had met only a few weeks previously, they were serious about each other and that meant getting to meet each other's family. So when she went to meet him the following evening, she invited him to tea on Sunday. She had begged her father not to mention his unlawful way of life and he had given her his word. She didn't trust him to keep to his promise but she just had to hope for the best.

'Yes, I'd love to come to tea on Sunday,' Harry said as they walked towards the cinema, arms entwined.

'That's good,' Lola said. 'I'll get it organised.'

'It's time I met your family anyway, especially now.'

'Why especially now?'

'Because things have been happening, my darling girl,' he told her excitedly.

'What things?'

'Good things,' he said, teasing her.

'Stop messing about and tell me what they are then,' she urged him.

'Well . . . my leave is coming to an end and I have a definite demob date. I've been thinking it through ever since I arrived home and I've decided exactly what I want to do as regards a job. I've been to see about it today,' he told her, his voice rising with enthusiasm. 'It was all very positive. I'm just the sort of bloke they are looking for, apparently, so I'm feeling much more settled now with a steady job to look forward to. In fact, I'm so positive about the future I feel in a position to ask you to marry me.' He stopped walking and took her in his arms. 'Will you marry me, Lola?' he said softly.

'Oh, Harry,' she said excitedly, 'Of course, I will.'

'I love you, Lola.'

'I love you too, Harry,' she said, holding him close.

'I am the type of person they want in their ranks,' he went on. 'Having done a stint in the army, I'm used to discipline.'

'What is the job, Harry?' she asked.

'I'm joining the Metropolitan Police,' he informed her excitedly.

Lola was shocked into silence. The job Harry was so pleased about meant the end of all her dreams of a life together with him. To bring a policeman into the family would be to betray her father completely. Harry would soon guess how Charlie earned his money and, as a policeman, would feel duty bound to take action. As much as she disapproved of her father, Lola just couldn't do that to him.

Chapter Two

'So, we'll get you an engagement ring as soon as you like,' Harry rattled on excitedly, his face wreathed in smiles. He was far too caught up in his own joy to notice any trace of negativity in Lola's reaction. 'Perhaps you might like us to go to a jeweller's shop in the West End together to choose one, unless you would prefer a surprise, in which case, you'll have to trust my judgement and I'll do my very best not to disappoint you.'

Lola didn't say anything.

'Whatever you want is fine by me, Lola, because you mean the absolute world to me,' Harry continued, joyfully in love and wanting only to please her. 'I've had a good bit of back pay recently so you can have something really nice. Oh, Lola, I'm so happy. I love you so very much.'

She remained silent, unable to say the words she knew she must now utter.

'Lola . . . what's the matter?' he asked, his excitement beginning to fade as her worried expression finally registered. 'You don't seem very happy. I thought you'd be as thrilled as I am for us to get engaged. We love each other, so surely it's the natural thing to do, isn't it?'

Still the silence, and now she was looking grim.

'You're beginning to scare me, Lola,' he said, looking at her closely, his voice gruff with emotion. 'So, what is it? What's the matter?'

At last she managed to find her voice. 'I can't marry you, Harry,' she said. 'I really am so sorry.'

He flushed, then turned pale. 'Can't marry me?' he said thickly. 'Why not? Whatever is the matter, Lola? We love each other, don't we? Or that's what I thought.'

She didn't reply at once. She had to choose her words carefully so as to leave him with no hope; she must avoid the possibility of his persuasion, which she didn't feel strong enough to resist. 'Well, yes, sort of, but not enough for such a huge commitment as marriage,' she lied. 'I can see that now.'

'What!' The colour drained from his face. 'So, what's the past few weeks been all about then?' he demanded. 'We've been absolutely besotted with each other.'

'You might have been. But not me,' she forced herself to lie. 'It's been a lot of fun – and I really like you a lot, Harry – but besotted, I don't think so.'

'You're lying,' he accused her, angry now because he was so shocked and disappointed. 'I know that you're not being truthful with me. Why are you saying these awful things, Lola? Why would you do this? I don't understand.'

'I'm not lying, I'm really not, Harry,' she forced herself to say. 'You've read too much into things, that's all. I've enjoyed our time together – of course I have – and I've absolutely loved being with you. It's been a lot of fun and I'm very fond of you. But marriage . . . oh, no, not for me at the moment.'

'I don't believe a word of it,' he said, his voice shaking. 'There's more to this than you're telling me and it has something to do with my joining the police. You were absolutely fine until I mentioned that.'

'You're wrong, Harry.' She forced herself on in an effort to convince him but her voice was trembling. 'How on earth could anything between us be connected to that?'

'I have no idea, but I'm certain that it has,' he said. 'Your attitude changed as soon as I mentioned it. Do you have something against coppers?'

'Of course not.'

'Then why . . .?'

'You're imagining things,' she lied. 'I'm sorry if I misled you about my feelings for you, I really am.'

'Not nearly as sorry as I am,' he said bitterly. 'But I know you don't mean it.'

'I do.'

'No, I just don't believe you,' he insisted. 'Something has happened to make you say these things. I'm sure of it. So please just tell me what it is and we'll sort it out together.'

'There's nothing to tell,' she said, on the brink of tears, but holding back so that he wouldn't guess the truth. She longed to be honest with him and giving him up was the most painful thing she had ever had to do. 'I wish you well with your new career, Harry, I really do, but I won't be part of it.'

'It's just a job,' he said miserably, all his excitement about the future now gone.

'That isn't true,' she said. 'You're really thrilled about it and it's much more than just a job to you, to anyone. Being in the police is a calling.'

'Maybe so,' he said, and she thought he was going to break down in tears but he managed to hold on to his self-possession. 'But I don't have to do it. There are plenty of other options open to me, other worthwhile careers that I could consider. Sure, I want to do something that matters, but you are far more important to me than any job. So, if you'd rather I didn't join the police, I won't. It's as simple as that.'

'But you really want to be a copper, don't you?'

'Well, yeah, but not as much as I want to be with you,' he said. 'So, as it obviously upsets you so much, I can do something else.' He looked at her. 'Is it because of the risks involved, the fear that I might get hurt? Is that the problem?'

'That sort of thing,' she fibbed.

'I suppose it could happen,' he said. 'But most policemen manage to survive and we'd both soon get used to the idea of the possible danger. But I can easily cancel my application if it means that much to you. You are far more important to me than any job. Just say the word and I'll change my plans.'

She was sorely tempted, but it could come between them later on, when he was older and realised that he had missed his chance. Anyway, it would be wrong to encourage him to give up something that obviously meant a lot to him. It really wouldn't be fair. 'No, don't do that. I won't change my mind. I'm really sorry.'

'Sorry doesn't go anywhere near what you've just done to me,' he said, angry now because he felt so helpless.

'Oh, Harry, I feel really awful about it.'

'Not half as awful as I do, I can promise you that.' He seemed broken but, as though suddenly managing to gather his dignity, he added bitterly, 'But I'll survive, Lola. I won't let this break me. I won't give you the satisfaction.'

'I don't want satisfaction. It isn't like that at all, Harry,' she said in a small voice. 'It might seem like it but it really isn't. You must know that I'm not that sort of person.'

'What is it all about then?' he demanded. 'For God's sake tell me so that we can deal with it together.'

'It's just . . . well, it's complicated.'

'Look, you either want to be with me or you don't, it's that simple.'

'It isn't.'

'Right, I've had enough of this,' he said, his voice gruff and shaky. 'Do you want to marry me or not?'

Lola took a deep breath. 'No,' she forced herself to lie, her voice trembling.

'Oh.' It was though she had slapped his face. 'In that case I won't waste another minute of my time with you.' He paused, staring at her with fury and hurt. 'You can't possibly know how disappointed I am in you, how devastated I am by your attitude. I really thought we had something special. That's how stupid I've been. But not any more; it ends now. Goodbye, Lola.' His voice was tight and bitter. He looked into her face as though searching for an answer. Then he turned and walked away.

She had to restrain herself from going after him because this must be a clean and lasting break and she dare not leave him with so much as a smidgeon of hope. That wouldn't be fair. For a few moments, she stood perfectly still, forcing herself not to follow him. Then she turned and began to walk home.

She couldn't face her family at the moment. She felt as though she hated her father for what he was, for what he had forced her to do, and she couldn't trust herself not to lash out at him and upset everybody. To go home wasn't an option while she felt like this so she headed to another house nearby where she knew she would be welcome.

* * *

'Well, that's a rotten blow for you,' said her good friend Doreen, having been told that Lola and Harry had broken up, but without any of the details. 'But you know the old saying about there being plenty more fish in the sea.'

Lola hadn't been able to tell her friend the truth about what had happened with Harry because Doreen knew nothing of Lola's father's illegal dealings, and that mustn't change. If Charlie chose to boast of his business, that was one thing, but Lola didn't want anyone to hear about it from her. If someone saw fit to tell the police, her dad would be sent to prison. There wasn't anyone Lola could confide in without betraying him. She had just told Doreen that she and Harry had had an argument and broken up. She had needed to tell someone even if she couldn't tell them the whole truth.

'Yeah, I have heard that saying but I really wanted that particular fish.'

'Go and get him back then,' suggested Doreen.

'There's more to it, Doreen,' Lola said. 'I can't tell you exactly what but, trust me, there is no going back.'

'In that case you'll have to find a new boyfriend,' suggested her friend.

'I can't even bear to consider that.'

'Then you'll have to live without one,' said Doreen. 'It is perfectly possible, you know. I do it quite happily for most of the time.'

'Yeah, I know you do, and I must do the same because I really don't want anyone else,' Lola said, but the future without Harry seemed bleak indeed.

'A new challenge, that's what you need,' suggested Doreen brightly. 'Something completely different to take your mind off things, especially men.'

'You're probably right, but you don't get offered many challenges when you work in a typing pool,' said Lola. 'The nearest thing to it is getting a late letter into the mail when the post room is closing for the day and they have done their figures. You have to literally beg the post girls to take it.'

'In that case you look for something worthwhile to do outside of work,' suggested Doreen. 'There are plenty of things out there to choose from. You'll recognise the opportunity when it comes along, and it will. You'll soon find something to take your mind off your broken heart. People do it all the time.'

'You've come over very wise all of a sudden,' said Lola. 'You sound about fifty.'

Doreen chuckled. 'Everyone seems to come to me with their problems, so sometimes I feel about fifty.'

'You're a good friend,' said Lola affectionately.

'You'd do the same for me if I needed it, I'm sure.'

'I certainly hope so,' said Lola warmly.

'You're home early,' remarked Lola's mother.

'Yeah, I've only been to see Doreen.'

'Where's your boyfriend tonight then?'

'I've no idea.'

'Oh, you've fallen out with him, have you?'

'I won't be seeing him again, if that's what you mean,' Lola said glumly.

'Oh dear,' said Rita, sounding genuinely sorry. 'That's a shame. You really seemed to like him.'

'I did. More than you can possibly imagine. But it hasn't worked out and I don't want to talk about it, Mum.'

'All right, keep your hair on,' Rita said. 'You should bring your friends home more often. It might make them feel as though you think something of them.'

'Oh, yeah,' said Lola with a bitter laugh. 'With Dad boasting about all his crooked deals, they're sure to be impressed, I don't think.'

'No one takes him seriously,' said Rita. 'It's just a bit of fun and everyone knows it.'

'His dodgy ways aren't "just a bit of fun", Mum,' said Lola seriously. 'They are illegal offences and one of these days someone is going to report him to the police if he doesn't stop boasting.'

'Ooh, I do hope not,' said Rita, as if she'd never thought of this before.

'Tell him to stop telling all and sundry about his crooked ways then,' said Lola. 'Better still, tell him to stick to the straight and narrow.'

'Since when has your father ever taken any notice of anything that I say?'

'There is that,' Lola had to agree. 'Perhaps you need to be more forceful with him, Mum.'

'It isn't in my nature,' she said.

'Mm, that is the problem,' Lola agreed. 'He's dominated you for so long, that's why. It'll be hard to break such a habit after all this time.'

'You're probably right,' Rita sighed. 'But your father and I have been married for a very long time and I'm used to the way things are. Obviously, I'd rather he didn't break the law but I can't change him so I just have to live with it. There could never be another man for me.' She paused and added rather mysteriously, 'Well . . . not that I would do anything about, anyway.'

'Is there someone you like then?' asked Lola curiously.

'Of course not,' denied her mother a little too quickly.

Lola wasn't entirely convinced but she just said, 'You don't need another man. You just need to stand up for yourself more with the one you've got.'

'I'm quite happy with the way things are between me and your father,' Rita said. 'The way they have always been. I certainly don't need advice from a youngster who knows very little about such things.'

Lola made a sudden decision. It wouldn't hurt her mother to know how far-reaching her husband's misdeeds were. 'Shall I tell you the real reason I broke up with Harry, Mum?'

'You said it didn't work out,' she said.

'I was telling fibs. It worked perfectly. In fact, he asked me to marry him,' she said. 'We absolutely adore each other but I had to make a choice. It was either him or Dad.'

'How do you mean?'

'Harry is about to join the Metropolitan Police,' she explained. 'If I were to marry him, which is what he wants, he would become part of this family and get to know the truth about Dad, especially as Dad makes no secret of his dodgy lifestyle. Being a policeman, Harry would feel duty bound to turn Dad in, I'm sure.'

'Oh my Gawd,' Rita said shakily. 'We can't have a copper in the family. Absolutely not!'

'Exactly! But giving him up broke my heart, Mum,' Lola said, fighting back tears. 'He means everything to me.'

'Oh, love, I'm so sorry,' said her mother, sounding genuinely sympathetic. She wasn't a hard woman; just completely in thrall to her husband, which meant that his needs came before anyone else's, even her daughter's. 'The only way you could do it is

31

to go away with your man, leave the area altogether, so that he'll never have to see your father.'

'I couldn't leave you and Frankie, and nor would you want me to,' Lola protested.

'You're right, I definitely wouldn't,' Rita agreed. 'But if it was the best thing for you, I'd have to put up with it. I know I'm weak as far is your father is concerned but I really do care about you and Frankie.'

'I know you do, Mum,' said Lola. 'Anyway, Harry is going in the Met so he has to be in London.'

'If I was a brave woman, I would work hard to persuade you to leave home and move to a different London neighbourhood to be with your bloke and away from your dad. But the idea of not having you around cripples me.'

'I won't leave, Mum, don't worry,' Lola assured her. 'Harry's family are local, anyway, so he wouldn't want to move away from here. And he would want to know why if I suggested such a thing. So, whatever I do, I can't escape from Dad's illegal dealings. They're casting a shadow over my whole life.'

'Yeah, suppose they would do,' her mother agreed sadly. 'You'll leave home to get married one day, of course, but I've always thought you'd stay local.'

'I probably will, but there's nothing like that in the offing at the moment so you can forget all about it. Harry is the only man for me, and if I can't have him I don't want anybody.'

'Aah, I'm so sorry, love. But you'll probably feel differently with time,' Rita said. 'We all alter our opinions as we get older.'

'Dad will always be a problem, though, because anyone I

go out with would be whiter than white. I wouldn't want to be with a crook. So I'll probably stay single.'

'I do hope not, Lola. I'd like to see you settled with some nice bloke. It's the natural way of things.'

'Yeah, I suppose it is, but Dad won't ever change, will he?'

'No, I don't believe he will,' Rita agreed, then paused thoughtfully. 'I am so sorry, Lola. I wish things were different and we were an ordinary family. I've tried many times in the past to get your dad to change but he doesn't take any notice of anything I say. So, I gave up in the end.'

Lola knew that she meant it. Mum was a good soul at heart; she was kind and affectionate, just lacking in courage, and dominated by her husband. Sometimes her submissiveness annoyed Lola but she tried to keep her feelings under control because she did love her mother very much indeed.

Rita was thinking that if it wasn't for the affection and moral support she received from a certain relative she didn't know how she would cope with the demands of her law-breaking husband. Her friendship with her brother-in-law Bert was purely platonic, but a real comfort to her and she thought the world of him. He was her rock!

When Harry left Lola he went to walk by the river, to calm his troubled mind and loosen the tension that was pulling tight inside him. He walked until his legs ached, then stopped at a pub on the riverside at Richmond. He wasn't feeling sociable so was glad that the pub was out of his own neighbourhood and there was nobody in there that he knew.

'Someone is thirsty,' remarked the friendly barman as he gave Harry the change from his first pint, which was being consumed at speed.

'Not thirsty, mate,' said Harry. 'Just drowning my sorrows.'

'Woman trouble, I bet.'

Harry nodded. 'What other kind is there?'

The man tutted sympathetically. 'You'll probably need a few of those then,' he said, referring to the beer. 'That's one good thing about woman trouble. It's very good for our business.'

'I suppose it would be,' said Harry. He wasn't feeling chatty and was glad that the barman moved away to serve someone else.

Harry went over his conversation with Lola again. He was absolutely convinced that there was some reason outside of their feelings for each other that had made Lola turn him down. Despite what he'd said to her in the misery of the moment he knew he could never love another woman as he loved her. He didn't want to be with anyone else.

The odd thing was she had accepted his proposal with delight at first, but changed her mind a few minutes later. She'd gone a bit quiet after he'd told her he was joining the Met. Some people were funny about coppers. But no, it wouldn't be that. She was far too sensible.

Something had put her off, though, he was sure of it. But if she loved him as he loved her, nothing would have made her turn him down. He knew somehow that there was no point in trying to persuade her to change her mind. She'd been absolutely definite.

As the beer calmed his nerves so his spirit returned. He didn't want any other woman so he would immerse himself in his new job. He wanted to be a good police officer so he would use all his energy to that end. Without Lola there would be nothing to distract him. The sooner he started work the better. He was going back to camp to get officially demobbed in a few days and then he could move on in his life.

But as Harry walked home his positive mood drained away. Without Lola there didn't seem to be much point in anything. He admonished himself: he was a very lucky man; he had come through the war unscathed; now a better life beckoned and he had a chance to make something of himself in the police force. He wasn't going to let Lola spoil all this for him. He did love her, though. So very much . . .

At the office a few days later, typing the letters from her shorthand pad, Lola could barely keep the tears away. She was still hurting from the break-up with Harry and she felt as if the pain would never go away. It was all very well for Doreen to talk about her finding a new challenge, but that wouldn't ease the ache in her heart, would it?

She supposed that her friend genuinely thought a distraction might help and she was probably right. But the nearest thing to a challenge she would find here was promotion from the typing pool to someone's secretary. That was the general ambition of the typists here, with marriage the glittering prize that would mean a husband to support them so they could eventually give up work. But if she couldn't have Harry she'd sooner stay single and make her own way in the world.

A tear ran down her cheek and landed on her pad. Oh, Harry, I love you so much, she said silently. Why did you have to spoil everything by joining the police force? But in her heart, she knew that it wasn't Harry who was the problem. Her father was.

As she got her letters typed and ready for signing, she wondered if she might be happier with a more general clerical job, perhaps in a smaller office where she would get to do more than just shorthand and typing. As a general clerk she would do filing and errands as well as correspondence. Some of it would be boring work and it would be a downward move, but it might be more to her taste, being more varied, which would take her mind off Harry. It could be worth considering.

Her parents heartily disapproved when she mentioned her thoughts over dinner that night.

'It's a ridiculous idea,' said her mother. 'After you went to night school for shorthand and typing for two years you want to give it all up and be the office girl again.'

'No, of course not,' said Lola. 'I'd still use my shorthand and typing but I think a smaller office might be more interesting. The work would be more varied.'

'If you want my advice, you'll stay where you are,' said her mother. 'You've got a good job. Don't throw it away to become the office errand girl.'

'Your mother is right,' said Charlie, who Lola knew would view the situation entirely in financial terms. His main concern would be that she had her pay packet on a Friday from which she paid her mother for her keep.

'Oh, well, it's just an idea,' she said. 'I heard someone on the wireless say that there are plenty of jobs about.'

'You can't believe what you hear on there,' said Rita.

'I don't see why not,' said Lola. 'They must get their information from people in the know.'

'I think Lola should do what she wants,' said Frankie, loyal as always.

'Thanks, kiddo,' she said, smiling at him. With the same honey-coloured hair and blue eyes as Lola, he looked a sweet kid, but Frankie was now showing signs of adolescence in quiet moods and rebelling against parental discipline, which his mum and dad didn't know how to handle. Charlie was nearly always too pre-occupied with his own interests to take any part in raising his kids and he left the discipline to Rita, who was always a soft touch. But despite this lack of parental guidance, Frankie was growing up to be a really nice boy and his sister adored him. 'I'll have a look in the job vacancies in the paper to see what's around. But don't worry, I won't do anything rash.'

'I should hope not,' said her father.

'I think I might aim for the West End,' Lola mentioned in a sudden burst of inspiration. 'The salaries are higher there and, as it's only a few stops on the tube, my fares won't be too much. I might as well take advantage of where we live.'

Her father brightened at this. 'Good idea,' he said, smiling at the mention of more money.

'I've got a few years' experience behind me so I should be in with a chance,' Lola continued. 'But I know the standard is high in West End offices.'

'As long as you don't hang about after work,' said her mother, concerned as ever for her daughter's wellbeing. 'Dodgy characters loiter in the West End.'

Lola laughed. 'I won't be in Piccadilly at midnight, Mum,' she said smiling. 'Anyway, I'm London born and bred – I'm used to going into the West End.'

'Yeah, I suppose so,' Rita agreed.

'What's brought all this job change business on, anyway?' asked Charlie.

'She's broken up with her boyfriend and needs something new to think about,' said Rita.

'Wouldn't it be simpler to just go to the pictures?' suggested Charlie, grinning.

'Oh, honestly,' said Rita, frowning at him. 'You men have no finer feelings.'

'That isn't true of me, Rita,' he said, laughing. 'You know how sensitive I am to your feelings. I always bring you a bottle of Guinness back from the pub.'

Rita tutted, Lola rolled her eyes disapprovingly and Frankie giggled. Lola despaired of ever being able to bring any decent, serious-minded person into this house. When the place wasn't full of crooks they had Dad's flippant remarks to contend with.

Later on, when her father had gone out, Lola sat listening to the wireless with Rita. Frankie was upstairs getting ready for bed. Lola found herself feeling stifled. She didn't want to be here listening to some boring play with her mother; she wanted to be with Harry. It was normal for a woman of her age to want her independence. Frankie would grow up and leave home, but she didn't see how she could do the same because of Mum. How could she leave her with her bully of a husband and his crooked mates?

Frankie breezed into the room in his pyjamas. 'I saved this for you,' he said, pressing an aniseed ball into his sister's hand.

It was sticky from his sweaty palm but it was part of his beloved sweet ration and had been given with love.

'Thanks, Frankie,' she said, a warm glow spreading over her, eliminating the gloom. Sweets were treasured in these hard times. 'I'll save it for later.'

He beamed at her. 'That's very strong willed of you. I wouldn't be able to save it. I'd have to eat it right away.'

'I'm a good example then,' she said.

Rita smiled but stayed quiet. She loved to see the siblings getting along. She wished things were different for them and they lived in a respectable house instead of one that had stolen goods hidden away in wardrobes and cupboards and the low life of the town on visiting terms.

She should have left Charlie years ago when she realised the extent of his illegal activities. He'd been law abiding during their early days together – always a bit flash, but he went to work every day in his job as a welder. Then he got to know a bloke in a pub with contacts in the black market and he'd got drawn into it. It hadn't stopped there either. He got involved in thieving as well, to the extent that he had even given up his regular job. She'd pleaded with him to go straight but all to no avail, and she'd lost hope long ago.

Rita kept up a united front with Charlie so that the children would think that she and their father were happy together, but she longed to get away from him, to have a normal life without fear. As things were at the moment, she lived in terror that the police were going to come and take him away. As much she had grown to dislike him, she didn't want him to go to prison. Even apart from the fact that he supported her, she hated the thought of his being confined with all the other villains.

And, of course, there would be the gossip to contend with. Paradoxically, too, he could still very occasionally make her heart beat faster as he had when they were young. There was just no accounting for human nature.

Although she hadn't made much of it to Lola, she was very upset that her daughter had had to give up the chap she was so keen on because of her father. But it was the only thing she could do under the circumstances. A copper in the family meant certain arrest for Charlie.

So all Rita could do was carry on until the children had left home and were living their own lives. She hoped that by then she would have the courage to leave. The idea terrified her, but the further she was away from Charlie the better. Anyway, that was all far in the future, especially as Frankie was only twelve.

'Why don't you go round to Doreen's, Lola?' she suggested now. 'Have a spot of company of your own age.'

'I think I will, Mum,' said Lola, relieved to get out of the house.

'I think I've found that challenge we were talking about,' Lola said to Doreen.

'Good. Are you going to climb up a mountain?'

'Of course not, but I am going to look for a new job – in the West End.'

'Ooh, good luck with that,' said Doreen with enthusiasm. 'Good pay up West, so I've heard, though I'll miss you around the office.'

'Hard work, too, I expect,' said Lola. 'But I'll be glad of something to take my mind off things.'

'I'll be interested to know how you get on,' said Doreen. 'You never know, I might follow you there. I could do with a bit more dosh in my purse.'

'I'll keep you posted,' said Lola, and they went on to look at the local paper to see what was on at the pictures with a view to going one night this week.

'Oh my word,' said Marg one evening when her son appeared in his police uniform for the first time. 'You look marvellous, Harry, doesn't he, Michael?'

'He certainly does,' agreed her husband proudly. 'You've got a lot to live up to, though, wearing that.'

'It's a bit scary,' said Ruby. 'You look like a policeman.'

'That's what he is,' said her mother, laughing.

'But he doesn't look like my brother.'

'You'll soon get used to it,' said Harry, but he did feel honoured to be a member of the Metropolitan Police, albeit a raw recruit at the moment.

'We're very proud of you, Harry,' said his grandfather. 'Ain't that right, Nell?'

'Ooh, not 'alf,' Nell beamed.

'I don't know if I will change into civvies at the station before I come home in future,' Harry said. 'I just wanted to give you a little preview.'

'We're very glad you did, son,' said Marg, to general agreement.

'You're a credit to us,' said Michael.

Harry grinned, enjoying the praise. His parents' opinion meant a lot to him but the most important person in his life was missing and he wondered if he'd ever get over losing Lola.

It didn't matter what he did, how deeply involved he was in any aspect of his life, she was always there on his mind.

A few miles away in her bedroom, Lola was thinking much the same about Harry. She had a job interview in the West End the following day with a well-known and prestigious company, and when she should be looking ahead to that, all she could think about was Harry and how much she was missing him.

If she got the job, which carried a higher salary and more responsibility, she hoped she would be too busy with that to dwell too much on the past. But she knew in her heart that thoughts of Harry wouldn't be far away.

Chapter Three

Although Lola wasn't unduly sensitive, she was quick to realise that the woman who was interviewing her for a job hadn't taken a liking to her. Having quizzed Lola at unnecessary length about her shorthand and typing skills, the chief clerk, Miss Soames, went on to explain the company dress code in an almost threatening manner.

'We are a very well-known and respected West End company in our field, and as such we insist on our staff creating a smart image, which means being suitably dressed in the office at all times,' said Miss Soames, casting a critical eye over Lola's white cotton blouse and summer skirt. 'Black skirts and stockings, always stockings. No bare legs, not even during one of London's rare heatwaves.'

As Lola went to speak the older woman, who was middle aged and drably immaculate in a high-necked navy-blue blouse with a dark grey skirt, her hair welded into symmetrical waves, beat her to it. 'I realise that we are still in the grip of clothes rationing but that doesn't alter the dress code here at this company. Our staff are expected to use the majority of their clothing coupons for smart office wear rather than outfits for leisure time. Work must be your priority. Our employers are top lawyers in their field and the company has a reputation to maintain, so we never let our standards slip. The clients would disapprove most strongly of that.'

'Yes, of course,' said Lola.

'The top brass here are extremely fussy about staff appearance,' she added unnecessarily.

This last remark was one too many for Lola. 'Surely the standard of the work is more important, isn't it?' she heard herself say, knowing as the words hit the air that any chance of a job here was lost.

'Well . . . obviously,' ground out Miss Soames, almost choking in an attempt to make her tone sufficiently cutting. 'But we back that up with a smartly dressed workforce.'

Lola played it safe and just nodded. She was longing to escape from this awful interview so she was pleased when Miss Soames said, 'I have a few more people to see. I'll be in touch when I've made my decision.'

Lola thanked her politely and left, guessing that she wouldn't get the job and feeling very relieved. She didn't fancy working under such a cold, dislikeable woman. There was no urgency about a new job. Her current position was perfectly adequate, and she was only trying to better herself in the hope that a more fulfilling occupation might take her mind off Harry.

The interview had taken place in an elegant old house converted into offices in a side street just a few minutes' walk from Marble Arch. Outside it was a glorious afternoon with low sunlight, the air tinged with the smoky scent of incipient autumn. As usual in the West End there were lots of people about, all hurrying this way and that, creating an air of bustle and energy that always struck Lola when she was here.

On her way back to the tube station to get the underground home, Lola passed a small parade of shops where she noticed an establishment called The Tulip Tearooms. As she had taken a full day of her annual leave and had the rest of the afternoon to herself, she had time for a fortifying cup of tea after the horrible interview with Miss Soames, so she headed for the tearooms' door.

It was the strangest café Lola had ever been in. Most places were run down after the war and this was no exception. But despite the shabbiness it had a peculiar elegance, with high-backed chairs and round tables adorned with lace-edged tablecloths, which had obviously seen better days but still had a touch of class about them. Table linen, like all fancy goods, was in very short supply in these times of crippling shortages. On one wall there was a large painting of a vase of tulips in a glorious shade of yellow.

'My father fancied himself as an artist,' explained a middle-aged woman who came to greet Lola. 'As a work of art, it is flawed, but as a reminder of Daddy it is a joy for my sister and me. It will always be centre stage here while we are running the place.'

Lola found her remark rather moving. This was obviously a family-run business and meant a lot to the woman. There were various old-fashioned photographs displayed on the walls, which Lola guessed had some past connection to the family. Despite the general dilapidation there was a nice feeling about the place, a warm atmosphere, and quite a few customers, which created a pleasant, sociable buzz.

The woman showed Lola to a corner table and left her

alone to look at the menu, which was basic, in keeping with the hard times. She reappeared a few minutes later for Lola's order. Definitely not a typical waitress. Even apart from the fact that she was so much older than usual for serving staff, she was somewhat odd in appearance; tall, middle aged and rather plain, with her hair plaited and wound around her head and her face devoid of make-up. She was wearing a dismal brown dress with a dull cream-coloured pinafore and looked as though she belonged in a bygone period of history. Lola wondered if she was the owner, and waitressing herself to avoid the expense of hiring someone, or if she liked to be involved. She sensed somehow that the latter was the case.

'Are you ready to order?' the woman asked with vowels more suited to a private school staffroom than a teashop, although this *was* the West End, Lola reminded herself.

'Just a pot of tea, please,' said Lola.

'May I tempt you to one of our scones?' the woman asked. 'They've only just come out of the oven,' she added.

Lola supposed they had a surplus and she wasn't really hungry, but the woman was oddly persuasive with a hint of warmth behind her cool brown eyes, so Lola said, 'Yes, all right then. Thank you very much.'

The woman smiled and went to fetch the order with an ungainly walk. She really was quite odd looking: tall with noticeably large feet and hands, her appearance not helped by her awful attire.

Lola sank into a low mood as she thought back on her job interview. Not an impressive performance and certainly not one that would win her the position. Since she'd broken up with Harry, she didn't seem able to do anything right. It was as though all the heart had gone out of her. She really must try harder to regain her zest for life before any more job interviews.

By the time the waitress returned with her tea and scone, Lola was deep in thought.

'I managed to find you a knob of butter,' said the woman, smiling, which softened her rather harsh appearance. 'I hope you enjoy your scone.'

'I'm sure I will. Thank you,' said Lola, too immersed in her own thoughts to pay much attention, though butter instead of margarine was a real treat, and she did notice friendliness in the woman's eyes.

Absently she spread the butter on the scone and took a bite. Now she did pay attention because it was absolutely delicious! She had never tasted a scone quite like it before. Light, creamy and with just the right amount of sweetness. It was so tasty it lifted her mood and she made a point of telling the waitress when she came over to ask if everything was to her liking. 'Perfect,' she said. 'The scone was lovely.'

'Thank you, my dear. I'm glad you enjoyed it. It's an old recipe passed down through generations of our family and now known only to my sister and myself,' she said.

'Your customers are very privileged, then, that you have such a gem.'

'We like to think so.' She paused then launched into an unsolicited account of herself. 'I'm Cissy Pickford and my sister Ethel and I run the tearooms together. It belonged to our parents originally.' She paused, looking downhearted. 'Sadly, both were killed in the Blitz, bless them.'

Lola nodded politely and introduced herself.

'Ethel and I are certain that our parents would want the tearooms to continue and stay in the family,' Miss Pickford continued. 'The place was closed during the war while we were all on war work so we have to build up the trade again from scratch.'

'With scones like that I shouldn't think it will take you very long at all.'

'Thank you. It's a challenge for us. We need something to do now that the war is over. We can't just sit about all day. That wouldn't be very interesting, would it?'

'I suppose not,' said Lola politely.

'The scone recipe goes back to my great-grandmother. People came from miles away for our scones before the war,' Miss Pickford said wistfully. 'Some came into the West End specially to pay us a visit. Of course, in these times of rationing we are limited in what we can offer, but we are looking forward to better days ahead.'

'I'm not surprised that people travel to come here,' said Lola. 'Your lovely scone certainly cheered me up. I've just been for an awful job interview so I was feeling a bit low when I came in.'

'Oh, really? What was so bad about it?'

There was something so compelling about her, Lola found herself relating the whole sorry incident.

'Sounds awful,' said Cissy, who was now sitting down at the table and listening with interest. 'We can all do without that sort of thing in our lives, can't we?'

'It certainly wasn't pleasant. Some people can make you feel so small, can't they?'

'They sometimes try, but they don't have much luck with my sister and me,' she said. 'We went to the sort of school where self-confidence is compulsory and it stays with you through life, which is just as well, as we are dealing with the public every day and it isn't always easy.'

Lola was wondering how a modest tearoom could support the sort of school that left you with a cut-glass accent when Cissy explained: 'Our parents owned several very successful restaurants in and around London before the war, some quite sizeable too. We were lucky enough to have rather a privileged upbringing.'

'Do you still have the other restaurants?'

'No, our parents sold them all except this one. They were afraid they would lose them to the bombs so thought the money was safer in the bank,' she explained. 'This was their first one and their favourite. The family home is upstairs, and Ethel and I live here. That's why we decided to reopen after the war. Everything is on hand and we know the business inside out. Our parents owned the building and we inherited it so there was nothing to stop us, especially as they left us their special recipes.'

Lola nodded politely, finding it difficult to imagine not having to work for the money.

'So, what was the job you had the interview for?' Cissy Pickford enquired.

'Clerical work,' Lola replied. 'I'm a shorthand typist, actually, although I wouldn't mind a spot of general office work too, filing and so on. But I definitely won't get that job, which is probably just as well as I don't fancy working for that awful woman.'

'It's quite a coincidence because we are looking for someone to run our office, as it happens,' Cissy said. 'We are both too busy baking and running the café to look after the paperwork, and things are getting out of control. Our gift lies with cooking, and office work is a real chore to us. So, we need someone to take it over completely: pay the bills, deal with the correspondence, keep the accounts in order for the accountant to do once a year. There wouldn't be much short-hand involved, but some typing is necessary and the work would be quite varied.'

'Sounds as though you might be offering me a job,' said Lola.

'Well, yes . . . Perhaps we could have a chat about it, if you are interested. We will offer a decent salary.' A group of people came into the café and those already there were needing attention so Cissy stood up. 'If you fancy the idea, would it be possible for you to come back later on, when the tearooms are closed? You can meet my sister then, too. As we live in the flat upstairs, we're on hand.'

Lola agreed to go back later on. She felt oddly excited, as though she had wandered into a strange new world, but one in which she could feel comfortable.

Lola's father was much less impressed. 'That's a diabolical liberty,' he raged when she told the family she was planning to go back to the tearooms when she'd finished her evening meal. 'Expecting you to trail all the way back to the West End. I hope they are going to reimburse you for the fare.'

'I'm sure they will if I ask them,' she said. 'She seemed a very nice lady. But as it's only a few stops on the tube I doubt if I'll even bother to mention it.'

'You must, Lola,' he demanded. 'They can't expect you to spend money on their account. But, personally, I don't think you should go back there at all. The job would be one hell of a downward move.'

'How do you work that out, Dad?' asked Lola.

'Isn't it obvious? At the moment you work for a big,

well-known and respectable company.' Family connections to a reputable company meant a lot to Charlie because he thought it covered his own questionable activities. 'And you're going to give it all up for some tinpot job in a backstreet café in the West End.'

'It isn't a tinpot job, at all,' she protested. 'It's a very nice tearooms and I would be in charge of the office; my responsibility and I could run it my way.'

'It's a backstreet café and you'd be the only one in the office,' he said. 'You're not going to be Secretary of the Year in that sort of set-up, are you?'

'I don't want to be Secretary of the Year, Dad,' she told him. 'I just want a job I'll enjoy, with decent pay. I think this one qualifies on both counts.'

'You don't know what the pay is yet.'

'That's true, and if it isn't enough, I won't take the job,' she said. 'But I am definitely going back to find out.'

'Oh, well, I can't stop you, I suppose,' he sighed.

'That's right, Dad, you can't.'

'That's enough, both of you,' Rita intervened, looking flushed. She hated any sort of altercation. 'Let's finish our meal in peace.'

'Sorry, Mum,' said Lola, while her father remained silent because apologies didn't feature in his vocabulary.

Frankie erupted into nervous giggles because the atmosphere had become so tense. Lola gave him a supportive wink. Her kid brother had a special place in her heart.

Lola found Cissy's sister Ethel to be equally eccentric. They both resembled figures from photographs Lola had seen of olden times. Ethel was a greyish blonde, but her hair was taken back into a bun so tightly that the colour wasn't really noticeable. She was a sweet soul, though, and the less vocal of the sisters.

'It would really help if you joined us,' she said to Lola in a soft voice. 'Neither of us enjoys clerical work. We have enough to do running the tearooms so the office work is a burden. We should have advertised for someone ages ago but we've been too busy with the tearooms to get around to it.'

'Well, so long as we can agree terms, I'll be happy to join you,' said Lola smiling.

Cissy gave her the terms, which were very acceptable, so Lola took the job and agreed to start when she had worked her week's notice in her present employment. She left feeling pleased with herself for the first time since she'd parted from Harry.

'I hope you know what you are doing,' said her doom-laden father over supper.

'I certainly do, Dad,' Lola said, smiling at him. 'So leave me to get on with it and stop worrying.'

'A café sounds good to me,' said Frankie. 'They might give you leftover cakes to bring home.'

'Trust you to think of that,' Lola said. Her brother's ferocious appetite was badly affected by food rationing. 'But don't worry, kid: if there are any perks, you'll be first in the queue.'

They all smiled, even her father.

'Sounds good to me,' said Doreen when Lola called on her and gave her an update later on. 'But won't you miss having young people around? From what you've said, the sisters are getting on a bit.'

'I hadn't thought about that,' admitted Lola. 'I've been so caught up with the job and the higher salary I haven't really got around to the basics. But they are ever such nice people and I think it will be fine. We won't be on top of each other. They'll be in the café and I'll be in the office. Anyway, you can't have everything, and I'll get used to it.'

'That's true,' Doreen agreed. 'It'll be lovely working in the West End too. You'll be able to look around the dress shops in your lunch hour and tell me about the latest trends.'

'I'll be wanting to buy all the fashionable things that I can't afford,' Lola said, grinning. 'Though it's a higher salary so I'll be able to buy more than I can now.'

'Lucky you – and the best thing about all this is that it's taken your mind off Harry,' said Doreen. 'I was right when I said you needed a new challenge.'

The new job hadn't taken Lola's mind off Harry at all. He was still uppermost in her thoughts and in her heart all of the time. But Doreen was happy thinking otherwise so Lola just said, 'Yeah, there is that.'

Harry was enjoying his job as a policeman enormously and knew he had made the right decision in joining the force. He was glad of the involvement because it helped to take his mind off Lola, though she was still there in his thoughts for most of the time. His initial, basic training was over, but there were other courses to come, as there would be throughout his career.

'What's going on over there?' Harry said now to his colleague Archie, an older, more experienced officer, as the two of them walked the early morning beat through Hammersmith and Harry noticed a man doing something to the door of a tobacconist's shop. 'He wouldn't be trying to break in at six o'clock in the morning, surely?'

'Never underestimate the mind of a criminal, son,' said Archie.

He and Harry ran across the road towards the wrongdoer, who spotted them and tore down the street. Harry followed speedily and very soon caught him.

'Oi, this is a dead liberty,' protested the man as Harry marched him back to his colleague, having told him his rights. 'I ain't doing nothin' wrong and you've got no right to manhandle me. I shall make a complaint about police brutality.'

'You can do that back at the nick,' said Archie.

'I bloody well will, an' all,' the suspect grumbled.

Harry and Archie escorted him to the police station and left him complaining to anyone who would listen when they returned to the beat. Sometimes there was very little for them to attend to on the early morning shift because there weren't many people about. But today they had another attempted break-in, a lost child, a cyclist riding on the pavement and, as always, people asking them the time. Then it was back to the station for a team meeting and paperwork.

Because he was on early shift, it was still light when Harry walked home, feeling as near happy as he could be without Lola in his life. He wondered how she was and what she was doing these days. Had she found another boyfriend? He really must try harder to forget her, although he knew that it was impossible. Maybe with more time he would think about her less, but forget her? Never!

*   *   *

On her first morning in the new job Lola wished she had never agreed to work there. The office was in a total state of chaos. There were invoices and receipts stuffed in drawers and cupboards, the daily takings book was barely legible and a mountain of paperwork covered the desk. Lola had been interviewed in the café, so this was her first sight of the office. It was a real shock and she really didn't know where to start.

'Bit of a mess, I'm afraid, my dear,' said Cissy brightly, in her posh voice. 'But I'm sure you'll soon sort it out, a bright gel like you.'

'Yes, of course I will,' said Lola bravely, although she was not at all sure that she could, or that anyone would be able to make sense of this muddle.

'I'll make you a cup of tea to help you along, and I might even find a biscuit or two,' said Ethel, and Lola felt her eyes burn with tears. The boss making the hired help a cup of tea on her first morning? It was such an unusual and kind thing to do. Lola was determined to make a success of this job somehow and restore order to their chaotic office.

'Thank you very much,' she said thickly.

'I knew you shouldn't have left the other job,' said her father when Lola told her family about her first day at The Tulip Tearooms over dinner, at which Uncle Bert was a guest, as he so often was. 'This new place doesn't sound at all professional. They might not have any money to pay you with on Friday.'

'Of course, they will, Dad,' she assured him. 'They are just a bit disorganised on the clerical side, that's all. The Pickford sisters have plenty of money that they've inherited, anyway, and the tearooms ticks over quite nicely, I think. There were a lot of customers.'

'I still don't trust them,' he said gloomily.

'How can you say that when you've never met them?' asked Bert. 'You haven't even seen the place.'

'It's a gut feeling. Anyway, I can easily get to see the place,' said Charlie. 'I'll go and have a look at the weekend.'

'So long as you don't go barging in there upsetting the ladies,' said Lola, whose working hours didn't include weekends, although the tearooms were open.

'As if I would.'

'Not half you would, and please don't, Dad,' said Lola, worriedly. 'They are refined ladies. They wouldn't take kindly to your brash attitude.'

'No, you mustn't go and cause a disturbance, Charlie,' said Bert. 'You don't want to embarrass Lola.'

'Anyone would think I don't know how to behave, the way you lot carry on,' Charlie objected. 'But I'll keep away, don't worry. Seeing as it won't make any difference to the way I feel. For what it's worth, I think you've made a big mistake, Lola.'

'You'll just have to live with it, Dad, because I am going to give the job a fair chance,' she said firmly. 'I made good progress today and I really enjoyed it. Once I got started it wasn't too bad and I'm arranging the office to suit myself as I'll be the only one using it. I wanted a job where I could use my initiative and I've certainly got that.'

'Well done, love,' said her uncle. He turned to Charlie. 'You should be really proud of your daughter, Charlie. She's a proper little gem and not afraid to try new things. I don't know why you are so down on her.'

'I'm not down on her at all,' Charlie denied. 'I want the best for her and I don't trust her judgement, that's all. She's young; she can't read people like I can.'

'You've never even met these women so you're not in a position to judge them.'

'I've heard enough about them to know what they are like,' Charlie insisted.

'Well, I think she's done the right thing in taking on this challenge.' Bert smiled at Lola. 'She's having a go and I admire her for it. Well done, love.'

'Thanks, Uncle Bert,' Lola said fondly.

'Well said, Bert,' added her mother, smiling at him.

'I think those ladies sound really nice,' said Frankie.

'If all goes well, I'll take you to meet them one day,' Lola told him. 'It's bound to be worth at least one of their lovely cakes.'

'Ooh, good,' enthused her brother.

'Oh, well, I can't sit here all night talking to you lot,' interrupted Charlie, looking sour. 'I've places to be, people to see.'

'Your crooked mates, I suppose,' said Bert.

'"Well connected" is the way I would describe them,' said Charlie. 'So, if you'll excuse me, I'll be off.'

He left the table and the others continued chatting, unconcerned by his departure. Charlie made his own rules and courtesy didn't play much of a role in his life. The rest of the family were used to it.

It was Saturday afternoon in the West End and Charlie was standing across the road from The Tulip Tearooms, observing the scene. There were plenty of people about and the tearooms seemed busy enough. Despite his promise to his daughter, he had intended to go inside and introduce himself to the two old girls his daughter worked for, but then something else had caught his attention and he'd changed his mind.

He'd come here purely out of curiosity. He'd heard so much about the place he thought he'd take a look for himself. He liked to keep a fatherly eye on his children's lives; it was no more than his duty. As it happened, it had proved to be a very worthwhile exercise. Not because of the tearooms – they looked perfectly legit – but because of what was next door. It was a jeweller's shop and looked as though it had once been a part of the tearooms, which meant that probably only one interior wall stood between the tearooms and a shop full of top-class sparklers. He'd had a look in the window and it was all high-price stuff. What a gift!

With his daughter working next door at the tearooms, access to the jewellers should be a breeze. It would take careful planning but there was no hurry. When the time is right, Charlie, me old mate, he told himself, when the time is right . . .

Brothers Charlie and Bert were having a pint together in the pub a few days later when Bert said, 'Don't you think it's about time you gave up all this dodgy stuff? Small-time crime and such.'

'Why would I do that?' Charlie asked.

'Because it's wrong, and one of these days the police are going to come knocking at your door.'

'Not on your life, mate,' Charlie said arrogantly. 'I've managed to avoid them for very many years, and there's no reason why they would catch up with me now.'

'I wouldn't be so sure of that.'

Charlie shrugged.

'Think of your family,' persisted Bert, who worried a great deal about his brother's sordid way of life. Despite Charlie's wrong-doings Bert still cared about him, and even more so about his family. 'Life won't be much fun for them if you're in the nick.'

'I'm not going to prison, mate. Not on your life.'

Bert sighed and sipped his beer. 'I can't understand why you do it,' he said.

'Isn't it obvious? So that me and the family can have a better life, of course.'

'But you don't do anything different from anyone else around here,' Bert remarked. 'I mean, you haven't moved to a better house; you don't shower your wife with gifts. In fact, you very rarely even take her out.'

'She isn't kept short,' said Charlie. 'No one can be showered with gifts these days anyway because there's so little to give. But you wait until I do a really big job. Rita will have the lot then: a big house, nice clothes, everything. We'll have a car. Rationing will end eventually so there'll be nothing stopping me.'

Bert sighed. He knew that Rita wasn't interested in any of those things and would much rather her husband led an honest life. 'You and your dreams,' he said. 'Is that why you do it? So that you can dream about the golden future?'

'Everybody should have a dream,' Charlie said.

'Maybe so, but preferably about something legal,' said Bert.

'You've always been a stick-in-the-mud,' said Charlie with blatant disapproval. 'Never wanted to take a chance. You're content with your boring job and low wages. I mean, who in their right mind wants to go out reading gas meters all day?'

'I do, and that is only part of my job at the gas board, as you very well know. Anyway, it's an honest living and I earn a decent wage,' said Bert. 'More than enough for what I need.'

'That's the difference between us,' said Charlie. 'I've always had that extra something that makes me want more and gives me the bottle to do something about it.'

'You see yourself as some sort of glamour boy, don't you?' said Bert. 'But you're not. You're just a small-time crook who is destined to end up in prison.'

'Never in a million years,' said Charlie, laughing.

Realising that he was wasting his time trying to reform his brother, Bert changed the subject to something that was close to both their hearts: football and their favourite team. All else was forgotten as they discussed their soccer heroes. A love of 'the game' was one thing they did have in common.

There was a heated argument in progress at The Tulip Tearooms, between the sisters. Lola was busy in her office but she could hear them at it hammer and tongs in the restaurant while they were laying the tables, prior to opening. The disagreement seemed to be about who was responsible for a batch of scones being overcooked.

'I told you to remind me to take them out of the oven at ten thirty,' said Cissy.

'I forgot, it happens to us all sometimes,' said Ethel. 'Anyway, they were your scones, your responsibility, so don't try to put the blame on me. You should have set the alarm. It was most unprofessional not to.'

'I didn't think I needed to as I'd asked you to remind me,'

her sister said. 'You are to blame, partly, anyway. You should have said something.'

'That is most unfair to blame me for your mistake.'

'Oh, I'm sick of you and sick of this place,' said Cissy in a sudden explosion. 'I'm leaving and you can have the bloody tearooms to yourself. Then you'll only have yourself to blame when things go wrong. I don't want to see another scone for as long as I live.'

'Don't be so ridiculous,' said Ethel. 'Mistakes happens to the best of us. Anyway, you are responsible for the scones you make, the same as I am when I'm baking them.'

These flare-ups were quite regular and Lola knew it was time for an intervention. So, she got up and went to the kitchen next door and made some tea, which she took through to them.

'Time for a cuppa, ladies,' she said.

'It will take more than tea, Lola,' said Cissy, scowling.

'It certainly will,' added Ethel.

'I know that. I just thought it might calm you both down. Anyway, you might as well have it, as I've made it,' said Lola. 'We can't let it go to waste.'

'No, of course not. Thank you, dear,' said Cissy. 'You are a very kind girl.'

'Hear, hear,' added Ethel, and the two women sat down at one of the tables with the tea.

Lola went back to her office, confident that all would be well between them within a very short time. Their arguments were frequent, but reconciliations never took long. They were a strange pair and their past seemed mysterious to an ordinary working-class girl like Lola. Men's names were mentioned and various well-known social occasions the ladies had attended in their youth. How two rich women with a tantalising past had ended up making scones for a living, Lola couldn't imagine. From her office work Lola didn't think they needed the money, so she assumed it was simply a love of the job. Most of the time they enjoyed it, you could tell.

Oh, well, they paid her wages and treated her really well so their circumstances were none of her business. They intrigued her, though, because she had never met anyone quite like them before. She had become really rather fond of them already.

Chapter Four

A good sense of humour was a huge asset in the police force; at least it was at Harry's nick, where the ribbing was merciless and nobody was spared. The banter was mostly of a male nature as there were very few female police officers working from this station, although Harry had heard that their numbers were beginning to rise elsewhere. He enjoyed the job enormously, though, and took all the teasing in his stride. The ability to smile in the face of adversity was essential in this profession because it could be grim at times. There were things a police officer had to see that the public were spared, often gruesome, terrible things: death, disaster and human nature at its worst.

But there was no other job he wanted to do and he was hoping to apply for the CID eventually, although he needed to prove himself as a uniformed copper for a few years first.

It was February 1947 and the current subject under discussion in the locker room, as the men came off duty, was Harry's single status.

'You should get out there and find yourself a good woman, mate,' said his pal Archie, otherwise known as PC Carter, who was forever extolling the advantages of the matrimonial state.

'There's no fun at all in being alone. You need a wife by your side. It's the best feeling in the world. You can't beat it.'

'That is one thing I really don't need at the moment, thanks very much,' said Harry. 'Absolutely not. It's the single life for me from now on. It's a damned sight simpler and much less painful.'

'Don't blame you, mate,' said another of the lads. 'Women are nothing but trouble.'

'That's defeatist talk,' Archie came back at Harry quickly. 'You can't be on your own for evermore just because of one setback.'

'I don't see why not,' said Harry. 'I'd sooner be single than dumped by some woman.'

'That will probably never happen again.'

'Too right it won't, because I'm steering well clear,' he said. 'Lola was the only girl for me, anyway. If I can't have her, I don't want anybody.'

'You're going to be a right miserable sod then, and we can't have that, can we, lads?' said Archie. There was a roar of agreement. 'You have to get back out there and find yourself a girl.'

'Not for me, thanks,' said Harry. 'Definitely a case of once bitten, twice shy.'

'All right then, let's leave women out of it altogether for the moment,' said the unstoppable Archie. 'But why don't we have a lads' night out sometime soon and discuss everything except Harry's lack of a love life over a few pints?' He paused, grinning. 'If I can square it with the missus, of course.'

'What was all that about you wearing the trousers in your house, then?' asked one of the men.

'I do . . . so long as I have the wife's permission,' Archie replied, causing a roar of laughter.

'I'll come for the booze and the company, but at the first mention of my non-existent love life I'll be gone, and that's definite,' said Harry.

'Right, everybody, Harry's love life is off limits, but let's have a boozy night out anyway,' enthused Archie. 'We need to find a night when most of us are off duty.'

They consulted the duty rota and the date was set for several weeks ahead. But as much as Harry enjoyed his fellow officers' company, he couldn't raise much enthusiasm for any sort of socialising these days. Nothing was the same since he'd lost Lola. However, the blokes were good mates and meant well so he would make an effort to please them.

'Surely you must sometimes come across men that you fancy,' Doreen said to Lola as they walked home from the cinema one cold night in March 1947, having just seen a film with Humphrey Bogart and Lauren Bacall called *The Big Sleep*. 'I mean, Harry couldn't have killed off your normal human instincts altogether, surely. It's natural for us to be attracted to people.'

'Well, it isn't happening for me at the moment,' said Lola. 'I have no interest whatsoever. If Gary Cooper walked into my bedroom stark naked, I wouldn't give him a second glance.'

Doreen thought that was very funny. 'I think you would, you know,' she said giggling, 'but you're safe in saying it as it'll never happen.'

'Exactly,' smiled Lola. 'But honestly, I am not looking for another romance at the moment.

'I suppose you get chaps showing an interest, though, don't

you?' suggested Doreen. 'Working in a café, you must meet quite a few of them.'

'I'm tucked away in the office for most of the time so I don't get to see anyone very much, but I do sometimes help out in the café, and yes, I do get chaps giving me the eye then,' Lola admitted. 'Posh types, some of them, too. They work in the nearby offices and it's quite a classy area. The tearoom is rather select, too, actually.'

'So, you might find a chap with a few quid in his pocket then,' Doreen suggested.

'I probably could if I was looking, which I'm not,' Lola answered. 'But some of them do give me that certain look.'

'And how do you react?'

'I pretend not to notice.'

'That's no good, Lola, although I suppose that would change if you were to see someone that you really fancy,' Doreen suggested.

'Possibly,' said Lola, vaguely.

'I know you think you'll never be interested in anyone except Harry but I'm sure you will in time. It's only natural.'

'We'll just have to wait and see what happens, won't we?' Lola replied.

'I know one bloke who really fancies you,' said Doreen.

'Who's that?'

'My brother's mate Keith,' she said. 'He's always talking about you.'

'Is he really?'

'Yeah, he thinks you're wonderful.' She made a face. 'Unfortunately for me, because I rather fancy him myself.'

'I'll be happy to stand back then. I've never thought of him in terms of a boyfriend anyway,' said Lola. She'd known Keith for years because he lived in the same area and they had all grown up together.

'There's no point in doing that,' said Doreen. 'You not being interested won't make him want me, will it?'

'It could do when he thinks things over, with me out of the picture,' suggested Lola. 'I mean, I like him and get on well enough with him when I see him around town or at your house, but he's never indicated anything other than friendship and that has certainly never occurred to me.'

'He probably doesn't have the nerve to say anything; he isn't the pushy type at all, bless him,' said Doreen. 'Don't let on that you know, for goodness' sake. He might be angry if he found out that I'd mentioned it.'

'My lips are sealed,' said Lola. It was nice to know that she had one admirer, anyway.

Lola was greeted in the hall by Frankie when she got home.

'Dad's drunk,' he informed her, looking worried.

'Oh, no, not again.' This wasn't a rare occurrence. 'What's he doing this time?'

'Acting really stupid, and Mum is ever so angry with him,' he said shakily.

'Oh, honestly, that flaming man,' Lola tutted. 'Don't worry, Frankie, we'll sort him out together.'

She found her parents on the sofa in the living room, her mother shrinking away from her husband's amorous advances. At least he was never violent in drink, just extremely annoying.

'Get off me,' Rita was saying. 'Go away and leave me alone. I mean it, Charlie.'

'Don't be like that,' he said in a soppy voice. 'You know very well that you like it.'

'There's a time and place for everything and I don't want you anywhere near me when you're drunk,' she said. 'So, go away and stay away until you're sober.'

'Aw, don't be so mean,' he whined.

'Don't make a fool of yourself in front of the children,' warned Rita. 'Just go away and leave me alone.'

'You heard what she said, Dad,' said Lola firmly. 'Go to bed, for goodness' sake.'

'I won't be told what to do by a slip of a girl,' he objected woozily.

'Don't bully Mum then,' she told him. 'Then you won't be.'

'Can't a man have a bit of loving with his wife in his own house?' he said mournfully.

'Not if his wife doesn't want it,' said Lola, but her father was looking so boyish and silly she thought she was going to laugh. In that moment she caught a glimpse of how at one time he would have been attractive to her mother. As drunk as he was, he noticed the softening of her mood and tried to use it to his advantage.

'Tell your mother not to be so hard on me,' he said, deliberately sounding pathetic.

'Tell her yourself, and just grow up, the pair of you.' She turned to Frankie. 'Come on, kiddo, let's go to bed and leave them to it.'

'Did we ought to, though, sis?' began Frankie as they left the room.

'Yes, definitely. Mum has to start fighting her own battles with Dad instead of leaving it to us all the time,' Lola said, surprising herself with her sudden decision. 'We'll help whenever we really have to, but she can sort this out herself. She needs to, Frankie, for her own sake, to build her self-confidence.'

'All right,' he said, having complete faith in his sister, and the two of them went up the stairs together.

Lola knew that the incident would be forgotten by her parents tomorrow and she was confident that she had done the right thing.

It was the big night out, and Harry and his mates were gathered in one of the town's pubs in civvies, full of beans and ready for some light-hearted recreation, the drink already flowing.

'Drink up, lads, and let's go and investigate what else the town has to offer,' said Archie, who was the self-appointed organiser. 'I formally declare this night out well and truly started.' He paused and wagged his finger. 'But no bad behaviour, lads. We're coppers, remember, in or out of uniform.'

There was a roar of agreement, then they headed out into the town. As the alcohol began to take effect, Harry started to enjoy himself. In this boozy mood he could forget his troubles and join in the banter with his mates. They went to one or two pubs, then found one with live music and dancing.

When they had ordered the drinks, some of the lads went off to find dancing partners; there were plenty of girls standing around waiting for invitations. Harry wasn't interested so he remained at the bar drinking with Archie.

'Why don't you go and find yourself a girl?' urged Archie. 'It's time you started enjoying yourself again and this is a really good opportunity.'

'Nah, I'd sooner stay at the bar with you and get quietly

plastered,' he said. 'That's enjoyment enough for me at the moment.'

As it happened, he wasn't given the opportunity because a redhead with a noticeably good figure came over and tapped him on the shoulder.

''Ello,' she said chirpily. 'Would you like to dance with me?'

'Not at the moment because I'm talking to my mate,' he replied. 'But thanks for asking.'

'That's a pity because I'd like to dance with you. And I don't usually take no for an answer.'

'Has no one told you the rules?' he said. 'The chaps usually do the asking.'

'I've never been much bothered by rules,' she said casually. 'So, come and dance with me. I'm pretty good on the dance floor so I won't tread on your toes.'

She was a brassy type, with lots of make-up and a dress so clingy she looked as though she'd been welded into it. She was attractive in an obvious sort of way, and her huge blue eyes were full of determination and mischief.

'What are you waiting for, mate?' said Archie. 'Go and dance with the lady.'

With more than a little reluctance Harry followed her on to the dance floor and they launched into a slow waltz. She was obviously more interested in being close to him than the dance steps, but she was very polite and introduced herself. Having asked him his name she told him that she was Essie and she was twenty-one.

'You're not short of confidence, are you?' he remarked.

'Never 'ave been, luckily,' she said, pressing herself closer to him. 'I know what I want and I go out and try to get it. I liked the look of you as soon as I clapped eyes on you, so here I am. What's the point of holding back if you know what you're after?'

'None, I suppose,' Harry said, beginning to relax a little and enjoy himself.

'Exactly,' she said brightly. 'So let's you and me have a good time together.' She looked up at him. 'But first I have to ask, are you married?'

'No.'

'Engaged?'

He shook his head.

'That's all right then,' she said, "Cos I never go after someone else's bloke.'

'That's very decent of you,' he said lightly.

'I like to have a good time but I always play fair,' she said earnestly. 'And I'm not here looking for a husband either, so you can relax.'

He laughed because there was something so amusing about her. He'd been locked in misery ever since he'd parted from Lola, so it was a relief to feel light of heart again. 'Such a thing had never occurred to me,' he said.

'It will have occurred to most of the girls here,' she said. 'Where else are they gonna get fixed up with a fella?'

'It applies to the blokes as well, I suppose.'

'Yeah, that's true,' she agreed. 'Posh people meet partners through family and business connections. The rest of us use the dance halls or the pubs.'

'Yeah, that's right.'

They fell into silence for a while as they danced. Then Essie announced, 'I work in a dress shop in the West End.'

'Oh, really? Do you enjoy it?'

'Not half,' she replied. 'Clothes are my passion and I get a good discount on everything I buy from our shop. We stock all the latest stuff too, so I've no complaints.'

'That's good. I think it's really important to be happy in your work.'

'What do you do?'

'I'm in the Met,' he replied proudly. 'A police officer.'

'Ooh, blimey,' she said, laughing. 'I've never been out with a copper before.'

'You haven't been out with me yet either,' he reminded her.

'I'll soon put that right, don't worry,' she giggled.

He laughed with her. She was good fun and he was really beginning to enjoy himself, helped along by a good few pints of best bitter.

They went to get another drink together in the interval while the musicians had a break, and everything felt jollier for Harry. He seemed to have parted company from his mates but he didn't mind.

He and Essie stayed until the last waltz and then he offered to walk her home. But Essie was far too much of a fun girl to go straight home. She introduced him to a secluded spot near the river, where they lingered for long enough to get to know each other a whole lot better.

They had both had quite a bit to drink but not so much that they couldn't function. For the first time since he had lost Lola Harry felt almost human again and it was such a good feeling. Eventually he saw Essie to her front gate and they agreed to meet again. He knew she would never be a serious girlfriend but he liked her and she made him laugh. Suddenly life seemed a whole lot brighter.

Harry took plenty of ribbing from his mates at the station the next day.

'Someone got lucky last night, then,' said Archie when they were in the canteen the following morning. 'She certainly wasn't shy, was she? I thought she was going to strip you naked on the dance floor.'

Harry laughed. 'She's certainly no shrinking violet.'

'Seems like a nice enough girl, though,' said Archie.

'Yeah, she's very nice, but only in small doses,' said Harry.

'Mm. You'd die of exhaustion with a girl like that if you saw too much of her.'

'Nice way to go, though,' said one of the lads.

'Not half,' grinned Archie.

Harry and Archie weren't on the earliest beat so by the time they were patrolling the streets the place was bustling with people heading to the station for the train to work in the City and the West End, and piling off the buses for their jobs in the local shops and offices. There weren't many private cars on the road. Even apart from the fact that petrol was still rationed, only the better off could afford such a luxury. But there were a few, as well as some vans and the odd horse-drawn cart.

The two officers ticked off a couple of delivery drivers for parking their vans on the pavement, spotted a boy stealing an apple from a greengrocer's stall and made him put it back, then let him off with a warning, and separated a couple of men brawling outside the fish shop. They had just moved on when the sound of a police whistle rent the air and they hurried towards it.

Lola had overslept and was late for work. The café didn't open until later, and her employers were easy-going about her hours, so long as she got all her work done. They were always busy baking in the kitchen at the back of the building when she arrived so they didn't know exactly when she got there anyway, but Lola liked to keep to the usual office hours and get in to work at nine o'clock or she feared falling behind. There was a lot of work in the office for one person to do.

She was running to the tube station in her high heels when she came across a crowd milling around near the station. There were people and police everywhere.

'Someone has collapsed,' she was informed by a woman in the crowd. 'They're waiting for the ambulance.'

'Could you move back, please, ladies and gents, so that the medics can get through when they get here?' said a policeman, moving along the edge of the crowd and roping the area off. 'There's nothing to see so you might as well be on your way. Haven't you got jobs to go to?'

The sound of the ambulance bell rattled through the air and people tried even harder to see what was going on. Lola was about to leave when through a gap in the crowd she saw a policeman rise from the ground, where he'd been attending to someone lying on the pavement, and speak to one of the medics. Her heart leapt when she saw that the policeman was Harry. Emotion overwhelmed her. Seeing him doing his job with such skill and confidence filled her with pride, even though she was no longer a part of his life. Oh, how she wished she was. How she loved him.

She was smiling with the joy of seeing him when he noticed her and stopped in his tracks for a moment, giving her a half-smile. Then, as though reminding himself that he was on duty, he looked away and spoke to the crowds. 'Come on, folks, the show is over. Nothing to see. The medics have the situation under control. Move along, please.'

Harry and Archie had been summoned by the whistle to help with the crowds who had gathered to watch the incident. There were too many people for the officers on that beat to handle on their own. Harry had been trying to comfort the man who had collapsed, but as soon as the medics had arrived he moved away to stop the crowds surging forward. That was when he saw Lola.

He was caught unawares and felt physically shaky at the unexpected sight of her, and he had to remind himself that he was on duty. But he knew in that split second that nothing had changed. He was still as much in love with her as the day he had walked away from her with a broken heart.

Lola had to stand on the train as it was the rush hour. But she barely noticed the crowds pressing against her and the smell of sweat and clothes that weren't quite clean. All she could think about was seeing Harry and how much she wanted to be with him. Was there any way around the problem of her father, apart from her leaving home? But even that couldn't guarantee anything. Harry would want to know her parents and as that wouldn't be possible, he would want to know why not. No, she must accept the fact that Harry wasn't for her. He probably had someone else by now, anyway. He might even be married.

Damn you, Dad, she thought angrily. Why can't you be an ordinary law-abiding citizen, like other girls' fathers?

She got off the train and headed for the tearooms with tears in her eyes.

When Lola got to the tearooms, Dilly, the neighbourhood cat, an attractive creature, black with white smudges and huge yellowish-green eyes, was outside waiting for her.

'You know you're not allowed in.' Cats gave Cissy the creeps so Dilly was banned from the premises. 'But, all right then, until the ladies come out from the kitchen. But then you'll have to go.'

Lola, who adored the animal, picked her up and carried her inside, kissing her soft silky fur. She was a comfort to her today.

Dilly clearly didn't have the same effect on Cissy.

'Oh, no, not you again,' she said when she and Ethel went into the office and saw the cat asleep on Lola's desk. 'How many times must I tell you, Lola? That cat is not allowed inside these premises.'

'She isn't doing any harm,' said Lola.

'She'll keep the mice away,' added Ethel.

'We don't have any mice,' said Cissy.

'Exactly,' said Ethel. 'They know she's around so they stay away.'

'Utter nonsense,' said Cissy. 'Put that animal outside.'

'It's a bit chilly out,' said Lola.

'No, it isn't,' said Cissy with an irritated sigh. 'It's a lovely mild spring day. Anyway, it has fur to keep it warm.'

'She's a "she", not an "it",' said Lola.

'Oh, really,' tutted Cissy. 'I am not having this conversation. Just put the damned thing outside.'

'She's all right in here for a while,' said Lola. 'She isn't doing any harm. And she really loves us all.'

'What complete rubbish,' said Cissy. 'Cats only care about themselves. It's a fact of nature.'

Although Cissy was warm hearted most of the time, she had retained an aloofness from her privileged past. She showed it with the cat and also with Roger, a war veteran who had fallen on hard times and lived on the streets near the tearooms. Lola would often buy him a scone and a cup of tea, and although Cissy didn't say anything, she clearly objected to having him around. But today she managed to stifle her irritation and allowed the cat to stay for a while. Cissy's good points by far outweighed her bad ones, and Lola was very fond of her. She and her sister were certainly good to work for. There was never any nagging. They simply allowed Lola to get on with the job without interference. She certainly blessed the day she had called into the café for a cup of tea.

'Right. Come on, Ethel, back to the kitchen. We've more baking to do before we open.'

Ethel nodded and the unusual pair hurried away, leaving Lola with an ever-growing feeling of affection for them.

★   ★   ★

Harry was still seeing Essie now and again but he kept things platonic because he knew he would never fall in love with her, especially since seeing Lola again. That one time the unthinkable had happened with Essie he'd been a little bit squiffy and off his guard. But he liked and respected her and didn't want to use her. She tried everything to lower his guard, but he had managed to resist. He knew he must stop seeing her but couldn't quite find the courage to tell her, especially as she made it clear that she would take him on any terms. He didn't want just to disappear from her life because that wouldn't be fair. He needed to be honest with her, but he knew she would be hurt if he rejected her, so each time he tried, he failed, and then he vowed to tell her the next time he saw her.

Although food for restaurants and cafés was not rationed, it was still in short supply, and owners of these establishments had to be creative and find other ingredients to replace those they couldn't get. They also had to stay friendly with their suppliers to get the traditional items. Cissy was brilliantly creative with the cookery, but not so good at being friends with people she didn't know or particularly like. This was where Ethel came into her own. She was naturally nice natured and could be sweeter than treacle if it meant getting an extra bag of flour or sugar.

So, when the Pickford sisters were asked if they could do a birthday party for twenty people to celebrate a sixtieth birthday, they knew that some sweet-talking would be necessary and also some creative cookery. However, they enjoyed a challenge, and it was good business, so they took it on with enthusiasm. They'd been booked with plenty of notice so they had time to prepare.

'It'll be the best birthday party in London,' said Cissy. 'A day for the lady to remember.'

'And good publicity for the tearooms,' added Ethel.

'Exactly.'

Lola entered into the spirit, too. She wanted the tearooms to do well, and not just because she wanted to keep her job. The sisters had something special to offer with their wonderful cookery and they worked hard, and they deserved success. She felt quite excited about the forthcoming party.

'So long as they don't expect you to help out in the café,' said her father over dinner when she told the family about the party.

'I hope they do,' said Lola. 'It will be a special occasion and I'd like to be a part of it.'

'You are a highly trained office worker, not a café skivvy,' he said.

'And they would never treat me like one,' she told him. 'But they might want me to help out. The other tables will still need looking after. It will make a nice break from my desk.'

'Well, in that case I think you're in the wrong job.'

Lola's temper flared. 'You're wrong, and I'm fed up with you criticising my employers. I'm happy in this job, Dad. I like the atmosphere, I enjoy the work, and I'm very fond of the people who employ me, so just give it a rest, will you?'

'Don't you dare speak to me like that.'

'Well, lay off me then,' she said.

Rita looked worried and Frankie had turned pink with nerves because he was more than a little scared of their dad.

Charlie scowled at her, but didn't say another word for the

rest of the meal. The atmosphere was awful. Lola was glad when it was over and her father went out. She helped her mother with the dishes, then went to see Doreen by way of escape.

Much to his annoyance, both of Charlie's children helped out at The Tulip Tearooms party. The sisters needed someone to help with the washing up, and as it was a Saturday afternoon and Frankie was always willing to earn some extra pocket money, he was happy to do it. The sisters took an immediate liking to him and it seemed to be mutual. Lola, who was doing a stint as a waitress, was proud of him.

She was also rather proud of her employers. The food was outstanding, despite the shortages: dainty sandwiches, the famous scones and little glazed fruit tarts. They had even managed to make a birthday cake. The visitors were full of praise. Lola guessed that this wouldn't be the last party the ladies hosted here. Once things got more plentiful there would be no stopping them.

Harry had noticed that Essie hadn't been her usual exuberant self lately and she didn't look happy when he met her one evening.

'So, what do you fancy doing: pictures, pub or dancing?' he asked cheerfully. 'We could go to the West End, if you like.'

'I couldn't care less,' she said.

'Hey, what the matter?' he asked. 'It isn't like you to be so snappy.'

She shrugged.

'Essie, what is it? Have I upset you?'

'I'll say you bloody well have,' she said. 'I'm pregnant.'

'What?' he said shocked. 'But we haven't . . .'

'We have.'

'Only that one time . . .'

'That's all it takes.'

'Are you sure?'

'Of course, I'm bloody sure,' she said, on the verge of tears, her voice shaking. 'Do you think I'd come out with something like that if I wasn't?'

'I suppose not.'

'Anyway, you'll have to take responsibility so don't try to wriggle out of it.'

'Of course I won't let you down,' he said dutifully.

'I'll be chucked out of home once my mum and dad realise that I'm in the club,' she told him. 'They won't have an unmarried mother living in their house. It's far too much of a disgrace.'

Harry was still trying to adjust to the situation and she took his silence to be rejection. 'If you're thinking of turning your back on me, I can tell you now that I'll go straight up the copshop and tell them what a disreputable copper you really are. You'll be the talk of the station.'

'Give me a chance to get used to the idea, for goodness' sake,' Harry said. 'I've no intention of leaving you in the lurch, but I need to think.'

'What's to think about?' she asked. 'I'm up the spout, having your kid, so you owe it to me to look after us.'

'I know that, and I will.'

'I'm not going to be the guilty secret, hidden away,' Essie said. 'And that's definite.'

'I wouldn't expect you to.'

'You'll have to marry me.'

'Marry you?' he said, shocked.

'Can you think of another way that I can keep my respectability?'

'No, I suppose not.'

'That's what we'll do, then,' she said efficiently. 'I'll leave you to find us somewhere to live and I'll organise the wedding.'

'Wedding?' he gasped.

'That's right. That's what happens when two people get married. They have a wedding.'

'No need to be sarky,' he said, seeing a whole new side to Essie.

'Sorry,' she said. 'I'm really worried and it's making me a bit snappy.' She looked at him miserably. 'I've had a terrible time this past few weeks, waiting for my period that didn't come. I've been sick in the mornings and hiding it from my mum. It's been really awful, honestly.'

She looked very delicate to him suddenly, and his protective instincts rose to the fore. 'Ah, that's a shame. But don't worry, Essie, I'll take care of everything,' he said kindly. 'You won't have to face this on your own.'

'Really?' she said, smiling and looking relieved.

'Yes, really,' he assured her though he was feeling very trapped and longing to escape.

'Phew, that's a relief.'

'Good. Now I think we should go to the pub. I need a pint after that news.'

'Suits me,' she said, happy now that she had reassurance, and they headed for the town arm in arm.

Chapter Five

'Well, I can't say I'm not disappointed in you, Harry, after the way your dad and I brought you up to know the difference between right and wrong,' said Marg when she'd calmed down after he told her about the situation with Essie. 'But at least you are prepared to do the right thing by the girl without any prompting, so that's something in your favour.'

'I'm not doing it to gain favour, Mum. I just don't know what else I can do, to be perfectly honest,' he confessed. 'Essie isn't the love of my life and I certainly wasn't planning on getting married to her, but this has happened so I don't really have a choice.'

'Plenty of blokes would have scarpered,' said Marg.

'Oh, no, I wouldn't do a thing like that,' he said. 'I'm not that heartless. Anyway, it will be my baby so my responsibility. Essie is a nice girl. I wouldn't want to let her down.'

'What about her people?' she asked. 'Are they going to offer a helping hand?'

'Apparently not. She reckons they'll throw her out when she tells them she's pregnant and want nothing more to do with her,' he said. 'They are very strict and there isn't much love lost between them and their daughter.'

'Oh dear, what a shame,' said Marg. 'A woman really needs her mum at a time like this. But, in that case, you'll have to live here with us. We've got room now that your grandparents have gone to live with your auntie down at the coast. There's only me and your dad and Ruby. Your bedroom is big enough for the two of you and the little one when it arrives. For a while, anyway. It isn't perfect but it will do until you can get your own place.'

'Are you sure, Mum?' Harry asked. 'Wouldn't you be glad of some peace and quiet?'

'Plenty of time for that later on, when things get better generally and you can move into somewhere of your own. You won't get a place at the moment, not with the housing shortage as it is,' she said. 'It'll be years before it gets back to normal, I reckon. London was overcrowded before the war, and losing all those homes to the bombs has made things a damned sight worse. So, you're welcome to stay here with your new family for as long as you need to.'

Harry felt a burning sensation at the back of his eyes at his mother's immediate offer of help. She wouldn't be happy about the situation because she adhered to the strict attitudes of society and this pregnancy would be considered scandalous by most people of her generation. But she was putting her own principles to one side and offering to help, which couldn't be easy for her.

'Oh, Mum, that is so good of you,' he said, his voice breaking. 'I don't deserve you.'

'Probably not,' she said with a wry grin. 'But there's going to be a baby in the family and that's something to celebrate, whatever the circumstances. The wedding will have to be small because of the situation and with it being such short notice, but we'll do it with pride. We won't be able to have a swanky reception but we'll get a few bottles in and have the relatives round and have some sort of a do. We'll put the wedding in the marriages section of the local paper to make it respectable, as though everything is normal.' She paused for a moment. 'If that's all right with Essie and her people, of course.'

'Thanks, Mum,' Harry said, hugging her. 'I'm sure Essie will be fine with that. It's so good of you, especially as she's not expecting her parents to take an interest.'

'It's a shame about that. But never mind, I'm glad to help, son,' Marg said. 'This baby will be my first grandchild so I want things to be nice for it.'

'I'll tell Essie.'

'And I'll break the news to your dad. We need to meet Essie too,' she said, 'as we are going to be related.'

'Of course,' Harry said, reminded somewhat shamefully of the casualness of his relationship with Essie in that he hadn't even brought her home to meet the family yet. All of that was about to change dramatically and he felt quite nervous about it. But it was his own fault. He should have shown restraint; then he'd still be free. It was too late for regrets, however. He just had to get on and do what was right.

'Are you all right, Lola?' asked Cissy. 'You're very quiet today and you don't look very happy.'

'I'm fine, thanks,' fibbed Lola. 'Just a bit tired. I had a late night last night.'

'Out dancing, were you?' Cissy suggested smiling.

'No, nothing like that.'

'Oh, well, an early night tonight should fix it,' the older woman said helpfully. 'So, make sure that you are tucked in at a reasonable hour.'

'I will,' said Lola, and carried on filing some correspondence, knowing that it would take more than an early night to fix the ache in her heart.

After she'd finished work Lola didn't go straight home but called round to see Doreen.

'Blimey, you look rough,' said her friend. 'Have you been up all night or something?'

'Awake for most of it,' Lola replied.

'Why, what's the matter?'

'He's married,' she said thickly. 'Harry's married. I saw it in the wedding announcements in the local paper last night.'

'Oh, no,' said Doreen, putting her arms around her friend, who was struggling to hold back the tears. 'I'm so sorry. I know you were hoping that somehow you'd get back with him.'

'I thought by some miracle . . . I mean, I knew we wouldn't, that we couldn't . . . but this makes it so final.'

Later, when Lola had composed herself, Doreen said, 'I know that you're feeling really bad right now and you might think I am being hard on you but maybe this will prove to be a good thing in the long run. You'll have to face up to it now. He's married, out of circulation, not available to you. It's time you accepted it and started considering other people. Go out with other men. Give some of the blokes who come into the tearooms some encouragement when they show an interest. You could even give Keith a bit of hope. He'd ask you out like a shot if he thought you'd say yes. You never know, you might enjoy yourself.'

'You're right,' Lola agreed miserably. 'It's about time I had some fun.'

'That's the spirit,' said Doreen, wishing she felt as positive as she sounded. Her friend was really suffering and it would take more than a few nights out to cure her. But Lola didn't need to have that pointed out to her.

After Harry and Essie were married, he realised how little he had known her before. Then he'd only seen her for a few hours at a time and the mood had always been jovial because they had been out for the evening enjoying themselves.

Being married to her was a different thing altogether and a really miserable eye opener. Utterly selfish, she demanded her own way at all times, absolutely hated being pregnant and never tired of reminding him.

'I feel sick,' she wailed constantly. 'It's all right for you, Harry. Nothing has changed for you. I'm the one who's doing everything to make this baby and I'm bloody well fed up with it.'

'I do try to do what I can for you, but I can't change nature,' he reminded her; he was always running around after her, putting cushions at her back and trying to find things she fancied to eat, not easy with food rationing still in place. They had their own room but lived with the family, so Marg did all the shopping, cooking and housework with a little help from Ruby. Essie didn't lift a finger, had already given up work because she felt ill, and she complained constantly.

'I know you try to help, Harry, but you don't have to put up with sickness and heartburn and no end of backache, do you?' she pointed out miserably.

'Well, no, and I'm sorry about that, but there isn't anything I can do about it except try to make sure you don't have to do much,' he said. 'But I'm certain it will all be worth it when the baby arrives.'

'I dunno so much about that either,' Essie said, looking doom-laden.

'I'm sure you'll love it when it comes,' said Harry, wearied by her constant complaints but somehow managing to stay patient. 'We both will.' His life wasn't much fun now, but he didn't dwell on it since he had no one to blame but himself. Life with Essie was so difficult that he dreaded being at home, and his police work was his salvation.

'I bloomin' well hope so,' she said. 'But I wouldn't bank on it, as far as I'm concerned, because I don't have a maternal bone in my body. I've never wanted a baby.'

Her words worried him. He just had to hope that she had a change of heart when the child was born.

'Pregnancy is not an illness, Harry,' his mother reminded him one evening when Essie had gone to bed early, complaining about feeling sick.

'I know that, Mum.'

'So, why are you treating your wife like an invalid?'

'I have to because she feels so ill all the time.'

'Women do sometimes feel a bit off colour when they are expecting,' she said. 'I did when I was carrying you. But it's part of the process. The expectant mother doesn't have to be waited on hand and foot the whole time. You're worn out, especially as you're doing so much overtime.'

'I suppose I feel I have to make it up to her because I got her pregnant, and I need the overtime money with a baby on the way and all the stuff we'll have to buy.'

'I don't think you should blame yourself entirely for the pregnancy,' she said. 'I'm sure Essie was a willing party. She doesn't strike me as a shrinking violet sort of a girl.'

'No, that's the last thing she is,' he said. 'I suppose I'm just trying to make the best of things.'

'Well, you're certainly doing that all right, and I'm proud of you,' she said. 'But don't let her make you her servant.'

'Of course not.'

'She hasn't so much as washed a cup since she's been living here,' said Marg. 'She leaves it all to the rest of us, especially me. She has Ruby running around after her, too. And it isn't right. It'll do her good to do a few things instead of lying around all day wallowing in self-pity.'

'I'm sorry, Mum, if she's putting on you,' he said. 'I'll have a word with her about it.'

'I think that's a good idea, love,' Marg said. 'I mean, I don't mind doing it all but it's the principle of the thing. Anyway, she needs to get used to pulling her weight, especially as she's going to be a mother.'

'I understand,' he said, feeling thoroughly depressed.

Accepting that this miserable situation he was in was entirely his own fault didn't make it any easier to take. He'd tried telling Essie she should make more of an effort but she would fly into a rage and sulk for days. Of course, he accepted that the situation was worse for her because she had the pregnancy to cope with, which was why he made allowances for her bad temper. He felt as though his life had gone completely off course. He was married to a woman he didn't love and he knew the feeling was mutual.

Marriage had always seemed like a very special thing to him, probably because his parents had made such a success of theirs, so the way things were between him and Essie was a huge disappointment. He had no choice, however, than to keep trying to make the best of things and hope that at some point Essie might be easier to live with.

'We really could do with a man about the place,' said Ethel as she lifted some large boxes into the tearooms' kitchen. 'Someone to do the heavy lifting. I put my back out the other day moving a sack of flour. Then there's the maintenance: light bulbs and repair jobs about the place. We need help.'

'We don't need a man,' said Cissy. 'There's nothing a man can do that we can't.'

'Maybe not, but we have to struggle because we aren't built for heavy jobs. Anyway, there is more than enough for us to do in the kitchen,' said Ethel. She turned to Lola, who was making tea for her break. 'What do you think, dear?'

'I certainly think you need another pair of hands about the place,' she said. 'Why not have an odd-job man, who could do the jobs and the cleaning as well, to make it worthwhile? I know you like to do the cleaning yourselves, but the tearoom is doing well now so you can afford to have someone to do it for you. You could even have someone living in, so they were always on hand for things that come up . . . within reason, of course.'

The ladies were a curious mixture. They were very middle

class in manners and speech, but hated the idea of paying someone to do something they could do themselves. It was strange, given their upbringing.

'I can't say I fancy having a man about the place,' said Cissy. 'We would lose our privacy.'

'Only while he was working where you are,' said Lola. 'You could base him in one of the spare rooms at the back of the building, nowhere near the kitchen. You've plenty of space.'

'I still don't fancy the idea,' said Cissy.

'In that case you can do the heavy lifting,' said Ethel crossly. 'I'm fed up with straining my muscles.'

'All right, you let me know when you want something lifted and I'll do it.'

'Ridiculous,' snorted Ethel.

'I'll leave you to it,' said Lola, and made a hasty retreat with her tea.

The ladies had a habit of turning to her with their disputes, then each taking her sister's side against her if she gave her true opinion and it was at all critical. They could be childish within their relationship so Lola stayed well clear of their arguments. She was very fond of them both, though, and glad that she worked here. A little persuasion was going to be needed to get them to employ a much-needed odd-job man, but she had the perfect candidate in mind, the homeless chap she had got to know recently. All she had to do was convince them that he was right for the job, although, given the man's current situation, it wouldn't be easy. However, she could be quite determined when she needed to be.

★　★　★

'So, what was the matter with your last date?' asked Doreen when Lola called to see her to tell her about a chap she had been out with recently.

'Nothing, as such,' replied Lola. 'But I didn't feel comfortable with him.'

'You mean you didn't fancy him.'

'Exactly,' she said. 'He was nice enough, but not for me. I think I'll give up going on dates. I never enjoy them.'

'Don't give up the dates, just give up looking for another Harry,' said Doreen. 'Anyway, you've only been on a few. It's far too early to give up.'

Lola had taken Doreen's advice and accepted a couple of invitations out, one from one of the builders who was doing a repair job at the tearooms and the other from someone she'd met at a dance.

'Maybe I'll give it a rest for a while,' she said.

'That's defeatist talk.'

'So what if it is?'

'You're a young, attractive woman,' said Doreen. 'And you're wasting the best years of your life moping about for someone you can't have.'

'I'm not moping about.'

'Maybe not moping, exactly, but you're not going out enjoying yourself either,' Doreen pointed out. 'Just try one more. Let me fix you up with my brother's mate Keith, who I know is keen.'

Lola sighed. 'I'll get no peace until I agree, so go on then, get it arranged.'

Doreen gave a wide grin. 'I'll find you a boyfriend if it's the last thing I do.'

'It might well be, too, if I really don't like him.'

'You can't not like Keith,' Doreen said 'He's a lovely bloke; a war hero too. It might take a few days before I can get a message to him, though.'

'Take all the time you need,' laughed Lola. 'I'm in no hurry.'

'Oh, no, Lola,' said Cissy. 'We are not employing a tramp. It's bad enough having to pay an odd-job man but I draw the line at adding a tramp to the payroll.'

'Roger isn't a tramp as such,' said Lola referring to the homeless man who was often wandering around near the tearooms and whom Lola and Ethel had befriended. 'He is just a man who's fallen on hard times through no fault of his own, that's all. He's a war hero. He's been fighting for his country and now he has nothing, not even a place to lay his head at night. Someone should help him.'

'I'm sure someone will, but not us.'

'He's an educated man, actually,' put in Ethel. 'I've often had conversations with him. Very interesting he is, too.'

'You'd talk to anyone,' said Cissy in a critical tone.

'Yes, I would, and I don't mind admitting it,' said Ethel.

'No good will come of it,' said Cissy.

'You are such a snob, Cissy,' said Ethel. 'We are meant to communicate with our fellow humans. That's why we are given a voice. Even animals talk to each other in their own way.'

'We aren't meant to talk to every Tom, Dick and Harry,' said her sister.

There was a brief silence. Then Ethel said, 'Actually, Roger was a teacher of mathematics before the war. But the result of enemy interrogation when he was captured on active service shattered his nerves. It affected his concentration and he couldn't

93

do the job when he came back. His wife couldn't cope with his nerves and asked him to leave.'

'What a cruel thing to do,' said Lola.

'Yes, I thought so,' said Ethel.

'Anyway, he might have been a brilliant man before the war but he's a tramp now and we are not having a down-and-out working here,' Cissy insisted.

'It must be terrible, not having anywhere to live, though,' Lola put in. 'You can't get a job because you've no address so you've no income and you're forced to live on the streets. It's a vicious circle.'

'Awful,' agreed Ethel.

'I'm sure it is,' said Cissy in a sharp tone of disapproval. 'But he should go to the government for help. He can't expect ordinary people to help him.'

'He doesn't expect anyone to help him,' said Lola, her voice rising with feeling. 'But he can't help being hungry and he has to ask for food because hunger is a basic instinct and forces him to. I feel very sorry for him. I think we should all try to help each other. And you have plenty of room here, so he could live in one of your back rooms and work as a caretaker. Then you would always have him on hand for those jobs that are constantly arising: the lights fusing, the sink blocking and so on. It would be a comedown for him after teaching maths, but I'm sure he'd make a good job of it.'

'Oh, Lola, now you are taking it too far,' Cissy objected. 'Of course, he can't live here.'

'Why not?' put in Ethel. 'He needs a home and a job, and we can offer both.'

'That's all very noble, dear, but we have to be realistic about such things.'

'And the reality is that this man needs help,' said her sister. 'He's helped us by doing his bit for his country, now it's our turn to do something for him.'

'You're already helping him,' Cissy said. 'He won't go hungry with you and Lola around.'

'You can't expect us to refuse a starving man some food,' said her sister. 'That's just cruel.'

'That man is not coming to work and live here,' said Cissy. 'And the subject is now closed.'

'Why have you got such a down on him?' asked Ethel. 'You've never even spoken to him.'

'I haven't got a down on him,' denied Cissy crossly. 'I just don't think we should have a tramp around the place, that's all.'

'He wouldn't be a tramp if we gave him a job and a home,' said Ethel.

'He would always be a tramp to me,' said Cissy. 'Ugh, I can't bear the thought of having him here.'

Lola and Ethel exchanged glances to indicate that the subject would best be continued at another time, then Lola went to her office.

'So how did it go with Keith last night?' asked Doreen a few days later.

'All right until he got physical. Then I backed off,' replied Lola.

'Oh, no, not again,' wailed Doreen. 'You're getting really frigid.'

'I can't help it,' said Lola. 'I can't bear being mauled.'

'Unless it's Harry doing the mauling.'

'Exactly, and as he's very definitely unavailable I'm all set to be a dried-up old spinster.'

'Can't you make more of an effort?,' suggested Doreen. 'I mean, we all go out with blokes we don't fancy sometimes. You just grin and bear it and make sure you don't see them again.'

'Actually, I liked Keith. He was really good company. I wouldn't mind seeing him again, but without the snogging.'

'You won't get any bloke to agree to that,' said Doreen. 'Not unless you agree to be just friends.'

'No, I don't suppose I will,' said Lola. 'So, I'll grow old alone. But if Keith asks me out again, I'll go because I quite enjoyed his company.'

'That's what I call a step in the right direction,' said Doreen, sounding pleased.

'Don't get too excited,' laughed Lola. 'He probably won't ask me again.'

Keith did ask her again and she accepted. He said he wanted to talk so they went for a drink.

'I know this – us – is one sided,' he said as they settled at a table in the corner. 'You don't feel for me as I feel for you.'

'Only because I'm in love with someone else,' she explained. 'It doesn't reflect on you in the least.'

'Yeah, I heard that there was someone else,' he said. 'But as he isn't around why not give me a chance?'

'I enjoy seeing you, but it wouldn't be fair to you because I'm not looking for anything serious,' she said. 'I enjoy your company so it would be nice to see each other now and then. So long as you can accept it as casual.'

He grinned and he had a smile that seemed to light up his whole body. He wasn't traditionally handsome, having ginger hair and freckles, but he had the widest smile and his blue eyes shone when he smiled. 'Suits me,' he smiled.

The more Essie's pregnancy advanced, the more bad tempered she became. She didn't seem to be anticipating any pleasure in having the baby at all.

'A screaming kid and smelly nappies to wash, that's what I've got to look forward to,' she wailed as she got into bed one night.

'I'm sure there's more to a baby than that,' said Harry. 'People seem to get a great deal of joy from them. I'm no expert but I don't think they scream all the time.'

'I don't have a maternal bone in my body,' she said. 'So, it will all just be one big chore to me.'

'You can't know that for sure until the baby is here,' said Harry, ever the optimist. 'You might take to it right away. And even if it takes a little while you'll enjoy it eventually, I'm sure.'

'Stop being so bloody cheerful about it,' she said angrily. 'It's all horrible and my life is ruined.'

After months of listening to her complaining Harry had finally had enough. 'Stop moaning, for goodness' sake, Essie,' he said, his voice rising. 'A baby isn't what either of us had in mind at this time but it's happened and we have to make the best of things.'

'It's all right for you – you're not the one whose body has been invaded.'

'I realise that,' he said. 'But my life will change too. It already has, to a certain extent. I'm having to do lots of overtime so that we can give the baby a good start in life, and that will be ongoing. And having you moaning every time you open your mouth isn't exactly helping.'

'I don't care,' she said. 'It's all your fault and you've ruined my life.'

He wasn't in love with Essie but she did have the power to hurt him. He hated to think that he had ruined anyone's life. 'I'm sorry about that. But you weren't forced into anything.'

'I most certainly was,' she lied because it suited her mood to do so. 'I should have gone to the police and had you done for rape.'

The idea was so ludicrous, he laughed. 'Oh, Essie,' he said. 'You don't half tell some porkies.'

'It isn't funny,' she said, her temper rising.

'You're right about that,' he said. 'It isn't funny. It's bloody tragic . . . that you have let yourself believe something so wide of the mark. But you don't really believe it, do you? You're just lying to yourself because it's easier to take than the truth.'

'I don't know,' she screamed. 'All I do know is that I don't want a bloody baby. I want it taken away the minute it's born. You'll have to get it adopted.'

'We are not doing that, Essie,' Harry said, shocked at the suggestion. 'It will be our child, our flesh and blood. We will love it and look after it.'

'Shut up!' she yelled. 'I don't want to hear it and neither do I want a baby.'

A knocking on the wall from the bedroom next door quietened them down. 'Sorry, Ruby,' Harry called.

As he lay in bed, weary but unable to sleep although Essie was now quiet, he was pinning all his hopes on a change of heart in his wife when the baby was actually born. Surely her maternal instincts would kick in then and she would love her child when she actually saw it? Wasn't that how nature worked? He did hope so. But whatever happened with Essie, he was certain of one thing: this baby would be given the very best start in life he could manage. Nothing would be too much trouble for his child, as far as he was concerned.

Chapter Six

It was a series of misfortunes at The Tulip Tearooms in the autumn of 1947 that led to Roger, the homeless man Lola thought would be an asset to the Pickford sisters, becoming their live-in caretaker and general handyman. And what an asset he proved to be! He would turn his hand to anything: cleaning, plumbing, painting and decorating. He was even a huge help in the kitchen as he was a very capable cook. His scones didn't quite match up to those of the sisters, but they were perfectly adequate and would certainly suffice in a crisis.

Things had started to go downhill at the tearooms when Cissy fell sick with an acute attack of bronchitis. Soon Ethel was out of action with the same malady, leaving Lola to run the business alone. This was almost an impossibility as she had very little cooking experience, which meant she could make the sandwiches but had to buy in the scones and other cakes.

Given that she only had one pair of hands, it was a huge challenge, especially as she had the office to run as well. She was saved by Roger, who was available and willing to help, so Lola used her initiative and took him on.

Lola was delighted to get him off the streets by giving him

a steady job and accommodation in one of the spare bedrooms in the private quarters above the tearooms.

The sisters were both feeling too ill to care, and by the time they had recovered Roger had more than proved his worth and was settled into the job and a sunny room in the attic. He earned a reasonable wage so was able to pay his way and dress decently. Once the sisters got used to having him around the place, they both seemed to like him.

He was a similar age to them so that in itself was a bond. With regular meals and clean clothes his appearance improved and he looked rather distinguished with his white hair neatly combed into place.

As well as being an asset to the tearooms, he also became a very dear friend to Lola. She could confide in him about anything, knowing that it would go no further. As an educated older man and a father figure, he wasn't lacking in wisdom, and Lola trusted his judgement completely.

Living on the streets had toughened him up, but the atmosphere at the tearooms seemed to suit him and he was able to function normally, despite his bad nerves. Ethel already liked him and soon he and Cissy became very good friends. If the café was very busy, he helped out at the tables and was popular with the customers too.

From what Lola could gather, he had proved to be an asset in the home as well, and she often heard about some delicious meal he had cooked for the three of them.

'He works miracles with the measly rations,' Cissy was heard to say. 'He's a genius with the miserable amount of food the government allows us. It's high time we were finished with rationing.'

Having a job and a home boosted Roger's confidence and

he became unrecognisable as the hopeless figure they had once thought of as a tramp.

Predictably, Lola's father had something critical to say on the subject.

'You want to watch him,' Charlie warned. 'A man like that, who's lived on the streets, could have all sort of tricks up his sleeve.'

'But why would he want to trick us, Dad?' asked Lola in exasperation. 'His life is back on track. He has no need of tricks. Anyway, he fought for his country so you should show some respect for him.'

'Fighting for his country doesn't make him a saint.'

'No, but he's a good man and he's made a contribution to the freedom of this country,' she said. 'His nerves got shot to pieces in the process and he lost his wife and home as a result.'

'Humph, well, there is that, I suppose,' Charlie said grudgingly. 'But you never know what to expect from a man like that.'

'A man like what?' Lola exploded. 'He's a thoroughly decent sort of a bloke.'

'He does sound like a good sort,' added Rita in her usual tentative manner.

'He's taken you all in,' claimed Charlie. 'Gawd knows what he might have in mind.'

'I can tell you what he has in mind, Dad,' said Lola crossly. 'He just wants to work hard and live a decent life.'

'That's what he'd have you believe.'

'It's the way it is, Dad,' she said furiously. 'Some people want the simple life. Why do you always have to think the worst of everybody?'

'I'm a realist and I'm usually right.'

'No, you're not,' protested Lola. 'You're always saying nasty things about people, even your mates.'

'Oh, well, my mates are all villains.'

'Isn't that why you chose them, Dad?'

'Maybe,' he said.

Lola didn't say any more. She still hated the fact that her father mixed with criminals and was, of course, one himself. She didn't think she could ever accept it. It had already cost her the love of her life and that still rankled. She knew that she'd never stop wanting to be with Harry, but because of her father it couldn't ever happen.

Essie's pregnancy was nearly over and her temper was worse than ever.

'I am sick and tired of this awful existence,' she moaned one evening in early 1948. 'Look at me. I'm the size of a mansion house and I'm absolutely worn out, not to mention feeling ill all the time. The whole thing is a nightmare.'

'It won't be long now, dear,' said Harry's mother patiently. 'The baby could come at any time.'

'Could it really?' said Harry, who was in uniform ready to go on night duty.

'Oh, yes,' said Marg with confidence. 'When the pregnancy gets to this stage anything could happen.'

'How exciting!' he enthused.

'For you, maybe,' said Essie, her voice rising in irritation. 'There's nothing at all exciting about it for me, just hours and hours of pain to look forward to.'

'Is it really that awful?' asked Ruby, who was reading a magazine, the wireless barely noticeable in the background.

'Yes, it really is,' said Essie.

'How do you know?' asked Ruby. 'You haven't done it yet.'

'I've heard it's terrible from people who know, and the pregnancy is nothing short of a nightmare.'

'I'd better steer clear then,' said Ruby.

'Make sure you do,' said Essie.

'Don't frighten the girl, Essie,' said Marg sharply. 'It's the most natural thing in the world.'

'And the most painful.'

'If I could do it for you I would,' intervened Harry, hoping to offer his wife some support.

'Easy words when you know it isn't possible,' sneered Essie.

'I'll be off then,' he said, since there was no point in trying to comfort her when she was in this mood. 'See you in the morning.'

'Take care, love,' said his mother.

'See yer,' added Ruby.

Essie just turned and walked away. She had never shown Harry so much as a morsel of affection since they'd been married. She loathed her circumstances and never tired of making it obvious. Harry was hoping she might cheer up when the baby was actually born but he wasn't banking on it. She was a very unhappy lady and blamed him entirely for the miserable existence she was now forced to endure. Thank God he had a job he enjoyed. At least his work gave him some respite from his awful marriage.

'Is everything all right, mate?' asked Archie when the two men were out on the beat together a few days later.

'Yeah, sure,' replied Harry. 'Why wouldn't it be?'

'Dunno, but you don't seem very happy lately.'

'I'm all right,' fibbed Harry because he would never be disloyal to his wife by discussing their terrible marriage. 'Probably just a bit tired.'

'You have been doing a lot of overtime lately.'

'Needs must with a baby on the way.'

'Yeah, I remember doing the same,' said Archie. 'You must be getting excited now with the birth so close.'

'Not half,' Harry lied again. Essie had taken all the joy out of the expectation. If she was this bad tempered now, he dreaded to think what she would be like when the baby was actually here, with all the extra work and worry. He guessed life wasn't going to be easy.

Their conversation was interrupted by a disturbance across the road outside a pub. There was a fight in progress and people were gathering to watch. The two policemen hurried on to the scene and separated two young men who were apparently fighting over a woman. Their presence ended the fight so they didn't make any arrests, just sent the crowd on their way and continued on their beat.

Harry felt deeply depressed and wondered how he could have let his life go so seriously wrong. It's your own fault, mate. You should have shown restraint; then you'd still be single, he told himself. You wouldn't have the love of your life but at least you wouldn't be made to feel miserable every single waking moment by a wife who blames you for everything that's wrong in her life.

He knew he couldn't change things so he just had to put up with them.

*　　*　　*

Lola decided she must stop seeing Keith. She liked him a lot and valued his friendship but that was all it could ever be for her – a friendship – and she suspected that it was becoming more than that for him. It was little things – a tender look, a protective hand on her arm – small signs, but indications none the less. Ironically, had she felt differently her father wouldn't have been a problem because Keith was from a rough-and-ready family who didn't care what other people did. But she wasn't in love with him and she simply must tell him so.

But it proved to be more difficult than she'd expected. He was such a nice bloke and she didn't want to hurt him. So, she kept putting it off.

'Don't tell me you've still not done it,' said Doreen, in whom she'd confided.

'I just can't seem to bring myself,' Lola confessed. 'And I feel awful about it.'

'I should think you bloomin' well should, too,' said Doreen. 'You're leading him on.'

'No I'm not. I haven't given him any encouragement at all. I told him at the start I just wanted to be friends.'

'That was a while ago and the fact that you are still going out with him is encouragement in itself,' Doreen said.

'Mm, maybe you're right,' Lola agreed. 'I shall have a few serious words with him.'

'As soon as possible too,' warned Doreen.

Lola shot her a look. 'You seem very eager for me to do it,' she said. 'Are you still keen on him yourself?'

'That's got absolutely nothing to do with it,' Doreen said a little too sharply.

* * *

Harry had a rare night off and was sitting with his wife and parents listening to the wireless. Essie suddenly struggled to her feet and said she was going out for a walk.

'I'll get my coat,' said Harry.

'Just get mine,' she said. 'I want to go on my own.'

'But you're over your time,' said Marg, looking alarmed. 'The baby could come at any moment.'

'I'm sure it can hang on for half an hour while I get some fresh air,' said Essie. 'Anyway, I'm going on my own and that's that. So, you can all stop going on at me.'

'It's very cold out,' said Marg.

'I don't care if there's three foot of snow on the ground, I'm still going out,' Essie said, and left the house.

'She's a one-off your wife,' Marg remarked to Harry when Essie had closed the door behind her.

'I suppose she's feeling a bit restless,' he said defensively. 'It's understandable.'

'You're very loyal to her, son, and I'm proud of you.'

'She's my wife; the least I owe her is loyalty.'

'You don't get much back, though, do you?'

'It's just the way she is, Mum. We all have our funny ways. I try to make the best of things.'

'Of course you do,' said Marg, realising that she had over-stepped the mark in offering her opinion. Harry would never say a word against his wife, no matter how badly she treated him.

It was very cold out with frost forming on the garden walls and privet hedges, and Essie was shivering, despite her thick coat and woolly scarf. She wasn't sure why she had come out.

Walking wasn't exactly her favourite activity, especially while carrying all this horrid extra weight, and as the weather was so bitter the walk wasn't going to have a calming effect. She guessed that she was trying to escape – from the house, her husband, her life, pregnancy, approaching motherhood. She didn't want any of it but she was trapped.

Harry was a good husband in that he provided for her well but she didn't love him any more than he loved her. Most of the time she hated him for getting her pregnant. Still, he was having his comeuppance because he didn't want this marriage any more than she did. They disliked each other intensely.

But a girl had to have a husband, and he was good looking and had some standing in the community, being a policeman. Once she was rid of this damned pregnancy and could wear nice clothes again, she'd probably feel a whole lot better about things. Her mother-in-law would probably be keen to babysit so she'd get some freedom that way. Spring wasn't that far away with all the new lighter fashions. In fact, there was a dress shop just across the road so she'd go and have a look in the window to see what she had to look forward to.

Deeply immersed in thoughts of happier times to come, sunny days and pretty dresses, she stepped into the road without looking – right into the path of a bus.

Two of Harry's colleagues came to the house in their official capacity with the terrible news that Essie had been knocked down, was in hospital seriously injured and doctors were fighting to save her and the baby. They took Harry and his parents to the hospital in a police car. The driver really put his foot down but they were too late for Essie. She died just before they arrived.

'So sorry, Mr Riggs,' said the doctor. 'There was nothing more we could do; her injuries were too severe. She walked right in front of the bus, according to witnesses.'

'Oh . . .' Harry was too shocked to think properly. 'What about the baby?'

'The baby is doing fine,' the doctor said. 'The nurse will bring him to you when they've cleaned him up.'

'A boy? I have a son?'

'That's right, a healthy eight and a half pounds. Congratulations!'

Harry's emotions were frozen with shock, but when the nurse handed him a bundle wrapped in a shawl and he looked at the tiny pink face he was awash with love for his child and knew there was nothing he wouldn't do for him. The little mouth opened and out came a piercing scream.

'He's a nice healthy pair of lungs on him,' said the nurse cheerfully. 'I'll take him now and you can see him again later.' She took the baby. 'We're all so sorry about your wife.'

'Thank you,' Harry said numbly, and he went outside in the corridor where his parents were waiting.

'I'll look after the baby while you're out at work,' said Marg when Harry and his parents were all back at home. The newborn was to stay in the care of the hospital for a few days. 'And I'll help in any other way that I can.'

'Thanks, Mum.'

'Think nothing of it, love,' she said. 'He's a part of the family. We'll all help.'

'That's right, son,' added his father.

Essie's death was a terrible shock for Harry and he was still reeling from it. He hadn't been in love with her, but she had been his wife and she was far too young to die, so how could he not be sad? He didn't know why she had walked in front of the bus but he was certain it wasn't suicide. She had spent most of her time complaining about her life but she wouldn't have wanted to die. She was too full of life in her own aggressive way. He guessed she'd simply been pre-occupied with her thoughts and hadn't looked before stepping off the kerb.

Well, she hadn't given him much pleasure in life but she had left him with the greatest gift of all, their son, and Harry would do his very best to give the baby a good upbringing.

'Any ideas for a name for him?' his mother was saying.

'I think I'll name him Michael, after his granddad,' he said, looking at his father. 'Mikey for short.'

His father beamed. 'Oh, lovely. Thanks, son.'

'That's all right, Dad,' he said. 'Nice to keep it in the family, and I think another Harry might be a bit much.'

'Yeah, one of those is quite enough,' Michael said, joking.

Harry fell silent as he thought about the huge responsibility ahead of him, raising a child on his own. But before the thoughts had a chance to take root his mother said, 'You're not on your own, son. Little Mikey is a Riggs, one of the family, and we'll back you up all the way.'

'Thanks, Mum.'

He was choked with emotion. He was feeling sad about Essie and more than a little frightened of the huge responsibility ahead of him. But he had good support and he would do his very best for his son.

Because of the dramatic circumstances of Essie's death, it was reported in the local paper and Lola got to know about it.

'Are you going to see Harry to offer him your condolences?' asked Doreen.

'The ex-girlfriend turning up when he's just lost his wife? It wouldn't be appropriate, would it?'

'I don't think there are any rules in the case of a death,' Doreen said. 'But if you don't feel comfortable, forget it.'

'I don't even know where he lives these days, anyway.'

'You know his parents' address, though; he might be living with them because of the housing shortage. If not, they'll tell you where he lives.'

'Mm.'

'Think about it some more,' suggested Doreen. 'You're obviously not sure.'

'I don't want to intrude,' Lola said. 'Anyway, he has a baby so he'll be busy.'

Doreen shrugged. 'You weren't actually planning on seducing him, were you?'

Lola tutted. 'Of course not. Honestly, you don't half come out with some daft stuff.'

'Just trying to lighten things up a bit,' Doreen said. 'I know that when my uncle died people came from far and wide – relatives and friends the family hadn't seen for years. It's a kind thought, that's all.'

'Mm, I'll think about it.'

But she knew it was more than just a kind thought for her. She wanted to see him because she was still in love with him. Yes, she was sorry he had lost his wife, but she ached to see him for her own selfish reasons. And therefore she would stay away.

The funeral was over and people had stopped calling at the house. Harry's baby son was home from hospital and in the care of Harry's mother while he was at work. He knew that if he allowed it to happen his mother would take over completely and bring Mikey up, and he didn't want that. He had to hand the baby over while he went to work, but when he was at home he tried to do everything the baby's mother would have done. He made his bottle and fed him, changed his nappy and got up to him in the night, all of which was considered most unmanly. He took some ribbing over it from his mates at the police station.

'You shouldn't tell them if they are going to tease you,' said his mother.

'I'm not ashamed of what I do for Mikey, Mum,' he assured her. 'Anyway, you get used to a lot of mickey-taking in the force. It happens all the time and nothing's meant by it.'

'I suppose so,' she said. 'Anyway, I'm very proud of the way you are coping.'

Now, as he approached the police station on his way to work, someone else came into his mind and he had a sudden longing to see Lola. He'd never stopped loving her. All through his unhappy marriage she'd been on his mind. She was the love of his life and he would never forget her. He reminded himself that she hadn't felt the same and had turned his marriage proposal down. But that didn't stop him loving her.

Still, he had quite enough to contend with at the moment with a child to raise. He didn't need to remember old heartaches. He quickened his step as he approached the police station, full of enthusiasm for the day's work ahead of him. But, for all his determination to be sensible, thoughts of his lost love lingered in his mind.

An argument was brewing in the Brown house over dinner one evening in the early spring of 1948 when the family were discussing Lola's brother Frankie's future after he left school at the end of that term.

'He'll do all right working with me,' said Charlie.

'He wants to do an apprenticeship to be a car mechanic, Dad,' Lola reminded him. 'You know that.'

'There's no money in that,' said her father. 'You get much better pay in a factory, and he can come out with me after work to earn a few bob more.'

'No, Dad, you're not dragging him down into your seedy deals of an evening. He's too young to go in a pub, anyway.'

'I'm good mates with the landlords where I go,' he said. 'They'll let him come in.'

'No, I won't let you do it,' said Lola. 'You know how much he wants to do the apprenticeship. He's mad about cars.'

'They'll have him working for nothing,' said her father.

'They don't pay much when you are learning, it's true,' she said. 'But once he's qualified, he'll be able to earn well. Now that the war is over there'll be more cars on the road. It's a growing trade.'

'And he'll earn buttons for three years while he learns.'

'It'll be worth it because he'll get good money after that.'

'Not that much.'

There was a sudden interruption from Frankie. 'I am going to do the apprenticeship, Dad,' he said, his cheeks flushed at this unusual opposition to his father. 'There's a garage in town that is interested in taking me on. I'll be getting the forms soon. Once it's sorted, I'll be starting work at the end of term.'

'You've done all this yourself, Frankie?' said his sister, impressed.

'One of the teachers has been helping me,' he said. 'He made some enquiries for me.'

'But you took the initiative in telling your teacher about it,' said Lola.

'Somebody came to the school to talk to us about what we are going to do when we leave. That's how it came up.' He turned to his father. 'This is what I want to do, Dad.'

His father scowled at him. 'You're entitled to your choice, of course,' he said. 'If you want to be scratching a measly living all your life it's up to you.'

'I want to do something that interests me.'

'Good for you, Frankie,' said Lola. 'I know exactly how you feel. I was like that until I got the job at the tearooms. I love going to work now. It's important to do something you enjoy.'

'Rubbish,' said Charlie. 'Work is work: a means of earning money. You don't expect to enjoy it.'

'Of course you do, Dad,' Lola argued.

'A lot of people don't,' he said. 'What about the poor buggers who collect the rubbish or mend the roads?'

'They would get a certain sense of fulfilment, I should think,' she said. 'It's a very worthwhile thing to do. But I accept that not everyone is as fortunate as me. I'm sure some people don't like going to work.'

114

'I can't wait to get there,' said Frankie, who would be fifteen in a few weeks' time.

'And long may it continue,' said Lola.

'I hope so too,' added Rita.

'I don't seem to have a say in this family these days,' Charlie complained.

'Frankie and me are not kids any more, Dad,' said Lola. 'We have our own opinions.'

'And don't I bloody well know it.'

'All part of life's rich pattern,' she said, laughing.

'I'm going round to see Uncle Bert later, to see what he thinks about my apprenticeship,' said Frankie.

'He'll be all for it,' said his father. 'He's a great believer in the straight and narrow.'

'Good for him,' said Lola.

'Oh, I know my brother can't do any wrong with you lot,' said Charlie. 'But I am your father, remember.'

'It isn't a competition, Dad,' Lola said. 'He's our uncle and he's always been good to us.'

Charlie sighed. 'I know.' He paused. 'Anyway, I'll be off. Things to do; people to see.'

And he left the others talking about Frankie's future career.

'Please tell me that you've ended it with Keith,' said Doreen, when she and Lola were walking to the cinema one evening that spring.

'I couldn't do it because he cancelled our date yesterday,' Lola said. 'He phoned me at work to say he couldn't make it.'

'Phone calls at work, eh? It's all right for some.'

'I know I'm very fortunate,' Lola said. 'As long as I get my work done, I can do as I please: phone calls, popping out to the shops. The ladies don't mind at all.'

'Lucky thing. Anyway, why did he cancel the date? Is he cooling off?'

'I don't think so. He told me he wasn't feeling well,' Lola said. 'He left work early because he felt rotten and called me from a phone box on the way home.'

'Probably just a cold or something,' said Doreen.

'I should think so, but he didn't go into detail.'

'Just think, though. He'll be able to go and see the doctor for free soon. We all will,' said Doreen.

'Yeah, Mum and Dad were talking about that. Some sort of health service that's starting up, isn't it?'

'Yeah, free doctors' appointments and medicine, and anything else do to with our health,' Doreen remembered hearing. 'Completely free for us all.'

'Comes out of our taxes, I suppose,' said Lola.

'Probably,' said Doreen without much interest. Neither of them was of an age to take an interest in such things.

'Anyway, as soon as he's feeling well again, I really will tell him, I promise.'

'You better had or you'll have me on your back,' said Doreen. 'I feel responsible because I sort of got you together.'

'I know,' said Lola. 'And I won't let you down. I'll tell him next time I see him.'

But somehow it didn't happen. Keith seemed so vulnerable when she met him a few days later, she couldn't utter the words. He was very quiet and looked exhausted. He was so pale his freckles seemed to stand out like dust.

'You really should have stayed at home in bed, Keith,' she said with concern.

'I wanted to see you,' he said earnestly.

'But if you're not well . . .'

'I went to work so I thought, if I'm well enough for that, I'm well enough to come out and see you,' he said. 'Anyway, I don't feel ill exactly, just very tired.'

'That's all right then.'

'Good,' he said with an attempt at a smile. 'Shall we just go for a drink somewhere? I don't feel up to much more than that, but I'll make it up to you, I promise.'

'Don't be silly; there's no need for anything like that,' Lola said, and it was at that moment she felt something deep inside her, a feeling of fondness for him. It took her aback because it was so strong and sudden. She had always liked Keith and felt a kind of sympathy for him because he had suffered in the war, she knew, having been taken prisoner. She wasn't in love with him – definitely not – but she did feel deep affection brought on by sympathy with the fact that he wasn't feeling well. She knew she couldn't tell him she didn't want to see him again at this point. It would have to wait until he was feeling better. He'd probably be perfectly all right in a day or two. It wasn't urgent. It could wait.

Chapter Seven

Lola could feel her life going off course but was powerless to do anything about it because she had a kind heart and a horrible thing had happened to Keith. He had been diagnosed with TB, so how could she end her relationship with him?

'It is very awkward for you, I admit,' said Doreen when Lola discussed it with her. 'But if you're not careful you'll end up marrying him out of pity.'

'Mm, I can see how that might happen and I'm determined not to let it. But I do feel very sorry for him so I am well and truly trapped, for the moment, anyway.'

'He has a good chance of recovery, though,' Doreen reminded her. 'I mean, it isn't like the old days when people nearly always died of that disease. There is new treatment available now. And he isn't holed up in a sanitorium. They can treat it successfully at home nowadays in a lot of cases. So, it isn't too bad for him.'

'It's still a long recovery period, though, and he's quite poorly at the moment,' Lola said. 'He'll be in bed for ages and he'll need plenty of support during that time. It's very depressing for him.'

'And you visit every evening after work, I suppose.'

'I feel I must,' Lola admitted. 'Some people still think it's contagious so they won't go within a mile of him. His mates are pretty good, but they don't go to see him every day so I feel duty bound to give him some company even if I don't stay very long. He keeps telling me I needn't, but I know he wants me to. Otherwise the only people he gets to see are his parents and relatives. He's an only child too, so it's very lonely for him. He needs plenty of company his own age.'

'Just make sure he knows that you are not going to be with him for ever.'

'I can't make too much of that at the moment, can I? Not while he's ill. That would be really cruel,' Lola said. 'He's very vulnerable and doesn't need any kind of rejection.'

'Are you sure it would really be so bad for him? I mean, you're not wanting to stay with him for ever, are you?'

'I think it would be a blow to him, as he seems so keen.'

'You're in a pickle then, kid,' Doreen said. 'The first thing you need to do is cut down on the visits.'

'But that would be too cruel at this stage of the illness, while he's feeling so rotten.'

'Sometimes you have to be cruel to be kind, Lola.'

'I can't do that to him while he's ill,' Lola insisted. 'It's having company that keeps him going.'

'If it's just a question of company, why don't I visit him sometimes instead of you, to give you a break? Would that help?'

Lola looked at her in surprise. 'Would you be willing?'

'Sure, if it'll help?' Doreen said brightly.

'It's certainly worth a try if you really don't mind.'

'I don't mind in the least. It isn't as if I don't know him.

Keith and I have been mates for years and I already go to see him now and again anyway, the same as all his pals. I'll just increase my visits. As long as he's happy about it.'

'I'm sure he will be, so thanks, Doreen.'

'No trouble at all, kid,' Doreen said cheerfully.

Initially Doreen's extra visits weren't welcomed by Keith, who wasn't happy to have Lola replaced by another visitor, and he made no secret of it. Doreen wasn't the sort of girl to take things quietly, however, so she spoke her mind.

'Look, mate, I know that you're ill and we're all very sorry for you, but Lola must be allowed to have some time to herself, if only to wash her hair and see her friends. As things have been since you've been ill, if she isn't at work, she's here visiting you. So, give her a break, will you? Stop relying so heavily on her.'

'Oh!' Keith was clearly shocked. 'I hadn't realised I was doing that.'

'I'm sure you hadn't,' Doreen said more warmly, sitting on a chair beside his bed. 'It must be easy to get wrapped up in yourself when you're ill and stuck at home in bed. You're a good bloke. You wouldn't deliberately put on anybody. I know that.'

'I hope I wouldn't, but I've done it without realising and I feel awful.'

'There's no need for that,' she assured him, her brown eyes resting on him, her dark hair arranged prettily about her shoulders. 'She's very happy to come, but maybe not every single night because she has some other things to do. But I'll come when she doesn't, if you like.'

Keith grinned at her. 'That is very good of you, but I don't want to put you out.'

'You wouldn't be. But you can decide about that after I've gone,' she said, then chuckled. 'Once might be more than enough. I'm not a particularly quiet girl.'

'I'm just glad you came,' he said.

'Ooh, you've gone all polite on me,' she laughed. 'Too much of that might make me nervous.'

'I don't believe you,' he said smiling. 'I can't imagine you being nervous under any circumstances.'

'Oh dear, am I that full of myself?'

'Not at all. But you are confident.'

'I'll try to tone it down a bit.'

'No need.'

'Anyway, how do you manage to pass the time during the day?' she enquired.

'Read, sleep . . . Mum sometimes comes in for a game of cards or a natter. Somehow the day passes. You do get used to it.'

'But you're really pleased to see someone of your own age in the evening, I imagine.'

'Not half,' he said. 'I look forward to it. People can't always come, of course. But most of the time someone manages it. I'm very lucky.'

'You must have done something right to have such good friends.'

'Indeed.' He paused, looking at her. 'Anyway, what about you? Not out on a date tonight?'

'No. No boyfriend at the moment.'

'I am surprised.'

'Don't worry, I'm working on it,' she laughed.

He smiled and the conversation just flowed. She was very glad she had come and she was enjoying herself.

'What about your job?' she asked. 'Will they keep it open for you?'

'Oh, yes, they've assured me that they'll want me back when I'm better,' he said.

'They'd be cruel if they didn't.'

He nodded. 'It wouldn't do much for their reputation if they got rid of me because of illness. It's a very long recovery period, though. I won't be able to go back to work for months.'

'We'll all have to make sure we come and cheer you up, then, won't we?'

'Thanks ever so much for visiting,' he said when eventually she made to leave.

'I've really enjoyed being here,' she said, and meant it.

'Hope to see you again soon.'

'I'll be back, don't worry,' Doreen said, getting up to leave, conscious of her tall, elegant figure and the swing of her long dark hair.

Well, she had really enjoyed her evening with Keith, she thought as she walked home. And to her astonishment she had sensed the beginnings of some sort of chemistry between them. Funny how she'd never really noticed what wonderful blue eyes he had before. Lola wanted out of that relationship, but would she still want that when she knew someone else was interested? There was nothing like competition to create enthusiasm!

'Are you sure you don't want to continue with Keith?' Doreen asked Lola the following evening when Lola called at her house on the way home from work.

'Not as a steady boyfriend,' she said. 'Definitely not. I'd like to stay friends, though, because he's a nice bloke.'

'Only I got on really well with him last night.'

'Don't tell me you still fancy him? After all this time?'

'I think I do,' Doreen said. 'There was definitely the beginning of something, but I don't want to think along those lines if you want to stay with him.'

'I don't.'

'Just making sure.'

'Do you think he felt the same about you?'

'There was certainly a spark between us, but it could just have been that he was glad of the company.' She thought about it. 'But no, it was definitely a real spark. Something for me to work on. If it comes to anything it will please both you and me. I gain a boyfriend and you get rid of one.'

Lola laughed. 'Put like that, it seems heartless.'

'No, not really,' Doreen reasoned. 'I get a bloke I fancy, he gets a new girlfriend and you get your freedom. So, everyone is happy. What's heartless about that?'

'Nothing is ever that simple, but we'll see how it goes,' Lola said. 'It'll be interesting to hear what he says about you.'

'Well, he isn't going to tell you he fancies me, is he? You are still his girlfriend.'

'Mm, I shall have to be subtle in my questioning,' said Lola.

'So how did you get on with Doreen?' Lola asked Keith when she visited later on that evening.

'Oh, she was all right,' he said, overly casual.

'You found plenty to talk about then?'

123

'Yeah, she's very easy to get on with. And it wasn't as if I didn't already know her.'

'It was a change for you, anyway.'

He nodded. 'I'm sorry I've been relying so heavily on you,' he said. 'I hadn't realised. Doreen gave me quite a ticking off about it, actually.'

'She does tend to speak her mind.'

'I was glad she mentioned it,' he said. 'You can easily get selfish without realising it when you're sick.'

'It's fine, really.'

'Anyway, she's going to come round sometimes now, so that will give you a break.'

'It will be nice for you too, to see someone else besides me,' Lola said.

He nodded and Lola could feel his stifled enthusiasm. 'I always enjoy seeing you, though,' he said.

'I know.' She squeezed his hand.

She knew without a shadow of a doubt that what Doreen had felt for Keith, he had felt for her in return. It was just a matter of time before they accepted it and broke the news to her. She looked forward to seeing her two friends get together at last.

Harry's son Mikey was six months old, sitting up and keeping the family entertained with his beaming smiles and happy noises. He made more miserable sounds, too, sometimes, but mostly he was a contented little soul, who was the image of his father to look at.

'He's quieter than you were at that age,' said Harry's mother one night when Harry was about to put his baby son to bed.

'Thank God for that too. You could be a little perisher at times. Isn't that right, Michael?'

'Not half. You had a voice on you that could be heard from here to Southend,' said Harry's father.

'So has Mikey,' said Harry proudly.

'He doesn't inflict it on us as often as you used to.'

'Just as well, by the sound of it.' It had been hard going at times when Mikey had been very little and Harry had been trying to juggle work with caring for him. As a newborn he hadn't given much back then; it had been all nappy-changing, feeding and trying to stop him yelling. But now he could sit up and chuckle, and Harry loved every moment of being a dad. Each day seemed to bring a new accomplishment for baby and a treat for his adoring relatives.

'He'll be running around before we know it,' said Marg.

'I can't wait,' said Harry.

'You'll have him kicking a football as soon as he can stand up, I reckon.'

'I certainly will,' he replied.

The love he felt for Mikey was a new experience and a shock to him because he hadn't realised that being a father would be so emotional and all consuming. It was an indescribable feeling of joy beyond any other. But there was also fear and worry, and a deep sadness that his son would never know his mother. Harry wanted to protect him from everything, but he knew that he couldn't. Harry realised that the strength of his paternal feelings would make him vulnerable for the rest of his life.

The lads at work still teased him. 'What's he done now?' they'd ask. 'Signed up to play for England?'

'Had me up half the night, more like,' Harry confessed one morning. 'I've been pacing the floor with him.'

125

'Not quite the little angel today then?' said Archie.

'Oh, yeah, he's still that,' said Harry. 'He always will be, no matter how demanding.'

'Let's hope he's sleeping through the night before you start studying for your sergeant's exam,' said Archie. 'You'll need your rest then, with all the preparation.'

'I'm sure he'll be fine by then,' said Harry. 'Anyway, I'll do the preparation somehow.'

The extra money wasn't the only reason Harry wanted to do the sergeant's exam. He was committed to his career and wanted to do well. Being a policeman was more than just a job to him and he was keen to progress.

'Well, you certainly took your time,' said Lola, when Doreen and Keith finally confronted Lola with the news that they had fallen in love and wanted to be together.

'We didn't want to hurt you.'

'I'm not in the least hurt,' she said. 'I'm glad it's out in the open at last.'

It was true. She was glad to be relieved of her commitment to Keith. But, seeing him and Doreen so happy together made her feel sad that she couldn't be with the man she loved. Everyone seemed to have someone, but she was on her own. She had good friends and a job she enjoyed so she mustn't complain. It was just that there was a feeling of loneliness deep inside her that sometimes seemed overwhelming.

Harry and Archie were called out to a domestic in the New Year of 1949. A woman who looked to be in her thirties was brandishing a kitchen knife and threatening to kill her husband with it. He was cowering away from her by the kitchen sink. The police had been called by a neighbour, alerted by the couple shouting.

It was a tricky situation for the two coppers because the woman was in a very emotional state and one wrong move from them could result in injury or even death for her husband.

'Why don't I take the knife?' suggested Harry. 'Before somebody gets hurt.'

'He'll be more than hurt when I've finished with him,' said the woman, who the neighbour had told them was called Mrs Granger. 'He'll be six foot under, where he belongs.'

'Why do you want to kill him?' asked Archie.

'He's been carrying on,' she replied. 'With one of the neighbours. Talk about rubbing my nose in it. It's bloody disgusting, and he's going to pay for it.'

'I haven't been carrying on,' said the man shakily. 'She's got the wrong end of the stick, as usual.'

'Why don't you give me the knife and we'll all sit down and talk about it?' said Harry.

'Nothin' to talk about, mate,' Mrs Granger said, waving the knife about dangerously. 'He's a liar and a rotten cheat, so he's gonna be punished.'

'I ain't cheated on yer. Not ever!' said the man nervously, his face glistening with sweat. 'I wouldn't do that.'

'You've been seen going into her house.'

'She asked me to help her unblock the sink. She needed a strong pair of hands. I was just being neighbourly.'

'And the rest,' said his wife.

She took a step towards him, but Harry grabbed her from behind and removed the knife from her hand.

'I'll report you,' she screamed at Harry, 'for attacking a member of the public.'

'I've got a better idea,' said Archie. 'Why don't we put the kettle on and discuss the whole thing over a cup of tea?'

Harry led the sobbing woman to a chair at the kitchen table while his partner put the kettle on.

From what Harry could gather, Mr Granger was telling the truth. He had just been doing the neighbour a favour. It was that sort of a neighbourhood. His wife was obviously very insecure and Harry felt sorry for her.

'It's all right for him,' she said, referring to her husband. 'He's out at work all day, getting up to all sorts of mischief, no doubt, and I'm stuck here all day on my own.'

'I don't get up to mischief,' insisted her husband. 'It's bloody hard work being at a machine all day.'

'Any kids?' asked Harry.

'No, we ain't never been blessed in that way,' said the woman.

'We're new to the area,' said her husband. 'Ain't hardly got to know anyone yet.'

'There's no one around during the day,' said his wife. 'All the wives go out to work.'

'Lots of married women have jobs these days,' Harry mentioned. 'Perhaps a little part time job—'

'She ain't going out to work,' interrupted her husband. 'I'm not having that. No, her place is at home. I'm not having people say I can't afford to support my missis. So, keep yer nose out.'

'It was just a suggestion,' said Harry.

128

'Not wanted,' said Mr Granger. 'I can afford to look after my wife, thanks very much.'

'Yeah,' added his wife. 'My husband is a good provider and I won't have you suggesting otherwise. I've a good mind to have a word with them at the station about your cheek.'

'It was just conversation,' Harry said, reminded of how careful you had to be in this job.

'Yeah, well, you mind what you say in future,' she said.

By the time the policemen left, things were calmer, Mrs Granger said she wasn't going to make a complaint against Harry and the couple seemed to be the best of friends again.

'It takes all sorts,' said Harry as he and Archie continued on the beat.

'It certainly does,' Archie agreed. 'And I've got a feeling that isn't the last time the nick will get called out to those two.'

'I think you're right.'

Dealing so much with villains, Harry found this side of the job very satisfying. The problems of ordinary people were interesting and brought the best out in him. But there was little time to reflect on this because they were being summoned by a police whistle already, and they hurried towards their next challenge.

'Well, what a rotten letdown,' said Lola to Doreen. 'Clothes rationing ends and there's nothing decent in the shops to buy.'

'Have you had a look in the West End?'

'Yeah. Only stuff you wouldn't be seen dead in. A few nice things in the small dress shops, but not many and they're quite expensive.'

'It said in the paper that clothes will be in short supply for a while,' said Doreen. 'Nice that we won't need coupons when they do become plentiful again, though.'

'Yeah, and at least it's a sign that things are getting better even though it doesn't actually look like it,' said Lola.

'I'll have a look down Shepherd's Bush market at the weekend,' said Doreen. 'If there's fashionable clothes to be had anywhere, they'll have them there.'

'At prices we can afford, too,' said Lola.

But the next morning at work something happened that put the clothing shortage right out of Lola's mind.

'I'll come straight to the point,' said a man called Sidney Bateman, who had come into the tearooms and demanded to see the owners. 'I am about to change your lives – very much for the better.'

'I really don't think so,' said Cissy, not pleased at being dragged out of the kitchen while she was busy baking. 'Now I don't wish to be rude but we must get back to work. We have a business to run here.'

'Not for much longer,' Bateman said, looking shifty with his dark hair heavily greased, as was his moustache.

She shot him a look. 'What do you mean?'

'I can offer you the chance to put your feet up and still have plenty of money.'

'How is that?' asked Ethel.

'I am going to buy this place off you.'

'I don't think so,' said Cissy. 'It isn't for sale.'

'It will be when I tell you how much I'm prepared to pay for it,' he said.

'Not a chance,' Cissy said. 'Anyway, our scones are legendary and the recipe is top secret. You'd never be able to match it and people would stop coming.'

'Scones?' he said in a tone of disgust. 'I wouldn't waste my time selling scones. No, this is a prime West End site, a place for entertainment. I intend to open a night club here. I can see that there is a basement. Perfect for a club. I already own several in London. Now is the time for me to expand even more. The good times are coming and I want to be ready for them.'

'As I have already said, we are not for sale, Mr Bateman,' Cissy told him firmly, 'and I would like you to leave now, please. We have work to do.'

'I would give you a very good price for it,' he persisted. 'You wouldn't have anything to complain about as far as that is concerned. Enough money to give you a decent standard of living for the rest of your lives.'

'We are not interested,' Cissy said, becoming irritated. 'Now will you please leave?'

Lola was listening to all this in her office next door to the room into which she'd shown Bateman when he arrived, and she thought it was time she intervened.

'Would you like me to get Roger?' she asked, standing beside Cissy.

'Yes, please, dear.'

'All right, there's no need to call in the cavalry,' Bateman said. 'I'll go, but you haven't seen the last of me, I can promise you that. Anyone would think I was trying to steal the place from you, and that's the last thing I have in mind.'

'Please just leave now,' said Cissy.

'All right, but I'll get this place one way or another,'

131

was Bateman's parting shot. 'I always get what I want in the end.'

Lola felt a shiver of fear at the threat in his tone.

'What was that all about?' Roger asked Lola when the ladies had gone back to the kitchen and he wandered into the office. 'The sisters seem really worried about some visitor they had.'

'A man called Sidney Bateman wants to buy the tearooms,' she explained. 'He has plans to open a nightclub here. Of course, they have no intention of selling it to him, but he was very threatening.'

'Was he really?' Roger appeared thoughtful.

'He certainly was. He sounded determined to get the tearooms off them,' she said. 'And I should think he's the type who could get really nasty.'

'He's already in the nightclub business so he wants to build his empire,' he said.

'You know him?'

'Not personally, but I know *of* him.'

'Oh,' she said, surprised. 'You don't seem the type to go out on the town.'

'I'm not,' he said, without further explanation.

'I'm really worried,' said Lola. 'Not because I would lose my job but because the ladies would be lost without this place.'

'They won't be going anywhere, don't worry,' Roger assured her.

'How do you know?'

'Because I am going to make absolutely sure of it.'

'But how?

'Never you mind how,' he said. 'Let's just say that you get

to see a lot of things when you're living on the streets. Especially in a wicked place like the West End of London.'

'Sounds like a man with a good eye for business,' said Lola's father that night when she told the family about Mr Bateman over dinner. 'That place would be a lot more profitable as a nightclub than a tearoom.'

'Trust you to take his side,' said Lola.

'I'm not taking sides,' he said. 'Just stating the obvious. Nightclubs are big business, especially in the West End.'

'It would be a shame if the ladies lost their tearoom, though,' said Rita.

'Not if this bloke is going to pay them well for the site,' Charlie argued. 'They'll be able to put their feet up. They're getting on a bit. Time to take it easy.'

'They are not in their dotage,' said Lola. 'And the last thing they want to do is retire.'

'They might not have a choice.'

'Roger is going to make sure they do,' said Lola.

Charlie raised his eyes in disdain. 'I'm sure a tramp is going to make a hell of a lot of difference,' he said sarcastically.

'He isn't a tramp,' Lola said angrily.

'You shouldn't be so nasty about people, Dad,' said Frankie. 'It isn't nice.'

His father gave him a stony look. 'You are getting too cheeky for your own good,' he said. 'Just because you go out to work doesn't mean you can be rude to your father.'

'I was only sayin' . . .'

'Well, don't.'

A silence fell. Then Frankie changed the subject. 'My guvnor reckons that even quite ordinary people will own a car in the near future,' he said. 'Especially when petrol comes off ration.'

'Rubbish,' said his father. 'Not one person in this street owns a car.'

'Not now, but they will do before too long,' said Frankie. 'And I'll be one of them.'

'Now we really are getting above ourselves,' said Charlie.

'There's nothing wrong with being ambitious, Dad,' said Lola. 'And they do say there's a new and brighter Britain coming.'

'For people with ambition,' he said. 'Not a bloody car mechanic.'

'Now that isn't fair,' said Rita angrily. 'Frankie is doing a good honest job, and he's doing well.'

'Oh, I've had enough of you lot ganging up on me,' said her husband. 'I'm going down the pub for some decent company.'

He left the house, slamming the door.

Oh well, thought Lola, at least a bit of family bickering has taken my mind off the situation with Sidney Bateman.

Chapter Eight

'You are looking very smart this evening, Roger,' Ethel remarked when their lodger appeared in a suit and a tie, his hair combed neatly into place. 'Going anywhere nice?'

'Just meeting a mate for a drink and a chat,' he fibbed. 'I won't be late back.'

'You get back as late as you like and make sure that you enjoy yourself,' said Cissy, who was knitting while she listened to the wireless. 'You won't disturb us. We are both heavy sleepers, as you know.'

'I'll do my very best to enjoy myself,' he said grinning. 'See you both later, or in the morning if you're in bed when I get back.'

'Cheerio,' the sisters chorused happily. They were both now very fond of Roger and wanted the best for him. But although they took a friendly interest in him, they were careful not to pry into his private life. They agreed that wouldn't be right.

Roger hated lying to the ladies but it was in their best interests that they didn't know where he was going on this particular occasion, he thought, as he headed along the crowded West End streets. They might not like the idea of him interfering in their affairs. But it was something he felt compelled to do on this occasion. They had been good to him and now it was his turn to help them.

'Do you think Roger is meeting a woman?' Ethel said to her sister.

'Surely he would have said so if he was,' replied Cissy. 'He's a free agent and has no reason to hide anything from us. His private life is none of our business and we've made that very clear to him.'

'Yes, that's true, but I thought he looked a little bit sheepish tonight. As though he wasn't being quite honest with us.'

'Probably because he values his privacy and doesn't much care to be questioned about his social life,' said her sister pointedly.

'I was only taking a friendly interest,' Ethel said defensively.

'Yes, I know you were, dear, but he might feel a bit stifled, living with two old women,' Cissy said. 'It's only natural he wants a private life and he expects us to respect that.'

'He's never shown any sign of it before,' Ethel reminded her. 'If he wants to be on his own, he just stays in his room and we never disturb him outside of work. We don't ask where he's been when he goes out.'

'I should think not. It's none of our business where he goes or what he does,' said Cissy. 'I just hope he has a nice time. He works hard and he deserves a bit of pleasure after what he's been through.'

'Yes, I know that, dear, and there's no need to make a performance of it.'

'I wasn't.'

'Yes, you were,' Ethel snapped. 'You always have to pick me up on everything I say.'

And so it went on. Bickering was as natural to them as breathing and they barely even realised that they were doing it.

Then Ethel said, 'Are you still worrying about that man who came to see us because he wants to buy the tearooms?'

'That Bateman fellow. Yes, I am feeling a little uneasy,' Cissy admitted. 'Obviously he can't force us into anything, but he seemed so determined – threatening, even. It has been playing on my mind rather a lot, actually. How about you?'

'Yes, I've been thinking about it too,' said Ethel.

'You wouldn't want to move away from here, would you, Ethel?'

'Oh, no, of course not! It's our home, our way of life. I couldn't bear to leave it. When we are too old to run the tearooms, we can still live here and rent the business out or get someone to run it for us.'

'I know that. I was just making sure,' explained Cissy. 'I need to know that we are together on this because that awful man will be back. I'm sure of it.'

'Yes, he did seem rather persistent,' agreed Ethel. 'But you can count on me for support. I am most definitely with you on this one.'

'That's good, dear,' said Cissy, but she was still feeling vulnerable. Mr Bateman had had a determination about him that had sent shivers up her spine. He was the sort of man who made sure he got what he wanted, one way or another.

*   *   *

'This had better be good,' said Sidney Bateman that evening as he faced Roger across his desk in the office at his nightclub, the distant sound of dance music drifting in from outside. 'You've got a bloody cheek, forcing your way into my premises. I don't see salesman of an evening. My people have told you that.'

'I'm not a salesman and I think you'll be interested in what I have to say,' said Roger.

'What is it, some new tipple that's guaranteed to double my bar sales?' Bateman asked, his bloodshot eyes narrowing suspiciously as he drew on a cigarette and blew more smoke into the already chokingly foggy room.

'No, nothing like that,' said Roger. 'As I've already told you, I'm not here to try to sell you anything. Quite the opposite in fact. It's more a case of stopping you from buying.'

Bateman shot him a look; his eyes narrowed. 'I see. So, you want to do down a competitor of yours. Is that what you have in mind?'

'I don't have a competitor,' Roger said calmly. 'As I have said, I am not a salesman.'

'Why the hell are you here then?'

'Personal reasons.'

'Get on with it then, for goodness' sake,' Bateman said irritably. 'I'm a busy man. I don't have all night to sit here listening to you waffling.'

'I've heard that you want to buy The Tulip Tearooms,' said Roger.

'Yeah, so what if I do?'

'I want you to abandon the idea.'

Up shot Bateman's brows. 'Oh, really? And how do you know my business?' he asked, not looking best pleased. 'Who are you?'

'I am a friend of the Pickford sisters,' he said. 'And before we go any further, I have to tell you that they don't know that I am here and I want it to stay that way.'

The man nodded but looked extremely disagreeable. 'So why are you here and what business is it of yours if they sell the tearooms to me?'

'The place has been in their family for generations and they don't want to sell,' Roger said. 'It's their home as well as their livelihood, and you are trying to bully them into selling it to you.'

'I am not bullying them. They will be very well paid when they hand it over to me so I am being perfectly fair. I am not trying to steal it from them. I will pay considerably more than the place is worth.'

'Money doesn't interest them that much,' Roger mentioned. 'I think they are quite secure financially. Running the tearooms is a way of life for them; that's why they keep going with it.'

'Money interests everyone, and I'll make sure that they have more than enough to get somewhere really comfortable to live,' Bateman said. 'They could even take on commercial premises somewhere else if they don't want to retire, possibly out in the suburbs or in the country somewhere, where property is cheaper than the West End and the pace is slower. But I need to be right here in the centre of things for the sort of business I'm in to make real money,' he said.

'It's another nightclub, is it?'

'That's right, but, as I say, I have no intention of cheating them out of a single penny. I will pay them very well.'

'And as I have said, they grew up in the accommodation above the tearooms and they really don't want to make a move for any price,' said Roger.

'Well, maybe, but it's time they had a change,' Bateman said, rising as though to indicate that the meeting was over. 'It'll do them good. Give them a new lease of life.'

'They are happy where they are.'

'They'll soon get used to their new place and be able to enjoy their old age with no work to bother them,' the night-club owner said dismissively. 'Anyway, you have taken up quite enough of my time so I'd like you to leave now.'

'Is there no way at all you will reconsider?' asked Roger.

'Absolutely none whatsoever,' Bateman said in a definite tone. 'I will be paying them another visit shortly. I'll get the tearooms one way or another.'

'Mm,' said Roger thoughtfully. 'In that case I will be getting in touch with your wife.'

Bateman stared at him, looking puzzled. 'My wife?' he said. 'What has she got to do with it?'

'I have some information that I know she'll be interested in.'

Bateman narrowed his eyes and sat down again. 'What on earth are you talking about?' he said. 'You know nothing about me or my family.'

'I know enough to put the mockers on your marriage,' Roger told him.

'Get out,' Bateman said. 'Get out now.'

'Sure,' Roger agreed. 'I'll go. I need to get home to get a letter written – to your wife. A letter that will put an end to your glamorous way of life.'

'Oh, yeah, and what might that be about?'

'What you get up to in the small hours while your wife thinks you are working hard at the club,' Roger said. 'When in actual fact, come ten o'clock, you are off in a taxi with a young woman most nights. All over each other. At least you were when I used to see you.'

'I don't know what you're talking about,' Bateman said. 'How dare you come out with all these ridiculous stories?'

'No stories, and you know it,' Roger said. 'I used to sleep on the streets, some nights within viewing distance of the back door of your club. I saw what went on. Of course, you didn't notice me. Homeless people are invisible to men like you.'

'So, you're a tramp.'

'I was a homeless person for a while, yes. But not now, and my return to the normal world is thanks to the Pickford sisters. So, I want to look out for them as they did for me.'

'Get out before I have you thrown out,' Bateman said, his face flushed and shining with sweat.

'I'm going. I need to get that letter written.'

'You wouldn't know where to send it.'

'Oh, but I do,' said Roger.

The other man narrowed his eyes questioningly.

'I have a pal who used to work at your club as a barman until you sacked him because you thought the young woman you were having an affair with had taken a fancy to him,' Roger explained.

'I don't know what you're talking about . . .'

'My mate is a lot younger than you and that made you feel insecure,' Roger went on. 'Anyway, he got to know quite a bit about you while he worked here, including where you lived because you used to send him to your house on errands sometimes with bits your wife wanted from the shops, or if you forgot your glasses or wallet or something. Thanks to your sacking him and having him beaten up, he went on a downward spiral and ended up on the streets for a while, which is how I got to know him.'

Bateman was beginning to look extremely uncomfortable. His wife was a powerful force in his life. She was from a moneyed background, which was why he had married her and how he had got started in business. But she held the purse strings, and without her by his side he didn't have a penny piece. The fact that this man seemed to know that was alarming. He could be bluffing and it was a lucky guess, of course, but dare he take the chance?

'So, what is it exactly you want me to do?' he asked, resignedly.

'Abandon your interest in The Tulip Tearooms and leave the Pickford sisters alone. That's all.'

The man's eyes widened 'I don't suppose I have a choice, do I?'

'Not if you value your marriage and all the perks that come with it,' said Roger.

'All right,' Bateman said, sighing heavily. 'I'll stay away from the Pickford sisters. Their tearooms wouldn't be much of an asset anyway.'

'Excellent,' said Roger. 'Don't even think of going back on your word because if you go anywhere near the sisters again, I shall get in touch with Mrs Bateman right away without discussing it with you again.'

'Just leave and don't come back,' snarled Bateman.

'Don't give me to cause to then,' said Roger, and went calmly on his way.

He was smiling as he walked home. There were times when you had to stretch the truth for the greater good and use guesswork. Most of what he'd said was true but he hadn't the least idea where Bateman lived or how to contact his wife. He could always do so through the club, if need be, but he was certain it wouldn't be necessary. Bateman had too much invested in his marriage to put it at risk.

Well, he'd done his work for the night and thought he deserved a pint before he went home so he headed for the local pub where he was sure he'd find some male company. He was very happy living and working with the ladies but he did need the company of his mates from time to time.

'You can rest easy in your beds tonight, ladies,' Roger said when he finally got home feeling pleasantly relaxed after a couple of pints and a spot of male humour with the lads. 'Because you won't be hearing from Mr Bateman again, and that's a promise.'

'You've been to see him, then?' guessed Cissy.

'I have indeed, and he's agreed to drop his interest in the tearooms.'

'Ooh, that's a relief,' said Cissy. 'But what did you do to him to make him agree? I hope there was no violence involved.'

'No, nothing like that,' Roger assured the sisters.

'How did you get him to change his mind?' asked Ethel.

'Just had a chat, man to man,' Roger said. 'So, all you have to do is forget about him.'

'Thank you, Roger,' said Cissy warmly. 'I don't know what we would do without you.'

'With a bit of luck, you won't have to,' he said smiling.

Roger felt unexpectedly sentimental. It was so nice to feel useful and he was very fond of the sisters, especially Cissy, for whom he had a real soft spot. She had no idea of his feelings and would probably be shocked to learn, so he would keep them to himself.

Doreen had some news for Lola when they went for their usual mooch around the shops one Saturday afternoon in summer, although she was more than a little apprehensive about telling her.

'I hope you won't be upset by what I have to say to you,' she said.

'Ooh, that sounds ominous. You'd better tell me what it is and you'll soon find out,' Lola answered.

'Keith and I are getting engaged,' Doreen said, sounding nervous.

'Oh, that's wonderful news,' said Lola. 'Surely you didn't really think I would be upset?'

'Well, he was your boyfriend before he was mine.'

'He and I were over long before you two got together, and I'm delighted for you,' Lola said, hugging her.

'Oh, that's such a relief,' said Doreen beaming. 'I am so happy, Lola.'

Lola meant what she said about being delighted for her friends, but an awful feeling of loneliness had crept over her. Everyone seemed to have someone except her. She was a young woman and longed for a normal love life like everyone else. But, thanks to her father, she couldn't be with the man she loved, even though he was now free. It was a fact and there was no point in getting miserable about it. She just had to accept it and get on with her life as best as she could. Maybe she needed a new project to distract her, something to immerse herself in.

What, though? She was happy in her job so didn't want to change that. She didn't want a boyfriend just for the sake of it. But she needed something worthwhile to concentrate on. Then the answer came to her. It wasn't a permanent solution but it would be something to keep her busy and occupy her mind for a while, and it was a worthwhile project. She'd speak to the ladies about it. Without their approval and co-operation it wouldn't be possible. The tearooms was their business, after all.

Harry enjoyed fatherhood more with every day that passed. Mikey was over a year old now, and his father was besotted with him even though he was a real handful. He was on his feet now, and so much so that Harry and his parents needed eyes in the back of their heads to keep up with him.

It was a joy to Harry that his parents were closely involved in the boy's life too, especially as Mikey didn't have a mother. That couldn't be changed, but having doting grandparents must make a difference. Being on shift work meant that Harry was around during the day sometimes so he was able to spend more time with his son than if he had a nine-to-five job.

So, things ticked over pretty well. But there was a missing element in his life that he was always aware of. He didn't have a special someone with whom to share his life and his son. Sometimes the loneliness was awful. There were always people around him, but not that special person. There had only been one woman he truly loved and he hadn't seen Lola for years. She was probably married with kids of her own by now. Oh well, you had to take what life sent you and he was luckier than most. He had a beautiful son and loving parents as well

145

as a job he enjoyed. Police work was often harrowing and always unpredictable but there was nothing else he would rather do. You couldn't have everything in life and he was very grateful for what he did have.

'I admire the sentiment, Lola,' said Cissy, when Lola pitched her idea to the sisters. 'But we are supposed to be running a business here, not a public assistance organisation.'

'Yes, I understand that, but we make a good profit the rest of the time so I thought we could afford to do a little something for charity.'

'She does have a point, Cissy,' said Ethel. 'I think we should do it.'

'A high tea on a Sunday afternoon, free of charge, for the homeless?' said Cissy. 'That's what you have in mind, then, Lola?'

Lola nodded. 'Only a one-off, not every Sunday, of course.'

'I should think not,' said Cissy. 'We'd soon go out of business if we did it every week.'

'Maybe every now and again,' suggested Lola. 'Once a year, perhaps.'

'Don't push it, dear,' said Cissy. 'Let's see how we get on with the first one.'

'We can do it then?' said Lola, delighted.

'Yes, you can get it organised,' said Cissy with a sigh of resignation. 'But keep it basic: just sandwiches and scones. First come, first served, and when they're gone, they're gone. No second helpings.'

'You are being a bit stingy, dear,' said her sister.

'Just trying to stop things running out of control,' Cissy

said. 'Lola can get a bit carried away with her charitable enterprises.'

'Only because there are so many people who have nothing, when we have lots,' said Lola.

'All right, dear,' said Cissy. 'No need to preach. We know how things work.'

'Sorry,' said Lola.

'Apologies aren't necessary,' said Cissy. 'We know you are very well intentioned. We just have to make sure that you don't get too carried away. The tearoom is only a small business. We don't have the huge resources of Lyons teashops. There is only so much charity work we can afford to do.'

'I understand,' said Lola.

'Those bosses of yours must be soft in the head to let you talk them into giving stuff away,' said Lola's father that evening over dinner, referring to the charity tea his daughter was organising. 'That's the most certain way to bankruptcy that I know of.'

'It's one event, Dad,' said Lola, 'It isn't going to break the bank.'

'Have you never heard of the slippery slope?'

'Of course, I have, and there's no danger of them getting on to that,' she said. 'The ladies are far too sensible. But they do like to do their bit for charity and I'm always ready to give them a reminder every now and again.'

'We'll see how long they stay in business with that sort of attitude,' he said.

'I agree with Lola,' said Rita. 'It'll just be a one-off. It won't bankrupt them.'

'And I suppose they've asked you to go into work on a Sunday afternoon,' he said.

'I offered,' said Lola. 'I wouldn't want to miss it for the world since it's my idea.'

'I hope they'll pay you Sunday rates,' he said.

'Of course they won't. I absolutely would not accept any payment at all,' said Lola firmly. 'It was my idea to do a charity tea so I'll happily work for nothing. That's what charity is all about, Dad.'

'Don't you dare work for nothing,' he roared. 'Once you start that they'll take advantage of you and there's no knowing where it will end.'

Lola put down her knife and fork and stared at her father. 'Why are you always so horrible about people?' she asked.

'I'm a man of the world and I know what goes on, that's why,' he said. 'You are just a slip of a girl who has seen nothing of life.'

'I wouldn't say that, dear,' put in her mother, mildly. 'She's a bright girl who works in the West End, and you get all sorts there.'

Charlie glared at his wife. 'Must you always go against me?' he snapped. 'Every single time we have a discussion in this house you take the other person's side.'

'I was just saying—'

'Well, don't,' he said. 'Keep your bloody mouth shut.'

An almost unprecedented interruption from Frankie halted the conversation. 'Can you all please stop snapping at each other,' he said. 'It's putting me off my food.'

There was a stiff silence, then Lola said, 'He's right. We shouldn't be bickering at mealtimes. So, let's change the subject.'

She turned to her brother. 'Sorry, kiddo. What sort of a day did you have?'

'Quite good,' he said with an uncertain smile, and the atmosphere gradually lifted.

Human nature could be very disappointing at times, Lola had found, and she felt very let down by it on the Sunday of the complimentary tea when people who clearly didn't qualify turned up, youths mostly, who had seen the notice and come for a lark.

'Ooh, cheese sandwiches,' said one young man, who clearly hadn't slept on the street and was dressed in a modern suit and a colourful tie, his hair greased with a fashionable quiff at the front. 'Just what I fancy. I love a bit o' cheese.'

'Oi,' said Frankie, who was helping out. 'This tea isn't for the likes of you.'

'Why not?' said the youth.

'You don't need it.'

'How do you know?'

'It's obvious that you're not living rough, so clear off,' said Frankie. 'This food is for homeless people.'

The intruder's mates pushed Frankie. Lola noticed what was going on and was about to intervene when Frankie suddenly squared up to one of the youths then grabbed him by the back of his jacket and marched him to the door of the café, which Lola held open, and helped him on his way out. Very much subdued, his mates followed. Her brother was really growing up, she thought, with a mixture of pride and sadness.

'Well done, Frankie,' she said.

He gave her a beaming grin and she realised that the incident had been a test of courage for him. He had passed with flying colours and she was so very proud of him.

'Come on, folks,' he said to the assortment of unfortunates seated at the tables. 'We don't want any leftovers. So, get eating.'

They needed no second bidding and the piles of sandwiches and cakes disappeared with speed.

'There's always hope while there are people like you and Frankie and the ladies,' said Roger, who had come along to help out.

'Oh, Roger,' Lola said, feeling emotional, 'what a nice thing to say. But you've left someone out.'

'Really? Who?'

'Yourself,' she said. 'You helped to organise it.'

'Oh, that,' he said, and, with his usual modesty, changed the subject.

Chapter Nine

'You'll never guess what our next-door neighbours have got,' said Lola's mother to the family over dinner one night with a mixture of excitement and envy.

'Is it a lodger?' suggested Lola.

'A puppy?' tried Frankie.

'Nope,' said Rita, obviously dying to spill the beans.

'We give up,' said Lola. 'So, tell us.'

'They've only gone and got a television set.'

'Ooh,' said Frankie enviously. 'The lucky things.'

'Have they really,' said Lola, also impressed.

'They had it delivered for Christmas, apparently,' their mother went on enthusiastically. 'The lucky devils. She's full of it, telling everyone and showing off like mad. She knows we're all green with envy.'

'Too right we are. I wish we had one,' said Frankie woefully. 'One of my mates at work has just had one delivered to their house. He said it's really smashing; just like being at the pictures in your own living room. Absolutely amazing!'

'Yeah, they are good,' agreed Lola. Television set owners were elevated to a higher social standing and sometimes invited those who didn't have a set in for an evening's viewing, with refreshments included. 'Doreen's auntie has just got one and we went round to see it the other night. It's really smashing.'

'Can we have one, Dad?' asked Frankie. 'Everybody is getting them.'

'Everybody isn't getting them at all,' said his father. 'Very few people have one, in fact. Anyway, I've heard the programmes are rubbish.'

'No one cares about the programmes. It's just so exciting seeing things moving about on the screen in your own living room,' Frankie informed him with authority. 'Anyway, it's being a television owner that really matters. You're behind the times if you don't have a set nowadays, and I'm sure you wouldn't be happy about that, Dad. You like to be first in the street to have anything new that comes in. I should think that the programmes will probably improve with time, too.'

'And you're an authority on the subject, I suppose,' said his father cynically.

'I know a bit about them, yeah,' Frankie said breezily. 'It's what everyone is talking about on the street. Anyway, Dad, you know that you like to stay ahead of the neighbours,' Frankie artfully reminded him. 'In fact, I'm surprised that you've let the people next door beat us to it.'

'Do you think I'm made of money?'

'No, of course not, but my mate at work, his family aren't rich or posh or anything, and they got one recently, so ordinary people are having them. I would chip in and help out, but I'm just a poorly paid apprentice.'

'Ooh, get out the sad violins,' said his sister, laughing.

His father was thoughtful. He had a lucrative bit of business coming up soon and he did like to keep ahead of the neighbours with material acquisitions. It gave him something to brag about in the pub and made him feel good about himself. 'You'll get your television set, boy. All in good time.'

'When, though?'

'You'll just have to wait and see, won't you?' said Charlie mysteriously. 'But we will be having one and that's definite. We can't have next door outdoing us, can we?'

'You gonna rob a bank then, Charlie?' joshed Rita.

'You don't need to rob a bank to get a television set these days, luv,' he said. 'You get one on the never-never.'

'Oh, I thought as much,' she said. 'I didn't like to ask her next door, and she wouldn't want to admit to it.'

'A lot of people get them that way,' Charlie informed her. 'But we won't because I know someone who can get us one cheap. But strictly cash on the nail.'

'What are you waiting for then, Dad?' challenged Frankie.

'Give me a chance, boy. I'm not made of money,' said his father. 'Anyway, what good would a television set be to you? You're never at home; always out with your mates of an evening, raking the streets and no doubt getting up to all sort of mischief. So, you'd never look at it.'

'I'd stay in more if we had a set,' Frankie said with a wicked grin. 'There you are, Dad, that's a good enough reason for you to get one.'

'Cheeky little bugger,' said his father.

'It's true, though, Charlie,' added Rita. 'It might encourage Frankie to stay at home more if there was something to occupy him.'

'It would be a five-minute wonder for him. He'd soon get bored with it and be off out again every night. He's young – it's what they do,' Charlie insisted.

'I wouldn't mind having one, though,' Rita said. 'And I definitely wouldn't get bored with it.'

Televisions sets were big business on the black market at the moment. There was a high demand and if you were in the know with suppliers you could earn good money in commission. Charlie had been doing very nicely out of their popularity so maybe it was time to get a set for the family.

'It would be nice for Mum,' Frankie pointed out craftily. 'Something to keep her company at home while you're out at the pub of an evening enjoying yourself.'

'I'm not out enjoying myself. I go out to do business so that you lot can have nice things,' said his father, who had big plans; a television set was just one of the luxury items he would be bringing into the house when the deals were right. After years of hardship and crippling shortages, popular items and new attractions were becoming available if you knew the right people. 'You'll get your television set soon enough.'

'When, though?'

'Wait and see.'

Lola was listening to this with a mixture of affection and tedium. It was very predictable. Still, it was better than wartime conversation about bombs and destruction. Not so long ago all they had wanted was to live through the night. Nowadays people hankered after the shiny new items gleaming in the shop windows, such as television sets and washing machines. She, personally, was more interested in the fact that clothes were no longer rationed, though there was still nothing very exciting to buy. But that situation would surely get better now that the country was really beginning to show signs of recovery. She did hope so because she enjoyed nice clothes.

'Tell 'im, Lola,' her brother was saying.

'What?' she said, startled out of her reverie.

'Tell Dad we have to have a television set because everybody is getting them.'

'I know of only one person that has one besides the neighbours,' she said, 'and that is Doreen's auntie.'

'Traitor,' Frankie said, but he was grinning.

The atmosphere was easy. At times like this Lola realised how lucky she was to have a loving family, albeit that her father was a crook and there wasn't much love lost between the two of them. But she was of an age to want to escape from the family and be independent. Most girls of her ilk made the change through marriage, so it would remain just a dream for now because there wasn't a man in her life at the moment. Harry came into her mind and she felt a horrible pang deep inside. She wondered how he was getting on. He was probably doing very well in the police. He was the sort who would put his heart and soul into anything he took on. Most likely he was married again, too, she thought miserably. It wasn't a good idea to think about him; it only made her feel sad. But he slipped into her mind uninvited and there wasn't much she could do about that.

'It's time you had a woman in your life again, Harry,' announced his father one evening when his son came downstairs after putting Mikey to bed. 'Someone to look out for you and be a mother to Mikey.'

'Not interested, Dad,' said Harry. 'Not at the moment, anyway. I'm doing all right as I am, thanks very much.'

'Everyone needs someone.'

'Maybe so, but I'm fine, really. I've enough to think about with work and being a dad.'

'Exactly,' said his father. 'It's all work and Mikey. You need some light relief. Someone to share it with.'

'Look, Dad, if a woman happened to come along that I liked and felt right with, I might consider the idea, but I am not actively looking for anyone. Mikey is my priority, and with the support from you and Mum he is having a good life. He certainly doesn't lack for love – or anything else, for that matter.'

'I know that, son,' said his father with emphasis. 'I was thinking more about you.'

'You can stop worrying because I am perfectly happy as things are.'

'Oh, well, it's your life, I suppose,' interjected his mother.

'That's right, it is, and while we are on the subject I might as well mention that I am really grateful to you both for your support. I don't know what I'd do without you. I mean, you've had your family and are at an age when you want a bit of peace and quiet. Instead of that you get a copper who works funny hours and a very noisy grandson living with you.'

'We're not in our dotage yet, thanks very much,' Marg pointed out quickly. 'And we love having you both here. Your dad was only thinking of you when he said you need a woman in your life.'

'Yeah, that's right,' Michael confirmed.

'You'd never get a place of your own at the moment anyway, with the housing shortage as it is in London, so stay here and let us enjoy having you and Mikey around for as long as it lasts,' Marg went on. 'Later on, when the country gets back on its feet and there is more accommodation available, that's the time to start thinking of making a move. Though Gawd knows when that'll be. Relax and enjoy your boy.'

Harry was overcome with respect and gratitude. His parents were such thoroughly nice people. 'Thank you both so much,' he said emotionally.

Basil came into Lola's life through the tearooms. In his mid-thirties, he was a rep for a high-class menswear company and was often in the West End on business. He often called in to the tearooms for a scone and a cup of tea. Smartly dressed, never lost for words and with a good sense of humour, he was a big hit with the Pickford sisters.

'Such lovely manners,' said Ethel dreamily.

'Yes, a rare thing indeed these days,' added Cissy.

'I hope you two aren't going to fight over him,' said Roger.

'Oh, no, he's far too young for us,' said Cissy.

'You speak for yourself,' said her sister, laughing.

'And he's too old for me, so that rules us all out,' said Lola. 'He's probably married, anyway.'

'No. He *was* married, but his wife died of TB some time ago,' said Roger. 'It came up in conversation the other day when I got talking to him in the pub.'

'Ooh, there you go then, ladies,' said Lola. 'He's available so don't waste any more time. You'll have to toss a coin for who gets first crack at him.'

'It isn't us he's interested in,' said Cissy, giving Lola a look.

'Exactly,' added Ethel.

'Oh, no, you can't mean me,' said Lola.

'You're the only one who hasn't noticed it.'

157

'Maybe I choose not to,' she told them. 'He's a nice enough bloke, but I'm not in the least bit interested in that way so I'm staying well clear.'

'A pity, really, because he has excellent prospects,' said Cissy. 'A good job, a car. I think he even has his own place.'

'Yeah, a flat in Kensington,' said Roger. 'He's very well set up. You could do a lot worse, Lola.'

'Those sorts of things don't interest me,' said Lola. 'If I don't fancy someone, a few material accomplishments won't change anything. He's far too old for me, anyway. Why are you all trying to fix me up all of a sudden?'

'Because it's the natural thing for a woman of your age to meet someone and get married,' said Cissy.

'We want the best for you,' added Ethel.

'It's good of you to care, but I can choose my own boyfriends, thank you very much.'

'Now we've upset her,' said Cissy to Ethel.

'No, you haven't, but you will if you keep trying to marry me off,' Lola told them. 'You might live to regret it too because a lot of men don't like their wives to go out to work, so if I do meet someone and get married, you could lose me as an assistant.'

'There is that,' said Cissy thoughtfully. 'So, we'd better leave off the subject.'

'Thank goodness for that,' said Lola lightly.

Unfortunately, the sisters were not alone in their quest to see Lola settled. Doreen was keen on the idea too.

'This Basil bloke sounds all right,' said Doreen. 'I think you should give him a try, Lola.'

'You make him sound like some sort of a special offer in a shop window,' laughed Lola.

'Available men are a bit like that when you're looking for one,' Doreen said.

'And there speaks a woman of experience,' smiled Lola. 'You didn't have to look far for Keith.'

'No. You dropped him right into my lap.'

'Because he wasn't right for me.' Lola sighed. 'Anyway, I'm not looking for anyone particularly. Just because you are all cosied up with Keith, you want me to be settled too. And I definitely don't feel that way about Basil.'

'That might come with time,' her friend suggested.

'I very much doubt it, but if he does ask me out, maybe I will go and see what happens. I don't want to lead him on, though, and you can't force these things.'

'At least you're going to give it a try,' Doreen approved. 'Some positivity at last.'

'I'm not a negative person, am I?' asked Lola worriedly. 'I do hope not.'

'You're not normally, but you have been lately when it comes to men, at least,' said Doreen.

'Only because I don't want to settle for anything less than the real thing,' Lola said, but she knew in her heart that she had had that once with Harry, and true love wasn't likely to happen again with anyone else.

Lola's brother Frankie had taken to spending his evenings aimlessly hanging around the neighbourhood with a group of friends, much to his father's disgust.

'The police should get the lot of you off the streets,' Charlie ranted.

'Why should they when we haven't done anything wrong?' asked Frankie.

'Nothing wrong?' said his father, furiously. 'There was a stabbing among one gang of youths somewhere in London. I read about it in the paper.'

'One incident, Dad,' Frankie pointed out. 'And it just happened to be a young bloke involved. It could have been anyone.'

'Most unlikely,' said Charlie. 'Where you get gangs, you get trouble.'

'Not in mine you don't,' said the boy. 'We just happen to like the same things so we hang out together. Anyway, mine isn't really a gang, it's a group.'

'Frankie doesn't have a smidgeon of violence in him,' said Lola. 'We all know that.'

'She's right, Charlie,' added Rita.

'I know that, and I wasn't suggesting that he would get up to anything dodgy. But the others might and he could get hurt or implicated. He's making himself vulnerable by mixing with those yobs.'

'I can look after myself, Dad,' Frankie assured him. 'We're not yobs and I'm not a little kid any more.'

'Maybe not, but being in a gang marks you out as trouble,' said his dad. 'Gangs have a bad reputation.'

'Very often misplaced,' said Frankie.

'But not always,' Charlie insisted.

'Frankie's a good boy, credit where it's due,' Rita said. 'Though I don't like the idea of you being at risk of violence just because you're out with your friends.'

'I'm not, Mum,' Frankie reassured her. 'Me and my mates keep well away from any sort of bother.'

'You're inviting trouble just by wandering around, wasting time. It looks like you're up to no good, waiting for your opportunity,' insisted Charlie.

'No, we're not, and I don't see why I have to stop seeing my mates just because some thugs are getting a bad reputation.'

'Good sense is the reason,' said his father.

'Well, I'll take my chances.' said Frankie.

'On your head be it,' said Charlie, while Rita's brow furrowed even more deeply.

'Don't worry, Mum, Frankie will be all right,' said Lola later on.

Rita was obviously worried about her boy, but Lola wasn't as confident as she was trying to make out. Her brother was a peaceful soul but the local hardened youths had a reputation for thuggery, so he would be an easy target.

'He can look after himself,' Lola added.

'I do hope so,' said her mother, sighing and looking worried. 'You have to let your kids grow up, no matter how painful it is. But I do worry about him.'

'I think we're all a bit concerned at the moment,' said Lola sympathetically. 'But this being in a gang will just be a passing phase. With a bit of luck, he'll soon grow out of it.'

'Let's hope so, dear,' said Rita, but she didn't sound convinced.

'There are groups of youths out in force tonight,' said Harry to his police colleague Archie one Friday evening a week or so later as they walked the beat.

'It's payday so they've got money to spend,' said Archie, watching a group of young men going into a coffee bar.

'So long as they stay in the coffee bars playing the juke box, they're no trouble,' said Harry. 'It's when they start to roam the streets looking for mischief that we have a problem.'

'Yeah. Still, at least they're not old enough to get served in the pubs,' said Archie. 'We'd really have trouble on our hands if they had alcohol inside them.'

'You're right there,' agreed Harry. 'And the army will soon sort them out. They'll have to do their two years' national service like every other eighteen-year-old bloke, like it or not. That'll make men of them.'

'But you don't have to do national service until you're eighteen,' said Archie. 'And some of these lads out now are just kids, fifteen or sixteen or so. They can cause a lot of trouble in a couple of years until the army gets its hands on them.'

'That's very true,' Harry agreed. 'So it's up to us coppers to sort them out when they misbehave.'

'Exactly,' agreed Archie.

'What shall we do now, lads?' Frankie asked his pals as they came out of the coffee bar.

'Let's have a wander,' suggested one of his friends. 'See what's goin' on in the town. Then we'll go in to another coffee place; see what they've got on their juke box.'

Frankie was pleased because he didn't want to go home yet. He loved being out in the town of an evening with his mates, wearing all the latest gear. It was exciting and made him feel grown up and a part of things. 'Yeah, that'll be good,' he said.

162

'What are you nippers doing out after dark?' asked someone, and Frankie looked up to see a crowd of older boys. 'Little kids like you should be tucked up in bed at this hour. The town at night is for grown-ups.'

'Which we are,' said Frankie.

There was a roar of laughter from the other crowd. 'Go home to Mummy and leave us to look after our own territory. We don't want children getting in the way.'

'We ain't children and we've just as much right to be here as you,' said Frankie. 'We're old enough to go to work so we're old enough to go out at night.'

'I don't think so, sonny,' said the older boy. 'This town after dark ain't suitable for nippers.'

'We're not nippers,' said Frankie. 'And we've every right to be here.'

The older boy, who had black, heavily Brylcreemed hair, said, 'I don't think so, kid. You lower the tone of the area – make it seem as though it's a place for schoolkids – and we take a dim view of that.'

'How many more times?' began Frankie. 'We ain't kids.'

'Now you're really getting on my nerves,' said the older boy, pushing Frankie. 'And I don't like being upset, do I, lads?'

'That's right, you don't,' chorused his friends.

'Oi, don't you push me,' objected Frankie.

'Try stopping me, big boy,' said the other lad.

Frankie lunged at him and they started wrestling.

Young men on both sides joined in and a brawl ensued, arms and legs flying. Then Frankie's attacker got to his feet and took something from his pocket. There was a hush as the blade of a knife gleamed in the streetlight. Frankie's attacker came towards him with the blade pointing at him.

'That's quietened you down, hasn't it?' he said as silence fell among the boys on both sides.

'Looks like a spot of trouble down the street,' said Harry to Archie. 'The lads are at it.'

'Yep, time to go and sort them out,' said Archie, and the two policemen ran towards the fighting.

The mere sight of the police sent the older boys hurrying on their way, but Frankie and his mates were too concerned about the blood gushing from the knife wound in Frankie's shoulder to leave.

'We were just minding our own business when they came up and started getting at us,' said Frankie to the policemen. 'We had to try and defend ourselves.'

'Not very successfully, by the look of it,' said Harry, seeing the blood oozing from Frankie's shoulder and blowing his whistle for assistance. 'We need to get you to the hospital right away.'

'OK,' said Frankie. He'd never been so pleased to see a policeman before.

Lola's father was out at the pub, and she and her mother were happily watching the new television set, when there was a knock at the front door.

'I'll go,' said Lola, and her mother didn't argue because the television was still a novelty and very much compulsive viewing for her.

Opening the door to see two policemen standing there, Lola was badly shaken but not so much that she didn't notice that one of them was Harry.

'Oh my God . . . Harry?' she whispered. 'What's happened?'

'Is this the home of Frankie Brown?' asked Archie.

'Yes, he's my brother,' Lola said shakily. 'What's happened to him?'

'There's been an incident,' said Archie.

Her legs turned to water.

'Lola? I'm so sorry. Is there anyone else at home with you?' enquired Harry.

'Yeah, my mother is here,' she said fearfully.

'Perhaps we could come inside then,' suggested Harry.

'Of course.'

Trembling all over, Lola opened the door wider and the two policemen walked in.

Chapter Ten

The medical team at the hospital decided to keep Frankie in overnight for observation as he'd sustained such a deep knife wound to his shoulder. Things were made even more dramatic for the Brown family by the presence of the police – though not Harry and his colleague – who had plenty of questions to ask of the boy.

'Never seen the geezers before in my life,' Frankie said of his attackers, fearing reprisals. The hostile gang were the sort of thugs who would target his family and friends if he spoke to the police about them. 'There were a few of them and they were all strangers. Must be from a different neighbourhood. They definitely weren't local.'

'You didn't notice anything in particular to mark them out then?' said the detective.

'No. I was too busy trying to defend myself,' Frankie replied.

'Mm . . . well, if anything does come to mind, you'll let us know, won't you?' the detective asked.

'Course I will,' Frankie replied without the slightest intention of doing so.

* * *

'Keeping quiet is the most sensible thing that Frankie can do,' Charlie said to Lola and Rita as they waited in the queue outside the hospital for the bus home. 'If he wants to avoid another beating.'

'I don't agree with you, Dad,' said Lola. 'Those louts shouldn't be allowed to get away with it.'

'Sooner that than the alternative,' he said. 'Those young thugs would welcome the excuse to give him another slapping if he opened his mouth to the cops. He could get even more seriously hurt.'

Lola realised that her father had a different set of values from his family because he mixed with such dubious types. But she supposed there was some truth in what he said, infuriating as that was. She couldn't bear to think of her brother's life being made a misery by a gang of violent louts. 'Even so, honesty is always the best policy. Surely there must be a way.'

'In a perfect world, there is sure to be,' Charlie agreed. 'But ours is far from that.'

'And it never will improve if we let thugs get away with bullying,' she said.

'Surely you don't want your brother to put himself at risk?' asked her father.

'Of course not,' she said. 'But it makes me angry that those louts get away with violence.'

'Look, Lola. We don't know exactly what happened so the least said about it the better,' said her father. 'Let your brother get on with his life and put it behind him.'

'Your dad's right,' said his ever-obedient wife.

Lola muttered something in agreement and accepted that it was probably the best thing for Frankie's safety. She hated the injustice of it, though.

Her thoughts turned to her recent meeting with Harry and how she'd felt when he'd turned up at the house. It had been a shock seeing him so unexpectedly, both physically and emotionally. He was even more attractive now with a few years and experience of life giving him an air of maturity. He knew how to handle himself and that added to his charisma. A stab of guilt coursed through her for thinking about her own personal feelings when her brother was suffering in hospital.

But she was only human and she had feelings. However, she had lost Harry long ago, she reminded herself sadly, and there was nothing to be done about it.

Frankie had worked a few weekend shifts at the tearooms, as well as at the tea party for homeless people, to earn some pocket money and was very well liked by the Pickford sisters. They were most concerned to know that he was in hospital.

'Give him these when you go to see him tonight,' said Cissy, handing Lola a paper bag full of scones. 'Tell him that Ethel and I will go to visit if he's in hospital for any length of time.'

'Thank you, ladies,' said Lola, touched by their concern. 'He loves your cakes and he'll be thrilled. He says that the hospital food is awful.'

'I believe it usually is,' said Ethel. 'Mass catering, you see. It can't really be helped.'

'Fortunately, I don't think he'll be in for long,' said Lola, who had left her office to come down for her morning coffee break.

'That's good news, anyway,' said Ethel.

'I doubt if the quality of the hospital food will stop him

eating it,' said Lola fondly. 'My brother has the appetite of a dozen elephants.'

A sudden scream from Cissy interrupted the conversation.

'What on earth's the matter?' asked her sister.

'That damned cat is in here again,' Cissy said as Dilly wound herself around the complaining woman's legs.

Lola made a hasty intervention, grabbing the animal and holding her against her shoulder, gently stroking her to calm her.

'Do my instructions count for nothing around here?' demanded Cissy. 'That moggy is not allowed inside this building. You know that very well, Lola.'

'Yeah, I'm so sorry.'

'Why do it then, if you're so sorry about it?'

'I, er . . . well, I just love having Dilly around,' said Lola. 'And I feel sorry for her, having to stay outside now that there is an autumnal nip in the air.'

'Any excuse to bring her in. Even on a warm summer's day she's in here when you know very well it's against my wishes.'

'She likes a bit of company—' began Lola.

'Take her home then, and keep her there if you like her so much,' the older woman came back at her.

'My father can't bear cats,' Lola said. 'He won't have one in the house.'

'I don't blame him either,' Cissy said forcefully. 'But that cat isn't staying here.'

'She doesn't do any harm, Cissy,' said Ethel, who also doted on the animal. 'And she is very sweet.'

'She is not sweet, not sweet at all,' bellowed Cissy. 'She is a horrid, flea-ridden moggy and she only comes in here because you and Lola feed and fuss her.'

'I think she is genuinely fond of us,' suggested Ethel.

'She's a blasted cat, Ethel,' Cissy snapped. 'They don't have emotions.'

'You don't know that.'

'It's a well-known fact.'

'She's entitled to some kindness, anyway,' said Ethel. 'And she needs food every bit as much as we do.'

'Let her hunt for mice then,' said Cissy. 'Isn't that what cats are supposed to do for food?'

'If they live in the wild it probably is,' said Ethel. 'But this cat lives in a civilised, built-up area, so is reliant on the kindness of people to help her out.'

The conversation was interrupted by the arrival of Basil, who swept in, looking as pleased with himself as ever.

'Morning, all,' he boomed cheerfully. 'Ooh, I've been dreaming about my morning scone and coffee throughout my last appointment. The thought of it kept me going through an awful meeting with a difficult client. But I managed to get an order out of him in the end. I put my stamina down to the lovely elevenses I get here.'

'Flatterer,' said Ethel, jokingly.

'He's got plenty of flannel,' added her sister.

'Essential in my job,' Basil said, laughing. 'A bit of flattery gets me everywhere in my line of work. I have to get the orders coming in or I don't eat.'

'Get away with you. I bet you've pulled in enough commission over the years to keep you in comfort for the rest of your life,' said Ethel.

'I've done all right, I won't deny it,' he said with a wide grin. 'I've certainly made enough to keep me in your lovely scones for a good long time to come. But I had that spell of war work when I didn't earn any commission. All over now, thank the Lord. I hated that job.'

Lola was watching him and wondering if she could ever love him in a romantic way rather than just feel a kind of friendly affection for him. He certainly had all the right credentials, even though, at about thirty-five, he was quite a bit older than the chaps she usually went out with. He was tall, dark and handsome, well dressed, articulate and funny. He was very keen on her, but she felt nothing for him other than the same sort of fondness she felt for the ladies. Perhaps what she needed was more time with him to get to know him. So when he came into the office on his way out to ask if she fancied a trip to the cinema that evening, she said she'd love to.

They saw *Sunset Boulevard*, and Lola was completely engrossed in the trauma of the ageing Hollywood film star.

'Quite moving, wasn't it?' she remarked as they made their way out of the cinema.

'It didn't do much for me,' Basil said. 'The best part was being with you.'

Oh dear, she wished he wouldn't make his feelings for her so obvious and tell her so often. It made her feel trapped and obliged to reciprocate, which she didn't feel able to do at this early stage. So she just said, 'You're so sweet,' and hoped he didn't continue along those lines.

He didn't and the rest of the evening was most enjoyable for Lola. They went for a light supper at one of the new coffee bars that had opened recently. It was bright and modern, with red upholstery, cream-coloured tables and the latest pop songs blasting out on the juke box.

'As well as the lovely milky coffee, I love the lightness of it in here,' Lola said. 'It's so contemporary. It really cheers me up. Lyons could learn a lesson from them.'

'Oh, no,' Basil said. 'It wouldn't be Lyons if they went all modern. Traditional is right for them.'

'I'd like to see everything brightened up,' she told him. 'We've had more than our share of drabness with all those years of wartime hardship and blackout.'

'Mm, there is that, but things are gradually getting better,' he said. 'In so many places contemporary is the current order of the day. Even some of the old-established firms I visit on business are modernising, with slimline furniture and painted walls in contrasting colours.'

'The whole country needs a boost,' Lola reiterated.

'Indeed,' Basil said, smiling. He seemed like such a nice bloke and really good company. She wished she could fancy him. She had been hoping her feelings would change with time, but if it didn't happen soon, she'd have to stop seeing him because a one-sided relationship wouldn't be right for either of them.

Doreen, who always took a close interest in her friend's love life, was angry with her about it. 'You should never have let it go on for so long if you knew you didn't fancy him,' she said.

'I thought I might with time. I still might, because I like him a lot.'

'Of course, you won't fancy him in time,' Doreen said. 'That sort of thing is a basic instinct.'

'You make it sound so simple.'

'It is. You either fancy someone or you don't.'

'It isn't always like that, Doreen. Every relationship is different,' Lola said. 'You do hear of love growing over time.'

'But you're not talking about love, are you?' Doreen replied. 'The physical thing is either there or it isn't. You can't make it happen.'

'I suppose people do sometimes have successful platonic relationships.'

'Of course, they don't,' Doreen stated categorically. 'Not young people, anyway.'

'What makes you such an expert?'

'It just seems obvious to me,' she said. 'I mean, there has to be some sort of spark in the first place, something to build on. I bet you had it in spades for Harry.'

'Oh, yeah, and I'll never have that again for anyone else. It was everything, loving him, caring about him so much it hurt,' she said. 'A once-in-a-lifetime thing.'

'You don't know that. It might happen again if you let it,' said her friend. 'You are so stuck in the past and on Harry. It's high time you put all of that behind you.'

Lola shrugged, then changed the subject because Doreen was getting heated. She could be very intense so Lola wasn't going to mention there was something not quite right about Basil. Things he said didn't always add up.

'How's the saving up going?' Lola asked. Doreen and Keith were saving up to get married.

'Hard going, but we're making progress.'

'Well done,' she said. 'Actually, I've been doing a spot of saving up myself.'

'For anything special?'

'Yeah, I want to get a motor scooter.'

'What?' said her friend, as though Lola had just admitted to wanting to drive a double-decker bus in the London rush hour. 'Why on earth would you want one of those when we live in London with plenty of public transport?'

'I thought it might be fun,' Lola said. 'They are very popular at the moment.'

'Maybe so, but that doesn't mean we all have to rush out and buy one.'

'Of course not.'

'I bet your mum is none too pleased,' Doreen said. 'Parents always panic when their children take to the road.'

'My brother is saving up for the deposit on a motorbike so she's too busy panicking about that to worry too much about me,' said Lola. 'A scooter seems quite tame in comparison.'

'I suppose it would do. But how can you afford a scooter?'

'The never-never, of course,' Lola said. 'I'll be paying for it for years.'

'Oh, Lola, are you sure that's wise?'

'It isn't in the least bit wise, but I'm prepared to do it,' she confirmed. 'I don't like the idea of taking on debt but it's the only way someone like me can have anything outside of living expenses and clothes.'

'You could save up.'

'I have, for the deposit, and that is quite hefty. If I wait until I've got enough for the full price, I'll be too old to ride it. Anyway, everybody is doing HP now.'

'I'm not,' said Doreen, who was naturally cautious.

'Lots of people are, though, and I'm about to join them,' said Lola. 'It's a gift to the working classes.'

'What about all the interest they charge?' Doreen asked. 'It's well known to be a rip-off.'

'Not if you go to a reputable firm,' Lola said. 'Anyway,

everything has a price. I'll never be able to have anything big if I have to pay cash, so this is the only way for someone like me. Of course, it isn't ideal, but we have to make the best of the life we are given.'

'Oh, well, if it's what you want.'

'It is. A scooter will be fun and it'll take my mind off not having a man.'

'You have Basil.'

'Yeah, there is that, and he is a dear . . .'

'But?' Doreen questioned.

Lola didn't reply at once. It would be a relief to talk to someone about her doubts about him; her suspicions that all was not as it seemed. But once the words were uttered, they couldn't be taken back. If she was imagining things, they were probably best left unsaid. After all, it was only the odd time things he'd said hadn't quite added up. Contradictory statements: the times when he'd said he was somewhere but then later had said something else. Even opinions that didn't match. Best to keep this to herself for the time being. After all, he was a nice bloke and he treated her well. It wasn't as if she was madly in love with him and planning on marrying him. She was fairly sure he had no such ideas either. For the moment it suited them both just to spend time together.

'But it's like I said,' she reminded Doreen.

'So, when are you getting this scooter?' asked Doreen.

'As soon as I can,' Lola said excitedly. 'I've managed to save quite a bit since I've been at the tearooms so I'll be able to make the deposit soon and my salary will cover the repayments.'

'You've obviously given it some thought, then.'

'Of course I have,' Lola replied, wishing Doreen would stop suggesting that she was irresponsible. 'Just think, I'll get fresh air on my way to work instead of being crushed on the tube.'

'Sounds like a good idea to me,' said Doreen, coming round to the notion. 'I'll be able to come for a ride on the pillion at weekends.'

'Sure. We'll go out to Windsor and Runnymede in the summer when you're not busy with Keith.'

'I can't wait,' smiled Doreen.

Lola was pleased that her friend was showing some enthusiasm. She tended to be too critical at times and it was very wearing.

'Are you two trying to kill me off before my time?' said Lola's mother when she heard the news. 'It's bad enough that Frankie is planning on getting a motorbike. Now you're getting a scooter. I'll never have a minute's peace when either of you are out of the house.'

'We'll be careful,' said Lola.

'Course we will,' said Frankie, without the slightest intention of taking care; he was far more interested in speed.

'Once we've been out a few times and come home safe and sound you'll feel more confident,' said Lola. 'And when we've taken you out for a ride you'll be as keen as we are.'

'Let's see what your dad has to say about it when he gets home,' said Rita.

At that moment Charlie was totally absorbed in his own affairs, in a quiet corner of his local pub with his cronies. His family was the last thing on his mind.

'The time is getting on, boys,' he said. 'We either start planning the job or we forget it.'

'We don't wanna forget it,' said someone.

There was a general roar of agreement.

'You say you're all for it, but none of you seems willing to commit,' said Charlie. 'We'll be too old to enjoy the money if we leave it much longer.'

'You speak for yourself, mate,' said Tubby, whose nickname spoke for itself. 'I ain't no old codger.'

'You will be by the time we do the job if we don't soon start getting things organised. We have to get it absolutely right, which is why we'll need plenty of discussion,' said Charlie. 'So, anyone who wants out, stand back now.'

Nobody moved.

'We ain't gonna be doing the job next week or next month even, but we need to start making plans,' said Charlie. 'So, suggestions everyone, please.'

There was a lot of noise. Everyone, it seemed, had an idea of how the perfect crime should be put into action.

Lola took to the road on her scooter in December and very exciting it was too. She'd done everything official and was loving the idea that she could miss the Christmas crowds on the tube by going to work on her new machine.

For the first time in her life, she felt as if she had achieved something as she sped through the traffic on her way to work. Her mother was a nervous wreck but Lola was confident right from the start. 'It's magic,' she said. 'Absolute magic!'

After a few outings on the pillion, Rita became a fan, and Doreen never said no to a lift. Lola's father wasn't so enthusiastic and seemed convinced she wasn't capable of handling it. Frankie thought the scooter was quite tame and still wanted a 'proper motorbike' but never said no to a ride.

The person with the most surprising reaction was Basil, and he showed another, darker side to his nature when he came round to her parents' house one evening.

'It's completely wrong for you,' he said, frowning deeply. 'The damned thing is a deathtrap. You could kill yourself on that. It isn't as if you need it. I can take you anywhere you want to go in my car. I'll even take you to work, if you like.'

'It's nice of you to offer, but I enjoy driving myself,' Lola told him, guessing it was the independence the scooter gave her that he didn't like.

'It's nothing more than a killing machine,' he said.

'Don't tell her that,' said her mother sharply. 'You'll shatter her confidence.'

Lola guessed that was what he had in mind, but she just said, 'No, he won't, Mum. I know when something is right for me and this definitely is.'

'Oh, well, it's your funeral,' he said, sounding bad tempered.

His attitude really annoyed Lola. Just lately he had frequently showed signs of possessiveness and she didn't like it one bit. Nor was she going to stand for it.

'Yes, it is,' she said. 'It's my scooter and my decision whether or not I ride it. Obviously, it isn't essential to my life. It's something I want for the fun of it as well as the convenience.'

'All right, no need to lose your temper.'

'You're the one who's doing that,' she came back at him.

'Now, now, you two,' said Rita. 'Save your arguments for outside.'

'Sorry,' said Basil.

'Yeah, sorry, Mum,' said Lola making a joke of it. 'I'll wait until we go outside before I give him a slap.'

There was a stony silence between them as they walked down the street, he refusing to ride pillion on her scooter. Lola felt stifled and knew she had to put him straight or end their relationship altogether.

'Don't ever interfere in my life again,' she said.

'I was only looking out for you,' he said.

'I'm a grown up and capable of looking after myself, thank you.'

'There's no need to take that attitude.'

'There's every need,' she said. 'You've just treated me like your daughter.'

'I didn't mean to upset you.'

'Well, you have, and not for the first time,' she said crossly. 'And it stops now, Basil. Either that or we go our separate ways.'

'Oh, Lola,' he said, sounding devastated. 'Surely you don't mean that.'

'I do.'

'But we're a couple and we get on well most of the time,' he said. 'I must mean something to you.'

'Of course, you do. But you're my boyfriend, not my father,' she reminded him.

'I'm only trying to be a good boyfriend and look after you,' he said.

'It's kind of you,' she said patiently, 'but I am only just beginning to escape from the authority of my parents and you are trying to replace them.'

'I never meant to.'

'Well, now that I've pointed it out to you, you can do something about it.'

'I most certainly will,' he said. 'I don't want to lose you, Lola. You mean everything to me.'

'So, stop stifling me,' she burst out.

'Oh,' he said, and it was as though she had physically assaulted him. 'I'm sorry. I didn't realise that was what I was doing.'

Now she felt awful, and a little frightened, too, by his vulnerability; of the power she had to hurt him. That was the last thing she wanted. He was a nice bloke, a good person, and she hated being mean to him. But his devotion to her was beginning to weigh heavy and the way he had been this evening depressed her. He was too clingy, too dependent on her feelings for him. It was a huge responsibility. But what was she to do? She was fond of him and didn't want to hurt him. So, for the moment, she would do nothing except discourage his tendency to dominate her and keep a close eye on his behaviour. It was all too easy to let things continue when you were comfortable with someone. That was probably the problem. She had always felt at ease with him until recently when he'd become so possessive.

'You're a good man, Basil, and I'm very fond of you,' she said with feeling.

'It doesn't seem like it,' he said huffily.

'Well, I am, I promise you, so let's go and enjoy the film, shall we?' she said, linking arms with him.

'Yeah, all right then,' he said dully.

Lola wasn't as happy as she sounded. Basil would be devastated if she ended their relationship, and she was fond of him so didn't really want to hurt him. But she was beginning to feel trapped and she didn't like the feeling.

'You shouldn't have let it go on for so long,' said Doreen when Lola discussed it with her the following night.

'I know, but I was enjoying going out with him until recently,' she said. 'There was no reason to give him up. He's a really nice bloke and I like him a lot – or at least I did until he started trying to smother me.'

'Didn't you notice before that he was getting a bit possessive?'

'He wasn't until recently,' she said. 'We've always had a good laugh together . . . until just lately.'

'Hmm. Awkward,' said Doreen. 'I suppose if you really liked him you wouldn't mind.'

'I don't think many women would enjoy it,' Lola said.

'Some women like to be dominated, so I've heard,' said Doreen.

'Well, I don't.'

'Could you talk to him about it, perhaps?' suggested Doreen. 'He might not realise he's doing it.'

'Mm, I suppose that's my best option, but I'm not sure how he'll take it, the way he's been lately.'

'Well, you can't let things go on as they are, that's for sure,' said Doreen.

Things came to a head between Lola and Basil a few days later when he objected to her going to the cinema with Doreen.

'I'll take you to the pictures if you want to see a film,' he said. 'We do things together, you and me. You've no need to resort to girlfriends.'

Lola was horrified at his attitude. 'I'm not *resorting* to Doreen,' she told him. 'I want to go with her.'

'Rather than me?'

'Well, in this particular instance, yes,' she said. 'She's my closest friend and I enjoy spending time with her. Most women enjoy their friends.'

'I take a dim view of that,' he said. 'I should be number one in your life.'

'It isn't a competition, Basil,' she said. 'I enjoy spending time with you both, though I'm not so sure about you if you're going to have this sort of attitude.'

'I'm your boyfriend; I should come first.'

'It doesn't really work like that,' Lola told him.

'How does it work then? With her being more important to you than I am?'

'Of course she isn't more important, but she means a lot to me and I will always put aside time to see her.'

'Even if I am not happy about it?'

She stared at him. 'Why on earth would you not be happy? Everyone has friends.'

'I should be the most important person in your life. You shouldn't need anyone else.'

'Of course I'll need other people,' she said, shocked by his attitude. 'I'm a sociable sort of person. I will always need people around me.'

'But you'll have me. That should be sufficient.'

'It isn't.'

'Well, it should be.'

'Oh, I've had enough this,' said Lola. 'You've shown a different side to your nature, a side I don't like one little bit. I'm going home . . . on my own.'

'But, Lola—'

'Don't follow me or try to see me again,' she said.

'But—'

'It's over between us, Basil,' she said, and headed off with a fast, determined stride.

Her confident manner hid the fact that she was trembling and close to tears. It wasn't every day she broke up with her boyfriend. She had had no prior intention of doing it, but now that it was done, she knew it was the right thing. She didn't love Basil enough to allow him to rule her life and that was obviously his intention. It had been happening for a while now and she had let it pass. But not any more!

Everyone was out, so Rita and her brother-in-law Bert were having a cup of tea and a chat in the kitchen.

'So, you reckon Charlie is up to something crooked again?' said Bert.

'Yeah, he's got that buzz about him. He's either planning something definite with those dodgy mates of his or mulling some sort of scheme over. Either way, it won't be legal.'

'I wish that brother of mine would stick to the straight and narrow, like the rest of us,' said Bert.

'Me, too,' said Rita. 'I hate all this dodgy stuff he's involved in. I've never been able to get used to it. I spend my whole life expecting the coppers to come to take him away.'

'I'm not surprised you feel like that, a law-abiding woman like yourself.'

'I should have married you,' she said lightly.

He shrugged. 'Well . . . the offer was there, but you chose Charlie,' he said.

She made a face. 'Gawd knows why.'

'I wasn't exciting enough for you,' he suggested. 'I was firmly set on the straight and narrow.'

'It wasn't that, Bert,' she said. 'I was young and Charlie could be very persuasive, as you know. A bit of a glamour boy, too. And, of course, I didn't know that he actually broke the law until after I'd married him. Scared the living daylights out of me when I first found out.'

'I bet.'

'I've never been able to get used to it and I've begged him to go straight, time and time again.'

'He never will, not until they lock him up.'

'Oh, Bert, don't say that,' she said worriedly. 'How would he cope with prison, and how would I manage without him? He's never let me go out to work so I'm completely reliant on him. I have no skills outside of this house.'

'Don't you worry about that,' Bert said. 'You're stronger than you think and you won't be on your own. I'll always be around.'

'Oh,' she said surprised. 'It's nice of you to say so. Thank you.'

'It will be my pleasure,' he assured her. 'It might never happen, but I'll be there for you if it does.'

'Thank you, Bert,' Rita said. Then she leaned over and brushed his cheek with an affectionate kiss.

Chapter Eleven

Nat King Cole was crooning 'Too Young' from Lola's portable radio, which she had in her bag on her motor scooter.

'I really like this song,' said Cissy, who was riding pillion. She and Lola were on their way to Shepherd's Bush market to look for tablecloths for the tearooms, having heard that there were some on offer there. News of a sighting of any popular commodity spread fast in these times of crippling shortages and punters had to be quick to beat the competition. 'The words are a bit soppy, but I adore the tune.'

'Well, I never thought I would hear you say that you like a pop song,' said Lola. 'Beethoven is more your sort of thing.'

'Indeed he is, so it's a surprise to me too, but this man's voice is just divine and perfect for the song.'

'And so say all of us,' laughed Lola.

'That's what comes of having a young thing like you working at the tearooms,' smiled Cissy. 'Our minds are opened to all sorts of new things.'

Lola laughed. 'I've been a good influence on you, then, have I?'

'I don't know so much about that,' said Cissy, smiling. 'But you've certainly livened things up.'

Much to Lola's surprise both the sisters had taken a real liking to her motor scooter, having been fiercely opposed to the idea of her having one when it was first mentioned. These little machines were very popular at the moment, especially with women, and Lola was enjoying hers enormously, all thanks to the easy availability of higher purchase. The scooter had been the perfect distraction after her split with Basil, allowing her to explore new places, which had boosted her self-confidence and gave her a feeling of independence.

She had felt compelled to end her relationship with Basil because he had become far too possessive and demanding but it had been really difficult because he had refused to accept it. He still appeared at her front gate occasionally, even now, behaving like a spoiled child and demanding that she reconsider her decision. Her father had sent him packing on several occasions and, unusually, she and her dad had been in agreement. Basil also visited the tearooms more than was comfortable for Lola. He waited for her outside after work and made a nuisance of himself. The sisters offered to make a complaint to the police, but Lola didn't want to cause trouble for Basil. Also, she didn't see why the tearooms should lose a good customer because of her. Thankfully, as time went on his annoying appearances were becoming less frequent, so she hoped that he was beginning to come to terms with her decision not to see him again.

But now, as Lola and Cissy arrived at the market, a crowd around one of the stalls indicated the whereabouts of the much-needed tablecloths. They were cream-coloured embroidered cotton, not large enough for family dining tables, but perfect for the small tables at the tearooms. Luckily, the seller let them have half a dozen.

'Oh, isn't it lovely being able to have something new and fancy again?' said Cissy excitedly, as she and Lola sat on a street bench examining their wares and drinking a cup of tea from a refreshment stall.

'Not half,' enthused Lola. 'Everything has been so short for such a long time; this is a real treat.'

'We've had years of shortages. Nothing nice to eat, and precious little of anything else.'

'Still, things are beginning to get better, and not having much has made us appreciate everything that little bit more.'

'Trust you to look on the bright side,' Cissy said.

'It's just the way I am. Also, we have the Festival of Britain to look forward to soon,' said Lola, ever the optimist. 'I wonder what that will be like. Will there be anything for us ordinary people to enjoy, do you think?'

'Well, the main purpose of the festival is to promote our country to the rest of the world, but I'm sure there'll be things that ordinary people will like because that's what most of the world is made up of, isn't it? Ordinary people.'

'A huge funfair on the banks of the Thames will please most people, I should think,' said Lola. 'That's the part I'm looking forward to most.'

'Yes, that will be something for you young things to have fun with,' said Cissy.

'Dad was saying that a huge amount of money has been spent on the festival and a lot of people are furious about it. They think the money should have been used for housing, as there is still such a terrible shortage.'

'Indeed, there is some bad feeling about that, and it's understandable with so many people unable to find a place to live,' said Cissy. 'But the decision has been made now and if the festival brings in lots of foreign trade and helps to put our country back on its feet, things in general will improve, including housing. So, we'll just have to hope for the best since there's nothing us ordinary mortals can do about it.'

'That's what I pointed out to Dad when he was complaining about it.'

'It's long past time we saw the end of rationing too,' Cissy mentioned. 'I don't think anyone thought it would go on for this long.'

'Yeah, I can't wait to go into a shop without my ration book,' said Lola.

'Meanwhile you've got the festival to look forward to,' Cissy reminded her.

'I wouldn't miss it for the world,' said Lola. 'I shall probably drag you and Ethel along too, at some point.'

'Roger might enjoy it as well,' said Cissy.

Lola smiled. A friendship seemed to be developing between Cissy and Roger lately and Lola thought they seemed really good together, though she doubted if there was likely to be any romance involved as they were both positively ancient. 'We'll go *en masse*,' said Lola, smiling. 'The Tulip Crowd.'

'You'll want to go with your young friends.'

'Yeah, them as well, but I'll probably go a lot more than just once,' she said. 'Depends what it's like.'

'We'll see what happens.'

'Most girls have a boyfriend to go with.'

'So might you by then,' said Cissy.

'I'm in no hurry,' said Lola. 'All that trouble with Basil has put me right off. I'd sooner stay single for the moment.'

Cissy finished her tea. 'Well . . . time we got back to work,' she said.

'I can't wait to show the others the lovely things we've managed to get,' said Lola.

In a happy mood, they climbed on to the scooter and headed back to work in Marble Arch.

There was an annoyance waiting for Lola back at the tearooms because Basil had come in for tea and scones. She guessed it was just an excuse to see her because there were several other teashops nearby that he could use. He just wouldn't give up, as far as she was concerned, and she knew he would make some sort of approach before he left.

Meanwhile there was a great deal of delighted squealing in the kitchen when she and Cissy showed Ethel and Roger the tablecloths. It was such a treat to have something new, and especially anything fancy. Then Lola made her way to her office to get on with her work, tense because it meant passing Basil.

'Fancy a film and a spot of supper tonight, Lola?' he called out predictably.

'I think you know the answer to that, Basil,' she said. 'But thank you for asking.'

'Won't you even think it over?' he persisted.

'No, Basil, I'm afraid not,' she said, and hurried into her office and closed the door. There had been a time when she would have welcomed him in for a chat, but now the Pickfords had made it clear, at her request, that the office was out of bounds to all but tearoom staff. Any kind words from her to Basil were seen by him as encouragement.

The whole thing was breaking her heart. She hated to see him unhappy, but he would be a whole lot sadder later on if she gave in to his pressure and took him back. She'd tried reasoning with him and explaining her feelings, but still he persisted. So, she must stay strong for his sake as well as her own. He was a good-looking bloke with fine prospects. There must be plenty of girls who would jump at the chance to be on his arm.

'So, Harry, sergeant's stripes on your uniform. We're so proud of you,' said his mother.

'Thanks, Mum.'

'You've always looked gorgeous all done up as a policeman in your uniform, and now with promotion as well.'

'I'm really looking forward to more responsibility,' said Harry, 'and you never know, it may lead to further promotion in time.'

'Yeah, of course.'

Harry had excelled in his sergeant's exam, but he still hoped to apply for the CID. The idea of being a detective had interested him even before he joined the force.

'We're very proud of you, son,' said his father, and, turning to his grandson, added, 'What do you think of that, Mikey? Your dad is going to be a detective one day.'

'Tectif,' said Mikey, who was now an energetic three-year-old with the same big brown eyes as his dad.

They all smiled. The boy was the love of their lives and brought joy into the house every single day. They didn't spoil him, though – not too often, anyway.

'We've got a treat in store for him next week,' said Harry. 'The Festival of Britain opens. The Funfair is the bit he'll enjoy.'

'He might be a bit too young to appreciate it but we'll see

how he gets on,' said Marg. 'There's sure to be some sort of roundabout or swings for the little 'uns. It's about time we had some fun and colour in our lives.'

'Absolutely,' agreed her husband.

Everyone said that the best way to arrive at the Festival of Britain was by boat on the South Bank of the Thames. So, one Saturday in May 1951, Lola and her friend Doreen caught a riverboat and arrived there, feeling somewhat awestruck by the splendour that greeted them. On what had been twenty-seven acres of derelict, bomb-damaged land there now rose a concrete paradise with the contemporary roofs of the Festival Hall and the Dome of Discovery spectacular in the sunshine. Above the buildings hung the Skylon, resembling a giant silver cigar suspended before takeoff to Mars.

'Oh, isn't it wonderful?' said Doreen, as they walked around admiring the many works of art and novelty structures.

The cafés had pink and yellow chairs, and sold coffee at the hugely inflated price of ninepence a cup. The girls splashed out on one cup each as it was a special occasion. They marvelled at the wonder of the artistic and imaginative things around them. Later on, they ran into the Pickford sisters and Roger, and spent some time with them before heading off to the funfair at Battersea, which was a threepenny boat ride away. Here they met up with Keith and Frankie and his mates. They went on as many rides as they could afford and took a stroll high above ground on the tree walk past a forty-foot paper dragon.

The whole thing was pure magic to these young people, so starved of colour for so long. The shine was taken off it somewhat for Lola because she didn't have a boyfriend to share it with, something that was emphasised by Doreen and Keith being very lovey-dovey. But she still managed to enjoy it.

They were looking at the Guinness Clock, whose miniature figures whirred into life every hour, when she saw him. Harry was here with a small boy she assumed was his son. The beaming smile on Harry's face when he spotted her warmed her heart and she knew that her instinctive joy in seeing him was reciprocated.

He came over, and Doreen and Keith made a diplomatic exit, arranging to meet Lola in a nearby café later on.

'So, this is Harry mark two,' she said, smiling at the boy.

'Yes, this is Mikey.'

'He's a fine lad.'

'Yes, I am very proud of him,' Harry said. 'He's the one thing I did manage to get right.'

'I'm sure there are many others,' Lola said.

'I doubt it,' Harry replied, and the unspoken implication hung in the air between them. She knew he had in mind the fact that they had broken up.

'Not everything that goes wrong is your doing, Harry,' she said.

'It sometimes feels like it, but I suppose it's the same for everybody,' he said.

'Oh, no, I don't think so,' she said. 'Some people think everything that goes wrong is someone else's fault. You must come across plenty of those in your job.'

'We get our share of blame shifters, it's true.'

They both turned their attention to the boy. 'He's fascinated by the little figures that come out of the clock so I don't know how I'll get him away. They only do their stuff every hour and they've only just done it so there will be quite a wait.'

She laughed. 'You'll have to tell him you'll come back later on,' she said. 'There's so much to see here he'll soon forget about this particular attraction.'

Harry smiled and nodded. 'Anyway . . . how are you getting on these days?'

'Fine,' she said.

'No little ones?'

She shook her head. 'No,' she said.

He took her hand and studied it. 'Not even an engagement ring?' he said.

'No, not even one of those.'

'I'm amazed,' he said. 'Obviously your choice. You wouldn't have lacked for offers.'

She shrugged and moved the subject on swiftly. 'So, how is the job going?'

'Fine,' he replied. 'I'm a sergeant now.'

'Oh, you're doing well, then.'

'The CID is my goal, but I have to do my time through the ranks. Not everyone wants to move out of uniform and some people do really well at it, but I wanted to be a detective from the very beginning.'

'Still enjoying it?'

'Oh, yeah, not half,' he said. 'The police is the only occupation for me. It has its ups and downs, like any job, but I wouldn't want to do anything else.'

'How about being a single parent?' she asked. 'I read about your wife's accident in the local paper, and about the baby, and I'm sorry. How does that fit in with the job?'

'I have a lot of help from my parents so I can't honestly say that I'm coping on my own,' he said.

'I see.'

'I'm a very lucky man,' he went on to say. 'I get to do the job of my dreams and I have a son I adore with his ultra-caring grandparents on hand if I need them. I don't mean to sound smug, but that's the way it is.'

Hearing this, Lola was glad she'd never tried to dissuade him from joining the police by telling him the real reason she had given him up. As painful as losing him was, the other option would have been worse in the long term. He could have been stuck in a job that wasn't right for him because of her and he might have grown to hate her because of it.

'I'm glad to hear that. It's nice when someone gets to do something they really enjoy for a living,' she said, and went on to tell him about her job at the tearooms. 'So, I have that luxury, too.'

They chatted easily for a while, then Harry said casually, 'Maybe we could meet up sometime.' He paused and gave her a half-smile. 'When my boy is in bed, obviously.'

All Lola's instincts cried out for her to say yes. But nothing had changed. He was still a policeman and her father was still a crook, so she couldn't afford to put herself in temptation's way. So, she forced herself to say in a definite manner, 'I don't really think it's a good idea to go back, Harry. Probably best if we remember each other as things were.'

'Oh,' he said, smarting with disappointment. 'I don't agree with you at all. We had something really special and we could have it again.'

'Or we could feel let down.'

'That's a very negative attitude,' he said sharply. 'But if that's the way you feel about it, I won't try to force you into anything. Absolutely not!'

She longed to tell him that she wanted to see him again so

much it hurt. But she had to be strong. To tell him the truth could send her dad to prison.

'It's probably for the best,' she said.

'Well, we'll be on our way then,' he said coolly, obviously hurt by her rejection. 'See you around sometime, maybe.'

And he marched off into the crowds, clutching his son's hand. She stared after him with tears in her eyes.

Harry was feeling shattered. Why didn't she want to see him? They were both free and he was certain she still had feelings for him. He could see it in her eyes. He recalled that it was she who had ended their relationship originally. This time, could it be because he'd once been married, perhaps? But he was free now so surely that couldn't be an issue. She was a modern woman and wouldn't be bothered by such things.

But she had made it clear that she wasn't interested in them getting together and he was very disappointed. If her attitude had been even slightly less adamant, he might have felt able to try to persuade her, but she had left no room for nego-tiation. It was as though she had pulled the shutters down between them and closed the door in his face permanently. After all this time she still had the power to hurt him.

Lola was still feeling upset by her rejection of Harry a week or so later, but she tried to keep busy to take her mind off it. She polished her scooter until it shone and even offered to help her mother with the housework to keep occupied. But still he filled her thoughts.

It didn't help that Basil was still bothering her. She'd been a little too gentle in her rejection of him at first, but when he'd persisted, she'd had to be more definite.

'I can be better,' he'd say. 'Just give me another chance. I promise you won't be disappointed.'

'Basil, you don't have to be better because there is nothing wrong with you,' she said. 'You are a good man; just not the right man for me. But plenty of other girls would want to be your girlfriend.'

'But it's you that I want.'

At times during this period that she had toyed with the idea of telling him the truth. That she couldn't love him in the way he wanted because she loved another, not through any fault of his own. But she was afraid he might cling on to some hope that he could make things better for her and change her feelings. So in the end she had been forced to get very firm with him.

'It isn't happening, Basil. You need to find someone else. Please don't try to see me again.'

'Oh . . .'

'Please, Basil, promise me.'

'I can't do that.'

'In that case I shall ignore you when I see you.'

'Oh, that really would be awful.'

'So, stay away then and find someone else.'

The firmness of her manner must finally have got through to him because he said, 'Oh, yeah, no problem there. I'm a good catch for someone. It was just that I wanted you. But that's life, I suppose. You can't always have what you want.'

And without another word he went on his way, leaving Lola feeling very cruel. Basil couldn't have the woman he wanted and she couldn't have the man she was in love with. How complicated life could be at times. And how very sad.

Lola's scooter was much more than just a provider of fun. It paid for itself in that it saved her money on fares, not just for her but also for family and friends, as she was always willing to provide lifts. She took her mother shopping and the Pickford ladies to the various women's groups that they belonged to. They were keen supporters of good causes. She had no shortage of company at the weekend either. Doreen's fiancé Keith worked on a Saturday so Lola and her pal headed off to Runnymede and other beauty spots. Lola even took them to the coast once or twice, but the seaside was a magnet for motorcycle gangs and tended to be rough, so they usually avoided it.

Apart from Uncle Bert, who loved to ride on the scooter and thought his niece was 'one hell of a girl', the men of the family were less keen. Her father still thought the scooter was a deathtrap and refused to go on it, and her brother said he wouldn't be seen dead on such a feeble apology for a motorbike. But for Lola life was hugely enhanced by having her scooter, so although she wasn't lucky in love, she considered herself to be very fortunate in many ways.

Most of her friends had steady boyfriends now, so weren't available at weekends, but this didn't stop Lola from getting out and about. Whereas she might not have gone out on her own without the scooter, now she consulted a map and took herself off to various beauty spots in and around London. There was nothing she enjoyed more than the feeling of freedom as she headed off.

One sunny Sunday afternoon she was riding through London, heading for Windsor. She'd once been on a school trip to see the castle, but now she was going to have a proper look and she was rather excited about it. The traffic was heavier than it used to be as more people got cars, but although her father complained about it rather a lot, it didn't bother Lola.

As she approached the tube station, she felt quite pleased that she could be independent and didn't have to take the train. Her scooter had opened up all sorts of opportunities for her and she was feeling rather pleased with herself.

Basil was going out for the afternoon too and was heading for the tube station. He was meeting some mates at Marble Arch and they were going to have a wander through Hyde Park and listen to the speakers at Speakers' Corner. There were always plenty of people about in and around Hyde Park on a Sunday afternoon, and his friends were hopeful of finding some female company. Basil would go along, but he wasn't really interested. His heart was still with Lola, even now, although it was a while since they'd parted. Her rejection of him had hurt him more than almost anything else he could recall. He had been besotted with her and staying away from her had been one of the hardest things he'd ever had to do. Somehow he'd managed it, but she was always on his mind. He didn't know how to stop thinking about her and wanting her. He just didn't seem able to do it.

Then he saw her on her yellow scooter, waiting at the traffic lights. Even with her crash helmet on he knew it was her. He recognised her immediately because her image was etched on his heart. All he could feel was utter joy at the sight of her, complete and pure delight. Instinctively he ran forward, waving his arms and calling her name.

Bert always went to tea with Charlie and Rita on Sunday afternoons. Sunday tea was a bit of a family institution, and Charlie and Rita and their family were Bert's closest relatives. He enjoyed spending time with them, though Charlie could be hard work because of his persistent talk of law breaking, but his wife was lovely company. This particular afternoon both the children were out but expected back for tea as usual, and Charlie was full of his latest and most wanted acquisition – a car.

'That's the way forward now,' he said with authority, having previously claimed, most adamantly, that motoring would never reach the working classes. 'Anyone with a few bob to spare is taking to the road.'

'Very few ordinary people have cars,' Bert pointed out.

'Those with the savvy to make a few bob are taking to the wheel,' insisted Charlie. 'You've only got to look at the increase in the traffic to see that.'

'I assume you won't be paying for yours with money earned honestly,' said Bert.

'Don't make me laugh,' said Charlie.

'I dunno so much about that,' said Bert. 'You only have to find the deposit. The rest is monthly payments, so I've heard.'

'No HP for me, mate,' said his brother. 'I want to pay outright.'

'Then you'll have to rob a bank,' said Bert, ''cos cars don't come cheap.'

'I've got it all in hand,' said Charlie. 'And when I'm ready

I'll have the dough. Don't you worry about that. It might not be next week or even next month, but this family is having a motor. We'll be the first in the street to have a car parked outside.'

Bert exchanged a look with his sister-in-law, then turned back to his brother and said, 'You'll get your comeuppance one of these days, you know.'

Charlie shrugged. 'So you're always telling me. But until then I'll enjoy doing things my way, thanks very much.'

'You won't be able to stop him, Bert,' said Rita. 'I've spent most of my married life trying and failing.'

'That's because I'm my own man,' Charlie said, as though his crooked lifestyle was something to be proud of. 'I do what I think is right.'

'Surely you can't think that breaking the law is right,' said Bert sharply.

'It's right for me, that's all I'm saying. So long as no one gets hurt.'

Bert raised his eyes in despair. 'The people you steal from get hurt because they lose their money.'

'They've got plenty,' said Charlie. 'They can afford the little bit I take. I don't steal from those who can't afford it.'

'And that makes you feel good about it, I suppose,' said Bert.

'I certainly don't feel bad,' said Charlie. 'It isn't fair that some people should have so much while others struggle.'

'You don't struggle.'

'I have done,' Charlie insisted. 'For years I had to get up early and slave away at a machine all day while the toffs have breakfast in bed brought to them by a skivvy. The system isn't fair. Things should be more equal.'

'Blimey, have you been reading socialist propaganda or something?' said Bert.

'Of course, I haven't,' said Charlie.

'Sounds like it.'

'Look, mate,' began Charlie, 'we all know that life isn't fair. Some people are born into money while others struggle. Us lot, we're all in the latter group so I make sure that me and the family can afford to live decently.'

'You're just making excuses to break the law,' said Bert.

'No, I'm not. I'm just trying to explain why I do it.'

'I've never heard such a load of old twaddle in my life. You should live within your means, like the rest of us do.'

'Oh, give over with the lecture, Bert. It's my business how I choose to live my life, so keep your nose out.'

'I'll put the kettle on,' said Rita, in the hope of calming the storm. 'It's a bit early to sit down to tea but we can have a cuppa.'

'That would be lovely,' said Bert, while Charlie fell into a sulky silence.

Lola was concentrating on the road ahead as she waited for the traffic lights to change, always careful to move forward as soon as they did because other road users were quick to anger if you were slow and held them up. Women scooter riders weren't popular with car drivers, who were mostly male; the majority thought they were a nuisance.

Suddenly there was a commotion on the kerbside. 'Lola, Lola!' someone was shouting and, looking to the side, she saw Basil grinning and waving his arms at her. The lights changed and the traffic moved forward, but Lola had lost her concentration and hesitated, causing a chorus of hooters and car drivers shaking their fists at her.

Flustered, she went to move forward, but wobbled and swerved into the path of an oncoming car. The scooter went over and she was flung into the road. She blacked out and knew no more.

Charlie and his wife and brother had just sat down for tea when there was a knock at the door.

'Who's that, calling at a Sunday teatime,' said Charlie irritably. 'It can't be one of the kids because they'd pull the key through the letter box. You'd better go and answer it, Rita.'

'You go, you lazy sod,' said Bert.

'It's all right, Charlie,' said Rita, who was so used to taking orders from her husband she barely noticed it. 'I don't mind.'

On opening the door her heart lurched when she saw two policemen standing there.

'Mrs Brown?' asked one of them.

'Yes,' she said shakily. 'What's happened?'

'Can we come inside?'

'Yes, of course,' she said numbly, full of dread as she showed the officers into the house. The police only came when something very serious had happened.

Chapter Twelve

With the return of consciousness came remorse, and Lola was full of it when her parents and Uncle Bert arrived on the ward to visit her.

'Sorry to give you all this worry,' she said tearfully; she was very shaken up by the accident but still aware of the effect it would have had on the people who cared about her.

'Don't you bother about us, love,' said her mother with typical maternal selflessness. 'Me and your dad and Bert are as tough as old boots. As long as you are all right, that's all that matters to us.'

'I'll be fine, Mum,' Lola assured her. 'I'm sure there's nothing seriously wrong. Just a few bumps and bruises.'

Her father was less sympathetic. 'It's that bloody scooter,' he barked, concern for his daughter manifesting itself in anger. 'I knew it would be trouble the minute I clapped eyes on it. The ruddy thing is a menace.'

'Now isn't the time to go on about it, Charlie,' said Bert. 'Not while your daughter is still feeling so shaken up.'

'It wasn't the fault of the scooter anyway, Dad,' said Lola.

'What else was it then? Tell me that,' he demanded.

'My driving, of course,' she said. 'A mixture of a distraction and carelessness on my part, I suppose. There is certainly nothing wrong with the scooter.'

'But it wouldn't have happened if you hadn't been on the damned thing in the first place,' he pointed out. 'It's nothing more than a deathtrap, as I've said all along. And don't even think of having it repaired. The scrap heap is the only place for that load of rubbish.'

'Don't go on at her,' urged her mother. 'She's in no fit state for the rough edge of your tongue.'

'Yeah, calm down, Charlie,' added his brother. 'You're not helping anyone with that sort of attitude.'

Even at this early stage, while still feeling shaky and with painful bumps and bruises in several places on her body, Lola was determined to get back on the road on her scooter as soon as she had recovered and the machine had been checked over. Although this mishap had frightened her, it hadn't made her want to abandon either her scooter or the independence it gave her. But now wasn't the time to talk to her father about it. She wasn't in a favourable position to put forward a decent argument with her body bruised and hurting. But she had loved the freedom the scooter had given her; the sense of being in charge. There was a knot of fear at the back of her mind at the thought of actually being on the road again but she couldn't let it beat her.

In her own mind she was sure the accident wouldn't have happened if Basil hadn't distracted her. Of course, she should have ignored him, but it was easy to see that in hindsight and she had only herself to blame. It wouldn't be wise to mention Basil's part in it to her parents. Her father would be furious and go after him and make things a whole lot worse.

Basil had seemed blissfully unaware of the accident, having

gone on his way just before it occurred. Had he, though? It had happened so fast Lola couldn't be sure if he knew about it or not. But it was easier to think he hadn't seen it because the alternative meant he had turned a blind eye. It was a horrid thought, but she had a niggling suspicion that he was perfectly well aware of what had happened and had chosen not to get involved.

But even as these thoughts settled, other, darker ones rose within her. Feelings that told her she had lost her nerve and didn't have the courage to venture into the London traffic again, despite her eagerness to do it. She struggled to banish her fears. Not many women of her age and class had their own transport and she'd been rather proud of the fact that she did. So, she mustn't let anything stop her once she had recovered.

Basil was, indeed, very well aware of Lola's accident and he was rather pleased about it. He'd watched from a safe distance and, having seen that she wasn't seriously hurt, he'd decided not to go to her assistance for fear he might get blamed for the accident for distracting her. Anyway, why should he help her when she'd not deemed him good enough to be her boyfriend? He saw his lack of co-operation as an act of revenge on her for ditching him. He was still a little shocked and offended about that. Women didn't usually give him his marching orders. Why would they when he treated them well, spent money on them, never took liberties and did his best to be entertaining company? But all of that hadn't been enough for Lola and that still rankled.

* * *

'We'd be failing in our duty as parents if we allowed her to take to the road on the scooter again,' said Charlie when he, Rita and Bert were on the way home from the hospital on the bus.

'She's over twenty-one,' his wife reminded him. 'I don't see how we can stop her.'

'I'll soon stop her, don't you worry about that,' Charlie said. 'I'll tell her that we are not prepared to put up with it.'

'I don't think you'll have much luck with that sort of attitude,' said Bert. 'She's a grown woman, and an independent one at that.'

'Yes, that is silly talk, Charlie,' said Rita. 'Of course Lola can ride a scooter if she wants to. Yes, it is a worry, especially after this accident, but we have no right to try and stop her. Anyway, she might want to steer well clear after this.'

'Mm, there is that, I suppose,' Charlie said thoughtfully, then surprised his wife by adding, 'we had better get it checked over while she's laid up. It will need it to be in good shape to sell it. And if we get it done, she'll be ready to get rid of it when she's back home.'

'If she wants to sell it,' Rita said. 'She hasn't said anything about that.'

'I'll be surprised if she wants to keep it after an accident like that,' Charlie said. 'Anyway, I'm going to put my foot down about it. She needs to get shot of it and I'm going to make sure that she does.'

A knowing look passed between Bert and his sister-in-law.

No one realised that Lola had had a very bad nervous reaction to the accident and was terrified of going back on the road on the scooter. Deeply disappointed in herself for what she saw as cowardice, she kept these fears to herself in the hope that she could overcome them. To add to her woes, she developed an infection and her hospitalisation was lengthened.

'It must be terrible being stuck in here,' said Doreen when she came to visit. 'I bet you're dying to be discharged.'

'No' was the truthful answer to that. Going home meant facing her fears, and Lola dreaded that. 'It isn't so bad in here,' she said. 'The nurses are lovely and everyone is very good to me.'

'You'd still rather not be here, though, I bet,' said Doreen.

'Of course,' said Lola. 'No one wants to be in hospital and I'll be glad to get back to normal. Apart from anything else, I'm worried about letting the ladies down. They've got a temp in to cover for me at the moment.'

'Your job is safe, though, isn't it?' asked Doreen.

'I should think so, but I need to get back to work as soon as possible.'

'I want you out of here too,' said Doreen. 'I miss my pal.'

Unexpected tears rushed into Lola's eyes. She and Doreen weren't normally sentimental within their friendship but they had known each other a long time and were very fond of each other. 'Same here,' she said thickly.

She couldn't even tell her soulmate, Doreen, how terrified she was of leaving the safety of hospital life because she was far too ashamed.

The evenings were autumn scented by the time Lola finally arrived home. And even then, it was a week before the doctor would sign her off to go back to work. A terrible row with her father erupted when she mentioned her intention to use the scooter to get there. Of course, he had no idea that she was absolutely terrified and deeply disappointed in herself about this. In her heart she knew that if she didn't use the scooter right away, she never would, so she had to do it.

'You want your brains tested to even consider getting on that thing again,' he said. 'You have no right to give me and your mum such worry. I won't allow it.'

'But, Dad—'

'No, I'm putting the damned thing up for sale.'

'You most certainly are not,' said Lola, who guessed her father's objections were more about control than genuine concern. He'd never been an affectionate father but he had always been a bossy one.

'I bloody well am,' he said. 'Why do you think I got it repaired?'

'I thought you were just being nice,' she said.

'I am being nice – by keeping you off that damned deathtrap.'

'But it belongs to Lola, dear,' his wife reminded him. 'I don't think you are legally allowed to sell it.'

'Of course, he isn't,' added Lola.

'Surely you must realise how dangerous it is,' said her father. 'It's put you in hospital. What more proof do you want?'

'It was my own fault. But I'll be more careful in future, Dad,' she said. 'I promise.'

'Humph.' He fell into a thoughtful silence. 'Well, I don't suppose there's anything I can do to stop you riding it, is there?'

'Not really,' Lola agreed, whilst wanting nothing more than an excuse not to ride. 'But I promise to be more careful.'

He shrugged his shoulders. 'I won't have a minute's peace when you're out on that thing.'

Lola longed to submit to his wishes, but she'd never forgive herself if she let this lack of mettle control her. She just hoped that once she was back on the road again her self-confidence would return. She had to try, at least! She planned to use her scooter when she went back to work and she couldn't allow herself to fail.

'You'll soon get used to it, Dad,' she said.

A boost to Lola's self-confidence came from an unexpected source. Ethel arrived at her house early on the morning of her first day back at work.

'I fancied a ride on your scooter,' she explained.

'You came here on the tube to do that at this time of the morning?' said Lola, amazed.

'No, I took the bus. There just happened to be one when I got to the stop,' she said. 'So, look sharp. Time to go to work.'

'Thank you,' Lola said, hugging her and feeling moved by the older woman's sensitivity in guessing that she might be feeling nervous. No one else had mentioned it.

'You're welcome,' she said. 'My sister and I didn't want to risk having you chicken out and take the tube. We know you'd never forgive yourself.'

'You're right, I wouldn't,' she said.

A few minutes later the two women were weaving their way through the London traffic. Lola had been quite shaky at first but was feeling better already, although she knew she had to give herself time to get used to it again. It was a caring thing Ethel had done and it had boosted Lola's confidence enormously. She knew she was going to be all right now. She'd proved that she wasn't a quitter.

It was Saturday afternoon and Charlie's mates had come back from the pub with him for a meeting about the jeweller's shop job they were planning. There were too many ears wagging in the pub. Rita had gone for a look round the shops, Lola was out with her friend Doreen and Frankie was doing some overtime at the garage. So, they had the house to themselves and could speak freely.

'So, you're planning on blowing a hole in the wall of the basement between the tearooms and the jeweller's next door?' said one of the spivs. 'And we go through and help ourselves to the stock.'

'That's right,' Charlie confirmed.

'But there are people living above the tearooms,' said the man. 'They'll hear it.'

'The accommodation above the tearooms is on two floors with attic rooms above that,' said Charlie, who had craftily gained information from his daughter by supposedly showing a friendly interest in her workplace. 'The occupants' bedrooms are bound to be on one of the upper floors. It will be one small explosion. By the time it registers distantly, all will be quiet so they'll think it was a long way away and forget about it.'

'Where do we get the explosive?'

'Billy the cracker in West Ham,' said Charlie. 'There's nothing he doesn't know about explosives, and he's got contacts so he can always get hold of them.'

'At a price, I bet,' said one of the men.

210

'We don't need anything big so it shouldn't break the bank. We'll have to pay cash on delivery, of course, but we'll be rolling in money when the job is done. I'm hoping to pay for a car outright and have plenty left over.'

'Won't the jewellery be under lock and key,' queried someone, 'in a safe or a safety deposit box?'

'I can't be absolutely sure, but I don't think so because they have strong security on the windows and doors,' said Charlie. 'It's only a small shop and security costs a lot of money. Anyway, we'll deal with that when we get to it. My guess is that they take a chance, especially as no one can get in from the outside because there are steel shutters in place. It would never occur to them that someone might get in from next door. Foolproof, mate. Foolproof.'

There was a roar of approval.

'How are we going to get into the basement of the tearooms?' asked someone.

'My daughter works there and they've given her a key to the main door because she sometimes gets in to work really early,' said Charlie. 'The old girls are getting on a bit and they don't get cracking until a bit later. They don't keep the basement locked because they keep a lot of stuff down there, so they're up and down to the basement all the time. So, all we have to do is open the main door.'

'But your daughter won't give you the key, surely?' suggested someone.

'Not bloomin' likely,' said Charlie. 'But she keeps it on the mantelpiece overnight so I'll get it when she's asleep in bed. We won't be doing the job until the early hours.'

'Well, you seem to have given it a lot of thought, Charlie,' said someone.

'Yeah, it's been in the making for a long time and if we pull it off it will change all our lives,' he said. 'Now we have to deal with practicalities. A getaway driver, for instance. Anyone know a good one?'

A couple of men answered in the affirmative so the gang of would-be jewel thieves continued discussing the job with increasing excitement.

'Everyone is Yank mad,' Cissy said to Lola one day in December when she and her sister and Roger were having a cup of tea together prior to opening. 'American films, Coca-Cola. And I hear of these burger bars opening, so soon there'll be no business for the rest of us.'

'That isn't right at all, Cissy,' said Lola. 'At the tearooms we aim for a different market altogether. We're essentially English. Hamburgers are American and a different thing entirely, and will mostly appeal to a younger market, I should think. I've no doubt they'll do very well but they are not competing with tearooms. I mean, can you imagine burgers putting afternoon tea at The Savoy at risk?'

'No of course not. And I'm glad of your optimism, dear,' said Cissy. 'It's just that we don't seem to be moving forward.'

'I didn't think we were planning to,' said Ethel. 'We're happy to just chug along.'

'We are, I suppose, but it would be nice to have some sort of an aim.'

'You could always introduce another line,' suggested Roger.

'A new kind of cake, you mean?'

'Could be a cake, or something savoury, perhaps as an alternative or an addition to the sandwiches in the afternoon tea.'

212

'Our sandwiches already have a wide range of fillings,' Cissy reminded him.

'Mm, I know. I was thinking in terms of some sort of savoury tart or pie or something.'

Lola had a thought. 'There is something that I've seen on café menus lately. I always keep an eye on what's being offered by the competition. It's called quiche Lorraine and it's sort of a cheese flan, I think.'

'We know what quiche Lorraine is, dear,' said Ethel. 'It's a savoury item.'

'I'd never heard of it before so I asked the waitress about it and she said that it's becoming quite popular. Well, I've seen it around, anyway.'

'Yes. It's delicious,' said Cissy, 'depending on who makes it, of course.'

'And it would fit wonderfully on our tea menu,' said Lola, her enthusiasm growing. 'You could either have a slice as an additional item, or remove something and have it as a replacement. I suppose you could even do little individual ones.'

'Too much pastry,' said Cissy. 'Large ones cut into slices would be better.'

There was a murmur of agreement.

'Well, Ethel, what do you think? Should we get our cookbooks out and start experimenting?'

'I think we should, dear,' her sister agreed excitedly.

'I suppose we ought to wait until food rationing finally ends,' said Ethel. 'It can't be much longer surely.'

'We can work on getting the flavour right in the meantime,' said her sister.

Ethel turned to Lola. 'Thank you, dear, for the idea,' she said. 'It's nice to know you look out for us.'

'Always,' said Lola.

As it happened, she wasn't the only one in a creative mood. Roger had been thinking too.

'We could do with a spot of music here at The Tulip, to add some atmosphere,' he said, glancing towards an elegant piano half hidden behind some potted palms. 'I've often wondered why the piano is stuck in the corner and never used.'

'Our father was the pianist in the family so we want to keep the piano for sentimental reasons, but it takes up a lot of room in the flat. That's why it's down here.'

'So, let's make use of it,' he suggested. 'I'm sure your dad would have liked the piano to be used.'

'The Tulip isn't that sort of a tearooms,' said Cissy. 'I mean, we are hardly in the same league as The Savoy.'

'What does that matter?' Roger asked. 'Some background music would go down a treat. Maybe at a weekend and just one afternoon in the week.'

'We'd have to pay someone to play it,' said Ethel. 'Cissy hasn't played since she was a child, and I was never a performer. We don't want to add to our outgoings, though.'

'I can knock out a tune or two,' Roger said. 'Music was my second subject when I was teaching and I had a few private piano pupils. I might be a bit rusty at first but I would soon sharpen up once I started playing again. And my salary would cover my fee so it wouldn't cost you anything extra.'

There was a stunned silence.

'Well, don't all look so stricken about it,' he said with a wry grin. 'I might not be Albert Hall standard but I'm sure I can manage a reasonable rendering of "We'll Gather Lilacs".'

They all laughed.

'Well?' he said. 'Have I got the job?'

'We'll think about it,' said Cissy, regarding Roger fondly.

'We'll have to get the piano tuned,' said Ethel.

'Definitely,' agreed Cissy.

They looked at each other and then turned to Roger, beaming.

'We'll book the piano tuner right away and make the arrangements to get started. Together we'll work out a timetable and discuss what you'll be playing,' said Ethel.

Roger beamed in return.

'And to both of you, thank you for looking out for The Tulip,' said Cissy. 'I don't know what we would do without you.'

'Hear, hear,' added her sister.

'You won't have to,' said Lola, feeling emotional. 'While you need us, we'll be here.'

'Agreed!' added Roger.

Lola was so proud to be a part of this establishment.

Harry was having a battle of wills with Mikey, who was having a tantrum. He had thrown one of his nursery rhyme books on the floor in a temper and was refusing to pick it up.

'I want to go to the park,' he said.

'Not until you pick the book up,' said Harry.

'You do it,' said the boy.

'Certainly not. You threw it down. You pick it up.'

'No,' said Mikey.

'I don't think you'll get him to do it,' said Harry's mother.

'He can be very stubborn,' added Michael.

'So can I,' said Harry. 'He's got to learn to do as he's told and to respect things, not chuck them around. It's my day off so I can wait all day if necessary.'

'You said you would take me to the park,' said Mikey, close to tears.

'I will when you pick the book up and tell me you're sorry for throwing it down.'

The boy stared at the floor in silence.

'We'll leave you to it then, Harry,' said Marg, turning to her husband. 'Get your coat.'

'I didn't know we were going out,' Michael said.

'Well, we are, so get a spurt on,' she said, and the couple made a diplomatic exit.

Harry's nerves were in shreds but he knew he had to stand his ground or have Mikey behaving like a spoiled brat again. The boy had some determination, though. This stubbornness had been going on for a while and Harry had had enough. But he couldn't back down. His love for his son was so acute it was actually painful. He'd never experienced anything quite like it before. He knew without doubt he would give his life for him if it were ever necessary. But at the same time, he had to instil discipline into situations like this or the boy would become impossible.

'So, what's it to be, Mikey: a go on the swings or an afternoon indoors waiting for you to do as you're told?'

The boy stared at the book. Harry saw a tear roll down his cheek and forced himself to ignore it.

'You know what you have to do,' said Harry, but he was aware that even at this tender age Mikey had pride and was having difficulty backing down.

'Shall I help you with it?' he offered.

Mikey nodded, but didn't look at his father. Harry got down on his hands and knees in a gesture of encouragement. Still Mikey didn't move. Harry didn't say anything. Then the boy hurriedly picked up the book, handed it to his father and stood back.

'Sorry, Daddy,' he said quickly.

'We'll say no more about it,' Harry said, remaining stern.

'Can we go to the park now, please?' asked Mikey in a small, very polite voice.

It was as much as Harry could do not to wrap his arms around him but he managed to stay in control and said, 'Yes, we can go now. Go and get your ball.'

'Yes, Daddy,' said Mikey, and headed off happily, leaving his father feeling shaky with emotion.

It had certainly been a battle of wills and an emotional episode. People had told him that being a parent wasn't always easy, but no one had ever told him that it broke your heart on a regular basis.

Roger was thinking of leaving his job at the tearooms. He didn't want to because he loved the place, but his feelings for Cissy made it difficult for him to be there. His love for her had grown slowly over the years but she showed no signs of reciprocation and that hurt.

'But you've never told her how you feel,' said Lola, when he came into the office one afternoon and confided in her. 'So how do you know how she feels about you? Cissy isn't the type of woman who would find it easy to talk about such a thing.'

'Exactly, that's why I don't want to bring it up,' he said. 'I don't want to embarrass her.'

'So, how will you ever know?'

'I won't, but I can't risk making her feel awkward,' Roger said. 'So, I have to leave.'

'That is one of the most ridiculous things I've ever heard,' Lola said. 'For all you know, she might share your feelings. But there is no way she will ever tell you unless you bring the subject up.'

'I know Cissy seems very confident – and she is about business – but I don't think she's had much experience with men,' he said.

'I wouldn't be so sure about that,' said Lola. 'I think both she and her sister had plenty going on when they were young.'

'Really?'

'Yes, really,' Lola said. 'Little things that they say, to each other mostly. I don't think either of them was short of male interest.'

'Oh.' Roger appeared rattled by this.

Lola looked at him. 'Why so surprised? You obviously find her attractive, so other men probably do too. And she might have been gorgeous when she was young.'

'Yeah, of course,' he agreed. 'It's just that she seems so out of reach for me. With her being my boss.'

'But we are more like a family here,' she reminded him. 'The sisters never pull rank.'

'No, that's true,' Roger agreed. 'But they are what they are – the owners of this establishment – and I work for them. So, it all seems a bit hopeless. I mean, I don't have anything to offer her.'

'You have yourself, and she relies on you,' said Lola. 'She always seems to be very fond of you but I have never spoken to her about it so I don't know how she really feels. You have brought a great deal to the tearooms and she would appreciate that. Not every contribution has to be a financial one, Roger. For all we know she might have a secret passion for you.'

'I wish,' he said smiling.

'She might, and even if she doesn't Cissy would be devastated if you gave in your notice.'

'Because I'm useful?'

'Yes. But also because she enjoys having you around, and that bodes well for other things,' Lola said. 'She's obviously very fond of you – anyone can see that – so please don't think of leaving.'

'I'll try not to,' he said.

'Good man,' said Lola, smiling at him. She was confident she had persuaded him not to hand in his notice. As for a future for him with Cissy, she didn't know but wouldn't be at all surprised if it came about. Maybe not right away, but one day, perhaps . . .

Ever since the battle of wits Harry had had with Mikey, the boy had been difficult. He wouldn't do as he was told, he was cheeky and downright disobedient.

'I can't understand it,' Harry confided to his mother. 'He is the sweetest child one day and a monster the next.'

'Yes, he is being naughty at the moment,' agreed Marg. 'They sometimes get like this when they are sickening for something but he's showing no sign of illness.'

'Far from it,' said Harry. 'He seems more energetic than ever.' He sighed. 'I feel such a failure as a dad. I should be able to make him behave.'

'Rubbish,' said his mother. 'You're lovely with him. All kids have times when they are difficult, but I must admit he's been especially naughty these past few days.'

That night Mickey woke in a fever. He was so ill that Harry

stayed with him all night and called the doctor the next morning, by which time the little boy had developed a rash.

'Measles,' pronounced the doctor after an examination.

'But he is really ill, Doctor,' said Harry, who had taken the morning off and been frantic with worry. 'It can't just be measles.'

'It is. Measles can make some children really ill,' said the doctor. 'Others just get a rash and feel a bit off colour. Your boy is in the former group, so give him plenty of liquids, keep him warm and wait for it to pass.'

'The best thing you can do, Harry,' said his mother when the doctor had gone, 'is to go to work.'

'I feel as though I shouldn't leave him.'

'Nonsense,' said Marg. 'He'll be perfectly all right with me.'

'It's hard on you, though.'

'If you think one small boy with measles will break me, you don't know me very well. So, get yourself off to work, for goodness' sake.'

So, Harry did as she asked, aware of how blessed he was to have such wonderful support.

'The trials and tribulations of fatherhood, eh?' said Harry's police partner Archie when they were out on the beat the next night and Harry was telling him about Mikey's measles. 'I couldn't count the sleep I've lost over my kids.'

'I didn't think I could feel this strongly for another human being until Mikey came along.'

'I'm the same with my kids,' said Archie. 'Mine are almost grown up now and I still worry about them.'

'I can understand,' said Harry. 'I can't imagine a day when I won't worry about Mikey.'

'Neither can I, mate. Even now I still fret about mine all the time.'

Harry was distracted suddenly. 'What's going on over there?' he said, looking across the street to a tobacconist's shop. 'I saw a flash of light, probably from a torch. There's someone in there.'

They hurried across the road. Immediately they could see that the lock on the door had been broken. They opened the door and shone their torches inside.

'Police,' called Archie. 'We know you're in here. So make yourself known.'

No response.

Harry called out. 'Come on, mate. You've been nabbed so come and face the music.'

All was silent. The two policemen made their way in, cautiously shining their torches. They heard a movement and then Harry felt a blow to the head and he slumped to the ground. The last thing he heard before he lost consciousness was Archie saying, 'You're nicked!'

'Well done, mate,' Harry said to Archie later, when he had recovered and was back on duty. 'It's about time that villain was banged to rights. He's got away with breaking and entering for far too long.'

'I couldn't have done it without you,' said Archie. 'Shame it cost you a knock on the head.'

'Yeah, not nice, but all in the line of duty.'

'I'll buy you a pint after work.'

'There's no need, mate, but I'll have a drink with you when we go off duty anyway,' said Harry, who enjoyed the camaraderie he had with his colleagues.

'Not rushing off tonight, then?'

'I won't hang about but I've got time to have a swift half with you as we're on lates, because my boy will have gone to bed long ago. I usually rush off to see him before he goes to sleep.'

'I used to do that when my kids were small,' said Archie. 'Nowadays they're often out of an evening.' He looked thoughtful. 'The time soon flies by, so make the most of him while he's little.'

'I do,' said Harry from the heart. 'Mikey means the absolute world to me.'

Archie nodded in an understanding manner.

'Have you ever thought of trying for the CID, Archie?' Harry enquired conversationally.

'No, never,' he replied. 'I enjoy being a plod. Always have. Why, do you fancy being a detective?'

'Yeah, I do as it happens,' he replied. 'I have from my very first day as a copper.'

'I've never fancied anything like that,' said Archie. 'Basic policing suits me fine. But if you have ambitions you should follow them up. When you feel ready, of course.'

'I need to get a bit more experience under my belt first, but that's my aim.'

'I hope it goes well for you,' said Archie. 'I'll watch your career with interest.'

Harry knew he had a good friend in Archie. The Metropolitan Police wasn't made up of angels, but the mates Harry had made in the force he would trust with his life. The job wasn't always easy but it was right for him and he was very glad he had joined. He was proud to be a part of it.

* * *

It was a few weeks later that Harry had some sweet coupons left on this month's ration so he called at the sweetshop to get some sweets for his son on his way home from work. He was on early shift so it was mid-afternoon.

'Two ounces of aniseed balls and two ounces of fruit drops, please,' he said to the assistant, handing her his ration book.

The woman, whose name was Mavis, smiled and nodded. She'd known Harry since he was a nipper. 'Just come off duty, Harry?' she asked.

He nodded.

She grinned. 'I didn't think you'd be buying aniseed balls to eat at work.'

'They're for my boy,' he said. 'But I might nick one or two. I'm very partial to an aniseed ball now and again.'

'I know you are,' she smiled, weighing the sweets and sliding them into a paper bag. 'I can't begin to imagine how many I've sold you over the years.'

'There have been a few,' he grinned. 'But we didn't have rationing when I was a lad.'

'That's true,' she said. 'It's well past time sweets came off the ration now.'

'Indeed.'

'Anyway, I'd better be on my way,' he said when he'd paid and taken the bag of sweets.

'Don't go dipping into them on the way home now,' she laughed.

'I can't promise not to pinch one or two.'

She smiled. 'See you, Harry.'

'See you, Mavis.'

Harry was smiling as he went on his way. It felt good to be among people he knew. His time away in the army had made him appreciate his hometown and his family. A woman in his life would make it complete, but there was only one woman he wanted and he couldn't have her so he'd stay single. He was well aware of how lucky he was. He had a fine son, whom he adored, and parents who meant the world to him. So, he wasn't complaining.

Chapter Thirteen

Cissy came into the office one Friday afternoon in early December 1952 looking worried.

'Lola, dear,' she began in a serious tone, 'the fog is very dense and you need to get home before dark. It's so bad they are even issuing weather warnings on the wireless. Apparently, it's the worst London fog for many years.'

'I can't go yet,' cried the diligent young woman. 'I still have some letters to type and get into the post.'

'They'll have to wait until next week, I'm afraid,' insisted Cissy.

'But they are important, you said so . . .'

'Never mind what I said earlier. Things have changed, and this really is one heck of a peasouper.'

'I'll be all right,' said Lola, young and strong and unworried by the weather. 'I'm a Londoner so I can cope with more than just a bit of fog. I'll have to leave the scooter here, though, if the weather is really bad, and take the train.'

'It *is* really bad, dear.'

'The tube will still be running even if the buses stop, so there's no rush,' Lola insisted.

'I think there is, so leave the letters and go home, Lola,' said Cissy, her manner becoming more forceful. 'Please stop arguing and do as I ask.'

'Oh,' said Lola, looking at her quickly, surprised by the sudden authority in Cissy's tone. 'All right. If that's what you really want.'

'It's necessary, dear, or I wouldn't insist. I want you to be safely indoors before it gets dark,' Cissy said. 'As your employers, my sister and I have a responsibility towards you.'

Roger appeared with Lola's coat. 'I'll walk you to the station,' he said.

'Oh, so there's been a conspiracy, has there? Honestly, what a fuss about nothing,' tutted Lola, though she couldn't help but be touched by their concern. 'It isn't as if us Londoners aren't used to a bit of fog.'

'It isn't just "a bit of fog", it's a nasty peasouper,' said Roger sounding serious. 'So, come on, don't hang about.'

'Oh, I see what you mean,' said Lola, as she and Roger went into the unrecognisable street, the swirling vapour stinging their eyes and throat. 'This is no little mist.'

'It certainly isn't.'

The walk to the station, which usually took only a few minutes, took them more than half an hour because they couldn't find it. Even the lights of the West End shops were barely visible. The smog seeped into their clothes and was so dense they were completely disorientated. It was a filthy, yellowish-grey blanket with sooty dust floating in it.

'I think I'd better come on the train with you and see you right to your door,' Roger suggested.

'There'll be no need for that, Roger,' Lola said firmly, not wanting to put him out. 'It's very kind of you to offer but I'll be absolutely fine. Honestly.'

'Are you sure?' He still sounded doubtful.

'Of course I am,' she assured him firmly. 'I'm young and strong, and the walk between the station and home I know like the back of my hand. I could do it with my eyes closed.'

'Well, all right then, but I'm not altogether happy about it. I'll never forgive myself if anything happens to you.'

'It's a fog, Roger, not an outbreak of war. Nothing will happen to me so stop fussing, concentrate on finding your way back to the tearooms and forget about me.'

'Well . . . only if you're sure,' he said, still sounding concerned.

'I'm absolutely positive.'

'All right then. But mind how you go.'

'You, too,' Lola said, and headed into the station, confident that when she emerged in Hammersmith the fog would not be anything like as dense as it was here in the West End.

A few people got off the train with Lola, but everyone went their separate ways so she found herself alone as she headed for home. There was a strange echoing silence with an occasional sound of voices in the distance somewhere. The fog was yellowish-grey here, too, and stung her throat and chest. Even with her scarf pulled over her mouth it still managed to get inside her. Her eyes were stinging too. It was bitterly cold and she was shivering.

When she got to the end of the road, she was surprised to

see from the street sign that she wasn't where she'd thought she was. How had that happened? She knew the area well, so how could she be lost? Half an hour later and with a couple more unfamiliar street signs, she accepted the fact that she was in unknown territory.

There was no one around either and the atmosphere felt eerie, with a creepy silence around her. She kept walking in the hope of seeing something familiar: a street sign that she recognised or houses that she knew. But all was unknown. To her annoyance she could feel tears burning. How could it be so empty and silent? This was London and she had 'got off the train at the right stop so she couldn't be far from home.

Then she heard voices; deep male voices.

'Help,' she called. 'Help.'

'Where are you?' shouted a man.

'Here,' she called.

'Keep shouting,' said the man. 'So that we can follow the sound.'

After what felt like hours, but was probably only minutes, two figures emerged out of the fog; two policemen.

'Oh, thank God,' she said, and it was a few seconds before she realised that one of the men was Harry.

'Lola,' he said, smiling at her.

'I feel such an idiot,' she said. 'But I can't find my way home.'

'I'm not surprised in this peasouper,' said Harry's policeman partner Archie. 'But don't worry, we'll soon get you safely to your door. What's your address?'

Fifteen minutes later Lola was at her front gate.

'Thank you, boys,' she said.

'Just doing our job,' said Harry.

'I don't know how I could have got lost so close to home, and yet you found it quite quickly.'

'You won't be the only one to lose their way in a fog like this,' said Harry. 'We're trained for this sort of thing.'

'Will you be all right now, miss?' asked Archie.

'Yes, I'll be fine, thank you so much,' she said, close to tears of relief.

As she turned her key in the lock, she realised that she was trembling and it wasn't just a reaction to the anxiety of being lost in the fog, as frightening as that was. It was the effect that seeing Harry had had on her. Even now, after all this time, he still had the power to set her heart racing, while he didn't seem in the least affected by seeing her. Would she ever really get over that man?

Harry wasn't as calm as he appeared. He was on duty so personal feelings had to be put to the back of his mind but he had been deeply affected by seeing Lola. Would he ever truly get over that woman, he wondered. Just the sight of her had sent him into a state of high excitement followed by sadness because they weren't together. Would he be cursed with these feelings for ever?

For a woman who claimed she couldn't abide cats, Cissy showed a great deal of concern when the tearooms' cat Dilly went missing.

'She'll be lost in the fog and frightened to death,' she said to Ethel and Roger over dinner that night.

'Cats have a survival instinct,' said Roger. 'She can look after herself.'

'But why hasn't she come home?'

'Who knows?' he said. 'Cats are a law unto themselves. We had one at home when I was a boy and he used to go off for days, then just turn up none the worse for wear. She'll be back.'

'I don't know so much,' said Cissy.

'If it'll ease your mind I'll go out and have a look for her after dinner,' he suggested.

'Oh, would you?' she said, sounding relieved.

'Course I will,' he said, smiling at her.

Ethel was watching this with a knowing eye. Her sister and Roger grew closer by the day. Ethel couldn't help but be pleased for them because they were so right together. Of course, she assumed they were both long past any sort of romantic notions, but they were lovely as close friends.

Her interest was diverted by a loud, demanding meowing from downstairs.

'She's back,' said Cissy, surprised at how pleased she was. 'I'll go down and let her in.'

'I'll come with you,' said Ethel.

Roger was smiling affectionately. Those two spoiled that damned cat rotten. He had to admit that he wasn't immune to her charms and many an evening she spent dozing on his lap. Thank goodness she was safely home.

The fog lasted all weekend, keeping people indoors. Lola couldn't even get to see Doreen. Her brother Frankie was miserable because he couldn't meet up with his mates. Most bad tempered of all was Lola's father, who was in the blackest of moods. He wasn't used to being confined to home.

'Now then, all of you,' said Lola's mother, sternly. 'There's nothing at all we can do about the fog. It will clear when it's ready, so stop being so miserable and accept the fact that you have to stay at home for a day or two. I don't want to see all these long faces about the place. You are warm and safe, so be content with that.'

'Sorry, Mum,' said Lola, which was echoed by her brother although their father stayed silent. What the rest of the family didn't know was that Charlie had been due at a meeting that night about the biggest job of his criminal career. The rest of the gang lived close to the venue so they would probably get there and have a discussion without him. He'd have to chase them up as soon as the fog cleared to get himself up to date. He hated to miss so much as a syllable of what was said. You had to stay one step ahead of things in his game and watch your back.

The fog, quickly named as the Great Smog, filled the papers and news bulletins, lasted all weekend until the following Tuesday, then dispersed quickly when the weather changed and a breeze sprang up.

'Thank goodness for that,' said Rita, relieved when the air was clear again.

'But you weren't affected by the fog, Mum,' said Lola. 'You had done the shopping before it descended, and you don't have to go to work.'

'I had to put up with you lot moaning because you couldn't go to work and yet you are always complaining when you do have to go.'

'That's human nature for you,' said Lola, laughing. 'We're never satisfied. I don't know how you put up with us.'

'At times, neither do I,' said Rita, but she was smiling.

'I reckon that husband of mine is up to something dodgy again, Bert,' said Rita to her brother-in-law one day in January 1953 when he called round for a cup of tea on his way home from work. 'He's got an air of excitement about him and he's as short tempered as hell.'

'Is he now?' said Bert. 'I hadn't noticed but I haven't seen him much this week.'

'I live with him and I don't miss a thing,' she said. 'Not that it does any good because I can't stop him, whatever he is involved in. He doesn't take any notice of anything I say. Just tells me to stop fussing.'

'He tells me to mind my own business if I say anything about his illegal goings-on.'

'He's going to end up in prison if he isn't very careful,' Rita said. 'He's been getting away with it for so long he's beginning to think he's invulnerable.'

'You're right, I reckon,' agreed Bert, worriedly. 'He'll only get away with law-breaking for so long. The police do know their job even though he thinks they are a bunch of idiots.'

'It's awful when you can see someone you care about heading for the edge of a cliff and you can't do anything about it.'

'I know the feeling,' said Bert. 'You still care about him then, after all he's put you through?'

'Of course,' she said. 'He's still my husband, no matter what he gets up to.'

'Oh.' Bert looked glum.

'Don't look so down hearted,' she said, patting his arm affectionately. 'You know how I feel about you. Us, you and me . . . that's a different thing altogether and no less important. But Charlie is still my husband, no matter what he gets up to, and I have to respect that. It's no more than my duty.'

'Yeah, I suppose you're right,' Bert sighed.

One day early in the New Year, when Lola was on her way to work on her scooter, she was pulled over by two policemen, one of whom was Harry.

'Your back wheel is wobbling,' said Harry's partner.

'Oh dear, is it?' she said, shaken by a police approach. 'I had no idea.'

'You need to get it seen to right away,' said Harry.

'I'll go straight to the nearest garage.'

'It's for your own safety,' said Harry.

'Yes, of course,' she said, breathless from the effect of seeing him so unexpectedly.

'Make sure you do, miss,' said the other policeman.

The two men went on their way and Lola headed for the garage, excited at seeing Harry, but sad too because they weren't together. Once again, she wondered if she would ever get over this man. Then she found herself wondering if there was any way they could be together but decided that there wasn't, not without risking sending her dad to prison. It wasn't a matter of her being too shy to approach him – not at all – she'd do it in a heartbeat if it wasn't her father's life she would be meddling with.

Harry probably had a woman in his life, anyway, she decided.

So she tried to squash her regrets as she rode onto the garage forecourt.

Lola's father was in the back room of a pub, one evening in January, with his partners in crime, mates of his, whom he'd known for years, small-time crooks who liked to think that they were high-class professionals in their attitude towards law-breaking.

'So, this job at the jeweller's needs to either get done or scrapped altogether,' said Charlie.

'We don't want to scrap it,' said one of the men. 'We've spent a lot of time planning it and it'll be rich pickings.'

'Yeah, you're full of chat but every time I suggest actually setting a date, you all back off,' said Charlie.

'Yeah, well, it's bigger than anything we've done before so I suppose it's only natural that we get cold feet,' admitted one of the men.

'Do any of you seriously want to drop out?' asked Charlie. 'Because now's your chance. I don't want anyone coming on this job half hearted. I need one-hundred-per-cent dedication. And if I can't get it from you, I'll look elsewhere. There's plenty of people who wouldn't say no to earning a nice juicy chunk of dough.'

There was a chorus of enthusiasm.

'Right, so we need to choose a date and work out what each of us will be doing. The job needs to be planned to the nth degree or we'll all end up in clink.'

Everyone started talking at once.

'Calm down, boys,' said Charlie. 'The first thing we need to do is choose a date that suits us all. It doesn't have to be right away so long as we actually get it set. We'll have something definite to work towards then.'

The men were so excited they were shouting out their choice of dates. This was more like it, thought Charlie. Enthusiasm and plenty of it. He'd finally got them keen enough to commit. Lovely!

Having Roger playing the piano at the tearooms was a huge success. As well as creating a pleasant atmosphere, the music also increased business, mainly because more special occasions were booked in. If people were going out for tea to celebrate a birthday or anniversary, they wanted it to feel like a celebration and music helped to create that.

Roger played songs from the shows, old classics like 'We'll Gather Lilacs' and also some of the popular tunes favoured by the young, such as 'You Belong to Me' by Jo Stafford and 'Wheel of Fortune', made popular Kay Starr. 'I Believe', made famous that year by Frankie Laine, was a favourite, and guests loved it when Roger played 'How Much is that Doggie in the Window?' just for a bit of fun.

Times were better for many people and they poured into London to see the sights and visit the zoo and the famous parks. As a result, all the eateries were doing well.

The Tulip had a party of thirty booked in for a sixtieth birthday party one Saturday in spring. It was a family group of various generations and they were a jolly crowd, in the mood to enjoy themselves. The sisters had made a wonderful spread for their tea with a beautiful birthday cake as the centrepiece, decorated with iced tulips.

Lola didn't work in the office on Saturdays but she came

in to help when they had a special event on. She liked to be a part of it and wouldn't miss it for the world.

Roger played light, background music while they were eating, but after they had cut the cake, someone asked for some wartime songs, especially those made popular by Vera Lynn. Guests from the other tables joined in 'The White Cliffs of Dover' and soon, everyone in the room was singing. When Roger played 'We'll Meet Again' there were very few dry eyes. The mood was lifted when someone started a conga line. Everyone joined in and they congaed all the way to Oxford Street.

'Well, I think we can definitely count that as a success,' said Cissy, when they had seen the last customer out and had closed up.

There was general agreement.

'A lot of it was down to you, Roger,' she continued. 'You did a brilliant job at the piano.'

'Hear, hear!,' added her sister.

'Thanks, ladies,' he said politely.

'How about I take you to the pictures tonight as a thank you?' Cissy continued. 'My treat. *The Greatest Show on Earth* is on. You've been wanting to see that.'

'A treat won't be necessary,' he said. 'I was only doing my job.'

'You made the occasion very special and I'd like to show our appreciation,' she said.

'It's very kind of you but—'

'Let her take you to the pictures, for goodness' sake, man,' said Ethel. 'She wants to do it.'

'Oh.' He looked at Cissy smiling. 'Thank you very much then,' he said. 'I'd love to.'

Lola was watching this with interest. It was nice that Roger

236

and Cissy were having an evening alone together and she was pleased for them. It had made her realise that love wasn't only for the young.

'Do you think Dad will ever get back on the straight and narrow?' Lola asked her mother one evening in early spring when they were in the kitchen clearing up after dinner.

'I wish he would, but I know he won't,' Rita replied. 'He's been at it for too long. He was already involved when I first got to know him.'

'It's never too late to change for the better,' said Lola.

'He doesn't see the right way as better,' said her mother. 'He thinks crime is the best way. To the people he mixes with it is. They think honest people are weak fools.'

'Why do you put up with it, Mum?' asked Lola.

'What else can I do? I made a commitment when I married him. Anyway, I would never leave my family.'

'Might you do it when Frankie and I have left home?'

'I don't know,' Rita said cautiously. She and her brother-in-law had discussed this subject many times. They had loved each other for years and Bert wanted her to be with him, but she couldn't bring herself to leave Charlie. Despite everything her husband had put her through over the years, she still had feelings for him. She couldn't say it was love, exactly, but it was something strong, which probably came from being with someone for such a long time.

'But surely—'

'It's private, Lola,' Rita said sharply. 'And I really don't want to discuss it.'

'Sorry, Mum.'

'It's all right, dear, but some things are best left unsaid and that is one of them, so please don't mention it again.'

Lola nodded and left the room. She felt sad for her mother and angry with her father.

When her father went out that night Lola followed him and caught up with him at the end of the road, out of sight of the house.

'What do you want?' he asked, swinging round after she had tapped him on the shoulder.

'I want to talk to you.'

'Not now,' he said irritably. 'I've got plans, so off you go home, please.'

'Meeting your crooked mates, I suppose.'

'What business is it of yours who I am meeting?'

'I'm your daughter, so of course it's my business.'

He looked around to make sure they weren't being observed, then grabbed her by the arm, pulled her forcibly into an alleyway between some houses and pushed her roughly against a brick wall.

'Don't you dare follow me out and accost me,' he said. 'Know your place.'

'Do you have any idea what it's been like for me, growing up knowing that my father is a criminal?' she said.

'I've always provided well for you,' he said. 'You've never gone without. Even when ratioing was on, you always had more than your mates.'

'I didn't want stuff that hadn't been legally come by.'

'I didn't hear you saying no when I came home with chocolate,' he said.

238

'I was just a kid,' she said. 'I didn't know anything about such things. When I got old enough to realise, I never took any of your ill-gotten gains.'

'Yeah. You were a sulky little sod.'

'I lived in fear of the police coming for you, or of my friends finding out,' she said.

'It was up to you if you wanted to worry about things that didn't concern you.'

'My whole life has had this shadow hanging over it because of you.'

'Oh, clear off and let me be on my way,' he said irritably, his face twisted with anger. 'You ungrateful little sod.'

He gave her a look of such fury she winced. Then he pushed her roughly aside and marched off down the street, a large man with a swagger.

She had never hated him more than she did at that moment. But at the same time, she felt sad that it had come to this. She had approached him on impulse and was glad she had. But all it had done was make her realise how hopeless the situation was. As much as she wanted to get away, she couldn't leave her mother and Frankie at his mercy. There was some relief in having told him the extent of her feelings although, as he didn't care, nothing would change.

Feeling a surge of compassion for her mother who had lived with this for so long, Lola headed home. She wouldn't tell Rita about the altercation with her father and she was damned sure he wouldn't. Mum would only be upset if she knew, and she had quite enough to contend with.

How could her father be so different from his brother Bert? Now there was a person she respected. He had always been supportive towards her and her brother, a quiet, law-abiding man with an air of strength about him. She got the impression that Mum was fond of him too. His presence in their family was a huge comfort to them all, except Dad, who saw him as a loser because he stuck to the straight and narrow.

Roger's piano playing at the tearooms grew in popularity and created a lovely atmosphere. It was only for a couple of hours twice a week and Saturdays, but the customers really enjoyed it.

'It cheers me up, and I just work here,' said Lola.

It was good for business because people began to see the tearooms in a more festive light and the party bookings increased.

'It's amazing the difference it's made,' said Cissy. 'I'd like to have music more often but it might be too much for Roger.' She paused, looking at her sister in a certain way.

'No,' said Ethel, who was an accomplished pianist but was too nervous to play in public. 'Absolutely not!'

'It would be good for the tearooms and you'd get over the nerves once you got used to it.'

'No.'

'But it's only background music, dear,' said Cissy. 'It isn't the same as being on a stage in a silent hall. You and Roger could take turns. It would be very good for business.'

'But we are just a small tearooms, not The Savoy,' said Ethel. 'We don't need music.'

'It's very nice to have it, though,' said her sister. 'It transforms the place.'

'It certainly does,' agreed Lola. 'Music creates a special atmosphere no matter how small the establishment.'

'You should play sometimes, Ethel,' said Cissy. 'You've always had a lovely touch, and it would take the pressure off Roger.'

'I don't play in public,' Ethel said. 'You know that very well.'

'Now is the time to start then,' said Cissy.

'I can't do that,' said Ethel.

'You could give it a try,' said Cissy.

'No, absolutely not,' protested Ethel. 'I don't have the confidence.'

But the following Saturday afternoon she was seated at the newly polished piano, playing very nervously at first, but gaining in confidence quite quickly. Lola had come in for an hour that afternoon to encourage her and was very glad she had because the atmosphere at the tearooms was magic.

What none of them realised was that a gentleman at one of the tables was uplifted by the music and enchanted by the creator of it. Ethel had an admirer in Frank Beasley, and he wasn't the type to hold back. A retired entrepreneur, he had always believed that life was too short for hesitation. Oh joy, he thought as Ethel played the introduction to 'We'll Gather Lilacs'.

'Well, well,' said Cissy with a half-smile to Roger and Lola. 'We've been deserted. My sister is going out to dinner with a man tonight. So it's just you and me, Roger.'

'Is it the man with the white curly hair, who was talking to her when she finished playing?' asked Lola.

'That's right,' Cissy confirmed. 'Apparently he's taking her out as a thank you for the music.'

'You'll have to come out to dinner with me, then, won't you?' suggested Roger.

'Oh,' said Cissy, turning pink. 'It's kind of you to take pity on me but I'll be fine on my own.'

'I'm not taking pity on you,' he said. 'I'm taking the opportunity to enjoy your company.'

'Oh,' she said, blushing furiously.

'I'll leave you to it then,' said Lola, smiling. 'See you both on Monday.'

She was feeling happy as she left the tearooms. It was about time those two got together. They'd been wanting to for ages. Thank goodness Roger had finally found the courage.

The big national event of the summer of 1953 was the coronation of Queen Elizabeth II. London was heaving with tourists, and the tearooms were busy all day with visitors from at home and all over the world. The Pickfords expanded their usual tea menu and provided breakfast and lunch too.

Lola was called upon to leave the office and help in the café and she enjoyed a spot of waitressing for a change. Roger and Frank Beasley, now both official boyfriends of the ladies, were also there to help out.

'I could get used to this,' Lola said to her employers as she was handed a tray to deliver. 'It's more fun than being stuck behind a desk.'

'Don't get any ideas,' warned Cissy. 'You're needed in the office. No one else would understand how to deal with our paperwork.'

'That is very true,' said Lola, because, whilst the ladies were excellent cooks they were not similarly gifted when it came to administration. 'But it's nice being out here among the people for a change. I'm enjoying it. The coronation has certainly created a lovely atmosphere.'

'The crowds are solid around the palace today, apparently,' said Ethel. 'I heard them talking about it on the wireless.'

'I'll be able to see it on television later,' said Lola excitedly. 'They are sure to show a recording of the ceremony for people who were at work when it was actually happening.'

'A television, eh?' said Cissy, her eyes gleaming. 'They seem to be getting very popular.'

'We are not having one, Cissy,' said Ethel firmly. 'Not while there are books to read.'

Although to many people the ownership of a television set was a wonderful thing, it was viewed as a mindless occupation by a certain section of society, of which Ethel was a part. Lola, however, could not agree.

Lola enjoyed being out in the fresh air and was a regular visitor to the local park, mostly because she liked to walk and also because she enjoyed being among all the different people who enjoyed this open space: young boys with their footballs; little girls on their bikes or with their dolls' prams; young adults playing energetic games; those with more years on the clock watching them. And, of course, the courting couples with eyes only for each other.

She was sitting on a bench one Sunday afternoon in the autumn sunshine when a small boy she recognised came tearing up. He went behind her and knelt down.

'I'm hiding from my dad,' he said, giggling and breathless from running. 'Don't tell him where I am. Promise?'

'I promise,' she agreed, smiling because the boy was as obvious as a kangaroo in the Co-op. She knew exactly who he was and felt a surge of excitement in anticipation of seeing his father. Even now, just the thought of seeing him again excited her like nothing else.

'Hello, Harry,' she said when he appeared.

'Lola,' he said, beaming.

'I think you might have lost something,' she said, grinning as Mikey's giggling could be heard.

'Yes, I've lost my little boy,' he said, playing along.

'I'm here! I'm here!' said Mikey, scrambling up and being lifted up by his father and smothered in kisses.

Lola felt quite emotional, seeing the love between them.

'Can we do hiding again?' asked the five-year-old.

'Give me a few minutes,' he said. 'Let me talk to Lola before you drag me off again.'

'She can play with us,' said Mikey.

And so it was that Lola found herself playing hide-and-seek in the park for the first time since she'd been little. It felt so good, so right to be with Harry and his son.

'So how have you been?' Harry asked her when they were sitting on the bench after the game, while Mikey ran around on the grass.

'Fine,' she said.

'Still got the scooter?'

'Oh yeah,' she said with enthusiasm. 'I wouldn't be without it. It beats public transport by miles.'

'I never really got over your rejection of me, you know,' he said without preamble.

'Oh.' She was lost for words for a moment. 'But you married someone else. And you have a lovely little boy.'

'And I love him to bits,' Harry said. 'But you were always the only girl for me. I was shattered when you turned me down.'

'Sorry.'

'No need to apologise,' he said. 'But seeing you again brings it all back.'

She wanted to be honest with him about her feelings for him. She wanted him back. But she said, 'I'll have to keep out of your way in future then.'

'Don't be daft,' he said. 'It's just me being stupidly sentimental. I'll get over it.'

She didn't want him to. Her selfish side wanted him to love her for ever. But she said, 'Of course you will. You're tough. You have to be, to be a policeman.'

'We do have hearts, you know, us coppers,' he said.

'I'm sure you do.'

The conversation was interrupted by Mikey, who wanted to play another game.

'No, we have to go home now,' said Harry. 'Granny will have tea ready.'

'Can we come again?' asked the boy. 'Can Lola come?'

Harry looked at her questioningly.

'Please,' said Mikey.

'I'm on duty Sunday next week,' said Harry, looking at Lola. 'But I could do Saturday afternoon, if you fancy a game of hide-and-seek. They've reopened the park café so we might even manage a cup of tea and a bun.'

'How can I refuse?' she said lightly.

'Three o'clock here, then?' he said.

She nodded, smiling.

'Yippee,' cheered Mikey.

'See you next Saturday then,' she said.

Walking home, she realised she hadn't felt this happy in ages. She was excited too. But in her heart she knew she had made a mistake. She shouldn't be encouraging him. He'd admitted he still had feelings for her. She'd hurt him once; she didn't want to do it again. But she so wanted to see him. And little Mikey. Just once wouldn't hurt, would it?

Chapter Fourteen

Lola's mood of elation quickly faded when she got home because her father was in a foul mood and was, as usual, taking it out on her mother.

'You need to smarten yourself up,' he said to his wife. 'I'm not having you sitting around the house in an apron and curlers when we're better off and living a different sort of life. We'll be mixing with the toffs then. People who know how to look good. They'll be calling in for drinks and that sort of thing. We'll need to match them and I'm not having you showing me up with your scruffy appearance. So, you'd better start making an effort right away so that you get used to looking half decent.'

Lola almost felt her mother flinch. After all these years Charlie still had the power to hurt her. But she stood up to him.

'I don't normally sit around in my curlers. I've got them in now because I'm going to the pictures with Lola tonight and I want my hair to look nice as I'm going out, and I'm wearing an apron because I've been busy in the kitchen, preparing food for you,' she said bravely, though her voice was trembling. 'Anyway, I don't know where you're gonna find all these toffs you're on about. They wouldn't want to spend time with a small-time crook like you.'

'They like bad boys with charisma and I've got plenty of that,' he said. 'Whereas you're boring and dowdy. And I don't want a dowdy wife.'

'You'd better find yourself someone else then, hadn't you?' she said with spirit, although her voice betrayed her again.

'Leave her alone, Dad,' said Lola.

'You keep out of it,' he growled. 'This has nothing to do with you.'

'She's my mother so it has everything to do with me,' Lola came back at him staunchly. 'I'm not going to stand by and let you treat her like a piece of dirt.'

There was a timely interruption when Uncle Bert arrived with a carrier bag. His presence gave Lola immediate comfort. Her brother wasn't around this afternoon and she could do with his support.

'I've brought you some apples off the tree in my garden,' Bert told them, putting the bag on the kitchen table.

'Thank you, Bert,' said Rita pleasantly, but her voice was still trembling. 'We'll enjoy those.'

'I won't,' said Charlie.

'Only if they're made into cider, eh?' said Bert, making a joke of it.

'Too sweet for my taste in any form, mate,' said Charlie ungratefully. 'I'm a best bitter man, you know that.'

'Lola and I are going to the pictures tonight, Bert,' said Rita with a swift change of subject. 'Do you fancy coming? The film is *Roman Holiday* with Audrey Hepburn. It should be good.'

'Sounds like a soppy romance, no film for a man,' said Charlie.

Bert could read the atmosphere in this house as well as those who lived there. There had been a bust-up, he could feel it. 'Actually, I wouldn't mind a night out at the flicks with two lovely ladies,' he said with a wicked grin at his brother. He looked at Rita. 'What time shall I call for you?'

'About seven should be fine,' she replied, feeling a little more cheerful.

Even the sex appeal of Gregory Peck and the undeniable charm of the delightful Audrey Hepburn on the screen couldn't hold Lola's interest entirely. Her mind was filled with thoughts of seeing Harry again. She wasn't so consumed with her own feelings as not to notice how much her mother was enjoying herself, though. She was like a different person from the woman who had been bullied by her husband earlier. She and Uncle Bert were chatting in whispers now and again throughout the film. They'd always got on well. She had a sudden thought. Could it be that perhaps there was more . . .? No, of course not. Mum would never look at any other man besides Dad. More was the pity!

On the way out of the cinema with the crowds, Bert said, 'Well, I can't treat you to a bag of chips as the fish-and-chip shops are closed on Sundays, but the pubs are open and we should be able to get served before they close. So do you fancy a drink?'

'I'd love one, Bert,' said Lola's mother, looking delighted.

But Lola felt the need to be alone with her thoughts. 'Thanks, Uncle Bert, but I think I'll go straight home. I've got work in the morning. You and Mum go and enjoy yourselves.'

'Just as you like, love,' he said, and they went their separate ways.

As she expected, the house was empty when she got home. Her father was probably at the pub with his dodgy mates. She made herself some cocoa and went to bed, allowing herself to anticipate her meeting with Harry.

After a week of Lola swinging between joyful excitement and painful reality, Saturday arrived. Meeting Harry in the park felt like a proper date to her, albeit that he had Mikey with him. Harry was even more attractive with a few extra years, his face firmer, and he had a confidence she hadn't seen before, which she guessed came partly from being a policeman. But he was still the same old Harry, warm hearted and funny.

They played ball and hide-and-seek with Mikey, then went to the café and had tea and cake. Once Mikey had finished his cake he asked if he could leave the table to play with a little boy who was kicking a ball outside.

'He's such a joy,' said Lola, as they watched Mikey hurry outside to join his new friend.

'Most of the time,' said Harry, smiling. 'But not so much at bedtime when he doesn't want to go. I reckon the whole of London can hear him shrieking then.'

'We don't,' she smiled.

'Count yourself lucky,' he grinned. 'It's enough to wake the dead.'

'You love every minute of it, though,' she teased him. 'I bet he can twist you around his little finger, policeman or not.'

'I will admit to the odd moment of weakness where my son is concerned,' Harry said with a wry grin. 'But I try to stay firm. He gets enough spoiling from his grandparents.'

'I bet,' Lola said, smiling.

They moved on to other subjects. It was all just light conversation until Harry blurted out, 'I'm still in love with you, Lola.'

'Oh, Harry,' she gasped. 'What are you saying?'

'Exactly what I said,' he explained. 'My feelings for you haven't changed.'

'But it's been years. You've been married, you have a child,' she reminded him.

'I am not married now, and time hasn't lessened my feelings for you,' he said. 'A father's love might be all consuming but it doesn't kill off feelings for other people.'

'All this time . . .'

'Yes . . . I never stopped loving you,' he said. 'And as soon as I saw you again, I knew nothing had changed.'

'But your marriage . . .'

'I had to marry Mikey's mother because she was pregnant, and I'm not proud of it,' he said. 'But it was you that I loved. Always. And seeing you again has brought it all back. I never knew why you turned me down. I never believed it was because you didn't love me.'

She wanted to throw her arms around him but she said, 'I could see that as arrogance.'

'Come on, Lola, I can't have imagined how it was for us back then,' he said. 'We were nuts about each other. It was the most wonderful time of my life.'

'Mine too.'

'So why?'

'It doesn't matter now, Harry,' she said. 'It's all in the past.'

'What about if I were to suggest we give it another try?' he said. 'See how we get on now, in the present. Now that we are more mature.'

251

A hot flow of excitement surged through her. She wanted that so much and she found herself wondering if there was a way she could be with Harry.

'I'm not sure, Harry,' she said.

'We're both single, so why not?' he asked. 'And don't tell me it's because you don't have feelings for me. I didn't believe it back then. And I won't believe it now.'

'You're right, of course, Harry,' she said. 'But—'

At that moment Mikey returned in tears. 'He won't let me play with his ball,' he wailed. 'That boy isn't very nice.'

'All right, calm down. I'll come and sort it out.' Harry looked at Lola. 'Duty calls, I'm afraid,' he said, rising and putting his arm around his son. 'I won't be long, Lola. Don't go anywhere.'

She nodded, smiling, glad of the chance to collect her thoughts. The beginnings of a new way of looking at things was beginning to form in her mind. Up until now she had always accepted that there wasn't a way forward for her with Harry. But could there be somehow? With feelings this strong after all this time, surely she was meant to be with him.

When he came back, Mikey now happily playing with the other boy, Harry said, 'Kids, eh? So, where were we?'

'You were talking about giving it another try.'

'And . . .?'

'I have complications in my life,' she said. 'I need to do some serious thinking.'

'I have responsibilities too, Lola,' he said. 'I'm not free to come and go as I please like I was when we were courting last time. Mikey will have to come first because he's still small and vulnerable. But I really do think that you and I deserve another chance and I would find a way to make it work if you were to say yes.' He became serious. 'I won't grovel. I have told you how I feel and now it's up to you. I won't try and force you into anything. It must be your decision.'

Despite everything, all the doubts and fear for her family, Lola felt deeply happy. After the awful way she had treated him, Harry still loved her. That simple fact brought tears to her eyes.

'I'm not playing hard to get, I promise you, Harry,' she said. 'But I have to deal with something before I can give you an answer. I'll tell you the next time we meet.'

'Maybe this will help you to make up your mind,' he said, leaning forward and kissing her on the lips.

They were interrupted by the reappearance of Mikey, who was having trouble again with his new friend.

Harry looked at Lola and raised his hands, laughing. 'See what I mean? My life isn't my own.'

She smiled. 'Go and be a good dad,' she urged him, and went with him to sort out Mikey's social life.

Mikey was at the centre of their attention from then on, until he got tired and became fretful so Harry decided it was time to take him home.

'I'll meet you in the evening next time and leave him at home with Mum and Dad so that we can have a proper adult conversation,' he said as Lola was about to leave. 'If you'd be happy with that.'

'Well, yes, I would like that,' she said. 'But I enjoy having Mikey around.'

'So do I, but we need some proper grown-up time together,' he said.

'You're right,' she said, knowing that she had reached a crucial time in her life and a decision had to be made.

'I've got Saturday night off next week so perhaps we could go for a drink together?'

'I'd like that,' Lola said.

'I'll see you outside the station and we'll decide where to go then. Will eight o'clock suit you?'

'Perfect.'

He brushed her cheek with his lips. Then, with Mikey on his shoulders, he headed home.

Lola went on her way, deep in thought. Whether or not to be with Harry must be her decision, but it was complicated and she felt the need to talk to someone about it and get some advice. It had to be the right person and she knew exactly who that was.

'In love with a policeman, eh?' said Uncle Bert when she had told him her story. 'Blimey, Lola, you couldn't have done a worse thing, as far as your dad is concerned.'

'I know, and I gave Harry up because of Dad originally, but he's come back into my life and I want to be with him so very much, Uncle Bert.'

'And you have every right to be with him, Lola,' Bert said. 'You shouldn't have your life ruined because your dad insists on breaking the law.'

'But if Harry became part of the family, which would happen if he and I got together, he is bound to guess what Dad is up to and he's the sort of man who would feel compelled to do his duty. So Dad would go to prison.'

'Yeah, that is a possibility,' Bert agreed. 'I've always believed it's only a matter of time before your dad gets nicked anyway. If you consistently break the law, there a fair chance you will go to prison at some point.'

'But what about Mum?' Lola said, worriedly. 'She's completely reliant on him.'

'Don't you worry about your mother,' Bert replied in a definite manner. 'If Charlie were ever to get locked up, I would look after her.'

'Oh, really?'

'Absolutely,' he said firmly. 'And you and your brother, even though you're both grown up now and are old enough to look after yourselves. I'll always be there for the whole family. You all mean the world to me.'

Tears rushed into Lola's eyes. 'Oh, Uncle Bert,' she said, hugging him, 'you are such a dear.'

'Don't go all sentimental on me, for Gawd's sake' he said thickly. 'You're the only family I have and I love the bones of the lot of you, including your dad, for all his faults.'

Lola swallowed hard.

'So, you be happy with this man of yours and don't give him up because of your dad,' Bert continued. 'But bring him home to meet the family.'

'I'd love to, but I feel as though that will be the beginning of the end,' Lola said worriedly.

'The alternative is to hide him away, and if he's a decent bloke and wants a future with you he won't want that,' he said. 'He'll be keen to get to know your family.'

'We haven't discussed the future yet,' she said. 'I know he's in love with me. But he does have a child to consider.'

'How do you feel about that?' asked her uncle. 'Taking on someone else's child is a big responsibility.'

'It won't be a problem for me,' Lola said. 'I want to be with Harry, and his boy comes with him. I am happy with that. But first I have to solve the problem of Dad. Harry is very law abiding, even apart from being a policeman. How will he deal with Dad's situation? If he turns him in, Dad will never forgive me for bringing Harry into the house.'

'Mm, I can see your problem, but it must be your decision, love,' Bert said. 'The last thing I want is for my brother to go to prison. But law breakers have to face the possibility of punishment and your dad won't get away with it forever, no matter what happens with you and Harry. He's been living on the edge for years. His luck is bound to run out eventually.'

'He might not let Harry into the house when he finds out what he does for a living.'

'Don't tell him,' said Bert. 'Not until Harry is well and truly over the threshold.'

Lola smiled nervously. 'That wouldn't work because Dad would explode and be really rude to Harry when he found out. And Harry is proud of being a policeman. He wouldn't want to hide it.'

'Mm, I suppose not.'

'Maybe it would be best if Harry never meets the family,' she suggested.

'That wouldn't be easy,' said her uncle. 'Your parents would want to know who you are seeing.'

'Mm, that's true.'

'One thing I will say, love,' said her uncle. 'Whatever you decide to do about Harry, and whatever the outcome is, I'll back you up one hundred per cent.'

'Thanks, Uncle Bert,' she said, hugging him.

Her father was at a corner table in the pub with his cronies and they were speaking in low voices.

'You all know what you've got to do, don't you?'

'We've been through it enough times, mate,' said someone. 'So, I reckon we ought to.'

'No need to get lippy,' said Charlie. 'It only takes one of you to slip up and we could all end up in clink.'

'He's right,' said another.

'If no one has any questions, this meeting is at an end so drink up and go home,' he said. 'Good luck, everyone.'

There was a babble of chatter and the men went their separate ways.

Lola's discussion with her uncle was still fresh in her mind and she lay awake in bed that night thinking about the situation with Harry from every angle. Her happiness with him came at a price for other people. Her father would be furious, which meant her mother's life would be hell because he always took his bad temper out on her. Frankie would also be affected because their father's moods impacted on the whole family.

Uncle Bert had said he would look after them and she trusted him to do that. But there were Harry's feelings to take into consideration as well as her own. He hadn't officially asked her to go to back with him but she knew he wanted it and they both needed to be together. So much so that it hurt, for her anyway. So she made a decision. When she saw him on Saturday night, she would tell Harry how she felt, and the problem of her father would be solved somehow. She knew that Harry would be pleased. He had made his own feelings very clear.

So, roll on, Saturday. It couldn't come quickly enough for her. Now that she'd made a definite decision, she felt very excited: nervous and worried about all the complications but happy too.

She heard the stairs creak as someone went downstairs. It was probably to get a drink of water, she thought drowsily. Oddly, she thought she heard the front door close. No, she must have imagined that. No one would be going out at this time of night.

She could never have guessed that someone had indeed left the house, having picked up the key to the tearooms from the mantelpiece where Lola always left it.

The next morning Frankie's voice was penetrating Lola's deep sleep.

'Lola, Lola, wake up. The police are here, something has happened to Dad. I think he's dead.'

'Dead . . . What!' she said, instantly awake, out of bed and into her dressing gown. 'Of course he isn't dead.'

'He is. I think.'

'Oh my God,' she said, hurrying towards the stairs.

Downstairs in the living room there were two police officers talking to her mother, who was sitting in an armchair, ashen faced. Charlie was indeed dead. The policemen told them the whole story. Apparently, Lola's father and his cronies had got into The Tulip Tearooms using Lola's key and had tried to gain access to the jeweller's next door through the interior wall, using various heavy tools to break it down sufficiently to climb through.

Part of the wall had collapsed, the debris falling directly on Charlie's head. He was dead when the police arrived, having been called by the ladies upstairs, who had been alerted by the noise. Charlie's mates had been caught as they tried to climb through the hole into the jeweller's.

'He must have taken the tearooms' key from where I always leave it on the mantelpiece,' said Lola, while Frankie went to fetch Uncle Bert at the request of their mother, who was tearful and trembling. 'How could he do that? I mean, to abuse the work situation of one of his own family. I don't know how I'll face the ladies.'

'They won't blame you,' said her mother.

'He was my dad,' Lola said, feeling sick and shaky. 'It's bound to rub off on me.'

'You knew nothing about it,' said her mother. 'And they will realise that.'

'I hope so,' said Lola.

Uncle Bert arrived and was absolutely devastated by the news. Charlie was his brother, for all his faults. But he concentrated on comforting Rita and was very kind to Lola and Frankie.

'It's a terrible shock for us all,' he said. 'But we'll get through it together. I'll be around and I'll do what I can to help.'

Lola's mother burst into tears at that, and it was all Lola could do not to join in.

'That's why I rejected your marriage proposal,' Lola explained to Harry that evening, when her mother and brother had gone to bed and Uncle Bert had gone home. 'Because my dad was a crook and I knew you would realise it pretty soon if you married into the family. You would have felt duty bound to turn him in and I couldn't do that to him.'

'I see. I always thought there was more to it than you were saying, but I was absolutely gutted.'

'I know, and so was I,' she said.

'I hope I'll have more luck next time I propose to you,' he said.

'When will that be?'

'I suppose now wouldn't be appropriate, would it?'

'I don't see why not,' she said. 'We don't need to tell people until after the funeral, when things have calmed down a bit.'

So, he got down on one knee to ask the question, and when they were next together with Lola's family they reined in their beaming smiles. This was a sad time, after all. Of course, Lola was upset about Charlie's death. He had been her dad, for all his faults. Her mother would need plenty of support from her daughter for a while and Lola would give it willingly. With Harry in her life she had new strength and could move to the future with her head held high. At long last she could be with the man she loved.

One sunny day a few months later Lola and Harry and their guests stood outside the church as wedding photographs were taken. Lola looked lovely in a long white dress and Harry stood handsome and proud by her side. Her mother and Uncle Bert were together. They spent most of their time in each other's company these days, and Lola had noticed a new confidence about her mother. She and Uncle Bert were good together and Lola was delighted. Frankie had a girlfriend, too, and wasn't at home as much as he used to be, so the whole family was evolving and re-forming in a new, good way.

Lola smiled up at her new husband as the camera clicked and caught the joy in both their faces.

We hope you have enjoyed reading
THE TULIP TEAROOMS.

Pam Evans has written over thirty delightful sagas,
all of which are available from Headline.

For further information visit: www.pamevansbooks.com.

BESSIE'S WAR

Pam Evans

It is autumn 1940 and, as the bombs drop on London, a close-knit community struggles to survive . . .

Working at the local post office, Bessie Green does her best to keep her customers' spirits up, but when a telegram arrives for her parents, there's nothing she can do to prevent the heartache that lies ahead.

Eleven-year-old Daisy Mason has been orphaned in a blast, and Bessie's sure that offering Daisy a home will help to heal her family's sadness. At first, Daisy finds it hard to settle and it isn't until her brother Josh comes back on leave that things start to look up. But the war brings further challenges for Bessie and her friends – with more hearts broken and loved-ones lost – before they can dare to dream of a brighter future . . .

www.pamevansbooks.com
www.headline.co.uk

HEADLINE

A BRIGHTER DAY TOMORROW

Pam Evans

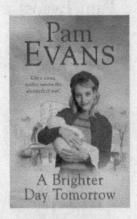

Despite air raids and rationing in wartime London, sisters Liz and Dora Beck find time for fun and laughter at the local ice-rink. Then a handsome American serviceman catches their attention, and so begins heartache between the sisters. Dora is increasingly jealous of her sister's blossoming romance with Victor. But when Victor is killed in a bomb attack, Liz makes a shocking discovery that upsets her whole family.

Forced out of her home, Liz finds support where she least expects it. And, with almost nothing left to lose, she hopes for a brighter day tomorrow . . .

www.pamevansbooks.com
www.headline.co.uk

HEADLINE

DANCE YOUR TROUBLES AWAY

Pam Evans

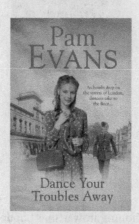

It is three years since the Second World War claimed the life of Polly's beloved husband George and not a day goes by without her wishing he was still alive. Polly is grateful that her mother is on-hand to look after her daughter Emmie while she works day and night to make ends meet. She can't help worrying about the future but at the Cherry Ballroom, where she works for her aunt Marian, Polly is able to forget her fears.

Then one night a handsome Canadian airman asks her to dance and in James's arms her troubles slip away. But the war cannot last for ever and James must return home, leaving Polly to face the future alone. That is until she is reunited with someone she never thought she'd see again . . .

www.pamevansbooks.com
www.headline.co.uk

HEADLINE

WHEN THE LIGHTS GO DOWN

Pam Evans

It is 1938 and the threat of war looms on the streets of London. But, when the lights go down in the cinema aisles, usherette Daisy Blake is transported to a world of glamour and romance.

Among the staff there is much merriment and Daisy soon falls in love with the handsome organist, Al Dawson. Then war is declared and, just after Al leaves for the frontline, Daisy discovers she's pregnant. Her mother is distraught; she doesn't think Al is right for her daughter and when Daisy's letters to him go unanswered, her mother encourages her to marry John, the cinema's projectionist, to spare her further heartache.

As the blitz rages over London and disaster strikes, Daisy's morale is boosted by her work, and her young son, Sam, brings her comfort and joy in the troubled times ahead . . .

www.pamevansbooks.com
www.headline.co.uk

HEADLINE

THE APPLE OF
HER EYE

Pam Evans

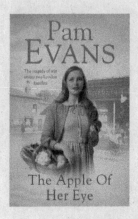

It is 1945 and April Green and her cousin Heather wonder if the war will ever end. Then tragedy strikes when the local pub in Chiswick takes a direct hit. April and her brother do all they can to help their grieving mother and, by tending her father's allotment, April discovers a passion for growing vegetables.

Meanwhile, Winnie Benson is facing the fact that her husband may never walk again and, until their son, George, returns from the Merchant Navy, Winnie must run their greengrocer's on her own. Once the war is over and George is home, things start to improve but rationing remains in force and April's supply of home-grown vegetables couldn't be more welcome. And, before long, George can't help wishing he was the apple of her eye . . .

www.pamevansbooks.com
www.headline.co.uk

HEADLINE